# When the
# Rainbow
# Goddess
# Wept

Also by Cecilia Manguerra Brainard

*Philippine Woman in America*
*Woman with Horns and Other Stories*
*Fiction by Filipinos in America* (editor)

Cecilia Manguerra Brainard

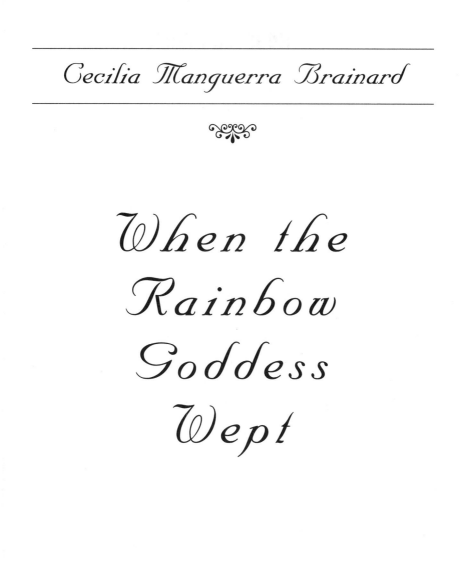

# When the Rainbow Goddess Wept

A DUTTON BOOK

Published by the Penguin Group
Penguin Books USA Inc., 375 Hudson Street, New York, New York 10014, U.S.A.
Penguin Books Ltd, 27 Wrights Lane, London W8 5TZ, England
Penguin Books Australia Ltd, Ringwood, Victoria, Australia
Penguin Books Canada Ltd, 10 Alcorn Avenue, Toronto, Ontario, Canada M4V 3B2
Penguin Books (N.Z.) Ltd, 182–190 Wairau Road, Auckland 10, New Zealand

Penguin Books Ltd, Registered Offices:
Harmondsworth, Middlesex, England

First published by Dutton, an imprint of Dutton Signet,
a division of Penguin Books USA Inc.
Distributed in Canada by McClelland & Stewart Inc.
An earlier version was published
by New Day Publications in the Philippines.

First Printing, September, 1994
1  3  5  7  9  10  8  6  4  2

This novel was first published as Song of Yvonne by New Day Publishers, Quezon City, Philippines, in 1991. Copyright © 1991 by Cecilia Manguerra Brainard. The chapter "The Crucifixion" was published in West/Word Journal, The Katipunan, and Fiction by Filipinos in America. The story about "Bolak Sonday" appeared in another form in Seven Stories From Seven Sisters: A Collection of Philippine Folktales, a Philippine American Women Writers and Artists publication, 1992. Copyright © 1992 by Cecilia Manguerra Brainard.

REGISTERED TRADEMARK—MARCA REGISTRADA

LIBRARY OF CONGRESS CATALOGING IN PUBLICATION DATA:
Brainard, Cecilia Manguerra.
When the rainbow goddess wept / Cecilia Manguerra Brainard.
p.    cm.
Rev. ed. of: Song of Yvonne. c1991.
ISBN 0-525-93821-4
1. World War, 1939–1945—Philippines—Fiction.    2. Girls—
Philippines—Fiction.    I. Brainard, Cecilia Manguerra. Song of
Yvonne.    II. Title.
PR9550.9.B73W48    1994
823—dc20                                                    94–4580
                                                                CIP

Printed in the United States of America
Set in Nuptial Script and Perpetua

Designed by Steven N. Stathakis

FOR

*Concepcion Cuenco Manguerra,*
*Mariano Flores Manguerra,*
*Mariano Jesus Manguerra, Jr., and*
*Lauren R. Brainard*

# $\mathcal{A}$cknowledgments

The author gratefully acknowledges the support of the California Arts Council, which made possible the writing of this book.

Special thanks go to my mother, Concepcion Cuenco, and my father, the late Mariano Flores Manguerra, guerrilleros and survivors of WWII, who told me endless stories about that war. For their firm support and belief in my work, thanks also go to my husband, Lauren R. Brainard; my brother, the late Mariano Jesus Manguerra, Jr.; my teacher, Leonardo Bercovici; my agents, Betsy Amster and Angela Miller; my editor, Rosemary Ahern; and Gloria F. Rodriguez.

# Part One

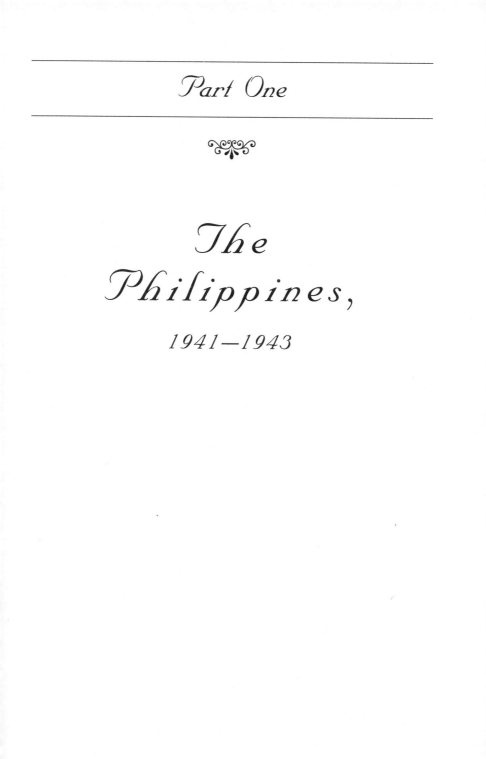

# The Philippines,
## 1941—1943

# Rumblings of War

❦

$\mathcal{M}$other Ignacia, fourth-grade teacher at Santa Teresa's School, made us pray for peace, and she kept our souls clean by taking us to weekly confession and Communion.

"If war should catch you with mortal sins in your souls, you will end up condemned, with chains, and you will roam the earth for all eternity," she warned.

It was a scary thought: I, Yvonne Macaraig, entangled with heavy chains, barred from heaven, barred even from purgatory, destined only to drag myself and the chains, and scare people away. There was a condemned soul who frightened the people in the house down the street from where we lived. He had borrowed fifty pesos and never paid it back, that's why his soul was not at peace.

To prepare us for the feast of the Immaculate Conception, Mother Ignacia talked about the Virgin Mary. "She did not have a speck of venial sin," Mother Ignacia said. "She was spotless, perfect. She did not commit concupiscence. Does anyone here know the meaning of the word *concupiscence?*''

No one replied. I, sitting right under her nose, avoided her eyes and looked down at my folded hands instead.

''Esperanza?'' Mother Ignacia's voice rang out. My first cousin stood up and looked around pleadingly. I stared back helplessly, wishing I had a clue to what this word meant.

''Not paying attention again!'' the nun barked. ''I'll have to talk to your mother about you.'' Backing up so she could survey her class better, Mother Ignacia said, ''Pay attention, class. *Com* means with, and *cupere* is to desire or to want—therefore,'' the nun pursed her lips, ''the word *concupiscence* means a strong abnormal desire. In short, class, it means lust. During your examination of conscience, girls, don't forget concupiscence. You don't want a bomb falling on your head and you ending up condemned. Reflect on the word *eternity*—that means forever and forever, not just a week, a year, or a hundred years—forever.''

For good measure, I included concupiscence in my list of sins. Esperanza and I had written down our sins on pieces of paper during recess. ''I'm not writing down concu-whatever-that-is on my list,'' Esperanza announced defiantly. ''I don't even know what it means.''

''It has to do with kissing and things like that,'' I ventured. ''You know, like what the lovers do in the back of the theater.''

''Then your father and mother commit sin all the time,'' Esperanza said. She was ten, a year older than I was.

I had to think about this for a while. ''But they're married,'' I countered, ''that doesn't count. Only those who aren't married commit that sin.''

''Mother Ignacia doesn't know anything. She's old and dried up. I hate her,'' Esperanza said.

''Anyway,'' I continued, ''I'm writing down concupiscence on my list. This is what I've got: bad thoughts, twice; late for Mass, once; talked and laughed in church, six; concupiscence, one.''

''You have to mention biting the host. That's bad,'' Esperanza said. ''You're always biting the host and one day blood will come out of that host. You'll see.''

Before Mother Ignacia herded us to the nearby church, and when Esperanza was not looking, I added "biting the host." There was no point, I figured, in taking chances.

There were two priests hearing confession: Father Ruiz, who was young and handsome and loved by the high school girls, and Father Odell, who was old with skin like parchment and lips that arched downward. We were in Father Odell's line.

Esperanza went in first and she stayed in the confessional for a long time. When she finished she stuck her tongue out. I entered the confessional and pulled my list out of my pocket. It was dark in there and I could not see my handwriting. I opened the door to allow a sliver of light in, but Father Odell shouted, "Shut that door!" I closed the door and stared into blackness. My list sat uselessly in my right hand and I finally crumpled it and stuffed it back into my pocket.

"Well?" Father Odell asked.

"Bless me, Father, for I have sinned, my last confession was last week. These are my sins," I began, then I panicked, completely forgetting what I had written down.

"Yes?" the priest said gruffly.

I cleared my throat. "Uh—these are my sins. I had bad thoughts, six times, and I was late for Mass, two times. I talked and laughed in church, three times; and I committed concupiscence—twice."

"What?" Father Odell shouted.

"Twice, Father, twice."

"You committed what?"

"Sins, I committed sins, Father."

"I know you committed sins. Who has not committed sins. All men commit sins. But you had bad thoughts, then what?"

"Oh, that—concupiscence—that means lust, Father."

There was a long silence and I thought the old priest had fallen asleep, when I heared a pained sigh. "For your penance, say five Hail Marys and three Our Fathers. Bad girl." Then he slammed shut the window.

I later learned that Father Odell had also called Esperanza a bad girl. "He's mean," we agreed. Esperanza, whom Mama accused of having "a mouth," continued, "And he even smells like a goat. I'll never confess to him ever again, even if I end up dragging chains for all eternity."

Papa and Mama and Lolo Peping—our grandfather—picked us up after school. "We had confession," I said, throwing my bag into the backseat of the '39 Ford, where Lolo Peping was dozing. He was our mothers' father. Because he was old and addled, he often called us by his daughters' names.

"Don't wake your Lolo Peping. How was confession?" Papa asked with one hand propping up the pipe in his mouth.

Esperanza rolled her eyes upward and slumped into the seat. "He called us bad girls."

Papa shook his head. "Girls, don't listen to everything the old priest tells you. You are good girls. Very good girls—well, most of the time you are good girls."

Esperanza and I giggled and sat back, feeling better about ourselves. "Are we going for a ride?" I asked.

"Papa has to see Max down at the pier," Mama said.

"Where the prostitutes are?" Esperanza asked.

"The ideas you girls get! It's just a bar, and they're bargirls," Mama insisted.

"Bitong says the girls there are good-time girls," Esperanza continued. "When he goes there, he pays for the drinks and the girls drink them fast and they have quick hands."

"That's enough, Esperanza. Nando, you'd better talk to Bitong about his language in front of the children; and he hasn't been taking care of the garden—that man is so lazy. He does nothing but sit around polishing his boots. Esperanza, I hope you stayed out of trouble today, your mother's growing gray hairs because of you."

"The child was good, Angeling. Did you hear? They went to confession today. Their souls are lily-white," Papa said.

"Mother Ignacia says we must be ready at all times because there's no telling when war will come to Ubec. It's all over the rest of the world—in China, in Europe, everywhere," I said.

"Nando, Nando, did you hear that? Is that sort of thing good for the children to hear?'' Mama said. ''There will be no war in Ubec. What do we have to do with these Hitlers and Churchills? Isn't that right, Nando? Why, General MacArthur himself said he'll be dining at the Manila Hotel this New Year's.''

Grandfather stirred and mumbled, ''MacArthur? Murderer—a quarter of a million Filipinos, dead.''

''Pa, we're talking about Douglas, not Arthur MacArthur. Go back to sleep,'' Mama said.

Lolo Peping leaned against the door, mumbled a few more words, and began snoring.

Papa continued, ''Angeling, it's all right. The children are old enough to know those things. There are those who say there won't be any war, but it is prudent to be prepared.''

Mama began sniveling. ''Oh, Nando, I just can't believe it. Everything's been fine—the baby, Lourdes and her business, even Papa's been better.''

''Lolo Peping bought another sack of rice and more dried fish and mongo beans so we won't go hungry if war breaks out,'' Esperanza added.

''Laydan says she doesn't know where to put all that food,'' I said, remembering the cook's lamentations as she tried to stuff the food into the downstairs storage room.

Mama began sobbing.

''Now, now, Angeling, don't get yourself upset. We'll deal with things as they come.''

Esperanza and I looked at each other, then glanced outside. Mama was ''expecting,'' so she was very moody. Papa drove down Mango Avenue, past the house of the American family, and we giggled when we caught sight of the ten-year-old American boy, an albino with pink skin and white hair.

''He has cat's eyes,'' Esperanza said, ''that's why he wears sunglasses. He's going away.''

''Oh?'' Mama said.

''Yes, the American family's moving away in case war comes to Ubec. Too bad, I wanted to see his eyes up close.''

We stared at him until Papa turned around Fuente Osmeña plaza.

The huge dry fountain pointed at the cloudless sky. Vendors were arranging their wares around the grounds for the afternoon and evening promenaders. Papa continued down Jones Avenue toward the sea. He stopped by Monay's Bakery to buy sweet bread aptly called Pan Monay, which Esperanza and I happily gnawed on. Papa then drove past the old Spanish fort to the wharf.

Papa was an engineering professor at the University of Ubec, and he liked to teach. This afternoon, he lectured, "In olden days, Ubecans traded with Siamese, Chinese, and Borneans. The people lived in huts along the shoreline, right along here."

"When the Spaniards came they built that fort and the old church," I said.

"Very good, Yvonne," Papa said. "And when did the Spaniards arrive in Ubec? Esper, do you know the answer?"

"Ah . . . Magellan arrived in 1521."

"Excellent!" Papa said.

"He was Portuguese," I added, "but he sailed for the Spanish flag."

"Angeling, did you hear that? These girls are genuises!" Papa exclaimed.

Esperanza and I smiled at each other. Papa did that often just to make us feel good.

Outside, piers jutted out into the sea and ships rocked to and fro as the waves lapped the mussel-encrusted pier posts. The air was salty with a hint of tar. There were seedy restaurants, and Mama said you would get cholera from those places. Small hotels and bars lined the street. Papa slowed down and stopped in front of a bar lit up with colored lights. A huge red neon sign blinked above: SLAPSY MAXIE'S.

Sailors streamed in and out of the bar. Heavily rouged girls in Carmen Miranda-type dresses clung to the men's arms. No sooner had Papa switched off the motor than Nida, a big woman, burst out of the bar and rushed to the Ford. "Nando! Missus! Long time no see. Come and see the addition. There's a Norwegian ship in town so we're busier than hell, but I'm glad to see you." Nida wore a bright pink dress with a hibiscus print. She had ample breasts and hips. Nida had what people called, "a past," meaning she was once the mistress of the Chinese restaurateur Ong King Kin.

"Is Max in, Nida?" Papa asked. Max and Papa had met in America where he went to school and where Max boxed and drove a cab. Gadamit—Max liked to say, just like a New Yorker—gadamit to hell!

"He went to get more rum. We ran out."

"I have to talk to Max about something."

"Is it about the Japs invading? Max says MacArthur has formed a guerrilla regiment," Nida said.

"Just to be on the safe side," Papa said, and Mama burst into tears.

"War—oh, Nida, what'll we do if there's war?" Mama said.

"Now, now, Missus, I didn't mean to get you all riled up. It may never happen. Who'd want Ubec, anyway? This stinking little city? Manila maybe, because it's the capital and all, but Ubec? Don't worry about a thing. It's December, Angeling, we should be thinking of Christmas."

Grandfather suddenly woke up. "War? War? Damned Americans. Kill every single Cano. Butchers."

Nida stared at us with an expression combining bewilderment and amusement.

"Oh, Pa, go back to sleep, it's nothing," Mama said.

"War is a pit toilet," Lolo Peping continued. "I saw the Pasig River turn red from blood; I saw the damned Canos slaughter Filipinos like pigs—"

"Pa, that was forty years ago. It's 1941, the Americans are our friends now," Mama said.

"Don't be foolish, child. Americans are tricky people. That Cano Dewey told Aguinaldo they'd help him fight the Spaniards, and what happened? They betrayed him, that's what happened. And they tricked the Macabebes that way—Little Macs, the Canos called them. Damned traitors, may they rot in hell for turning against their own brothers."

"Instead of hell, it would be better, Lolo, if they're condemned forever and ever. They can drag chains for all eternity," Esperanza said. She nudged me and we giggled silently.

"Nando, isn't it time for us to go? It's almost suppertime. Poor Laydan's meal will turn cold," Mama said.

Papa started the car. "I guess we'll go, Nida. Just tell Max we came by."

"I'll tell him to see you," Nida said.

We lived on Colon Street in the old section of Ubec. Our two-story house cut the huge property in two. On one side was a courtyard with a stone well, a magnificent centenary flame tree, and flowering frangipanis and hibiscus bushes. A verandah with potted plants and an over-hanging bougainvillea vine ran along the full length of the house. The bedrooms, dining room, living room, and library were located upstairs, while the downstairs area and the other side of the property were work and sleeping quarters for the servants. An outdoor dirty kitchen with a wood-burning stove jutted out as a separate wing downstairs.

Ever since my grandmother died years ago, my mother and aunt had been taking care of my grandfather. He sometimes had the notion that my grandmother was alive and he would wander around Ubec searching for her. This afternoon, however, he was merely pulling weeds around the flame tree.

The maid, Lupita, who was keeping an eye on grandfather, sat with us around the stone well. Lupita came from an island called Payan, which virtually disappeared at high tide. The women's favorite pastime there was passing the fine comb through one another's hair to search for lice. Lupita liked Ubec, which she called a "big city." She especially enjoyed the vaudeville shows and the movies—she was crazy about Betty Grable and Susan Magalona. She also liked the radio soap operas, and the Friday evening Amateur Hour held at Fuente Osmeña.

"The well's due for a good cleaning," Lupita commented. "Probably next month."

"I can still see the little fish down there," I said.

"Catfish." Esperanza picked up a pebble and dropped it into the well.

"Don't do that, you'll dirty it up, and we'll be drinking the water and everything," I said.

"Last time they cleaned the well, they found a dead frog," Esperanza said.

"That's disgusting talk, Esper," Lupita said.

"I like it when they clean the well," I said. "Last time the men found some blue and white little vases. They were real old with Chinese scribbles. I still have one."

"I have mine," Esperanza said. "I put flowers in it. It's in front of the altar."

"Bah, you should pray, Esperanza. You're so naughty," Lupita said.

We had not noticed that Grandfather had moved toward us. "Look!" he shouted, pointing at the monkey chained to a bamboo pole. Momoy, as we called him, was grooming himself by meticulously picking imaginary fleas from his stomach. "Look!" Grandfather said once more. "Before man sinned, he was innocent, like that. Man's original sin wasn't eating the forbidden fruit; it was Cain's murder of his brother. Yes, indeedy, that was man's first sin." He nodded several times, then he looked at the sky and began counting.

The three of us stared up to see what had caught Grandfather's attention. There was nothing unusual, just the clear blue sky. I studied Grandfather, who was pointing upward, now counting in the hundreds.

"What's he doing?" Lupita whispered.

"He's counting," Esperanza said.

"The stars," I ventured.

"Could be," Esperanza said.

"But it's daytime. There are no stars up there." Lupita appeared puzzled.

"Lolo," Esperanza called out, and Grandfather paused and looked at her. "Are you counting the stars?"

"No, *hija*, I'm counting all the dead, but you have just made me lose count. Now I have to start all over again." He looked up and started from one all over again.

"He's crazy." Lupita scratched her head as Lolo Peping resumed counting.

"Don't call our grandfather crazy," Esperanza said.

"He's certainly different."

"Eccentric, that's what he is, eccentric," Esperanza declared.

"That's right, eccentric," I added, but later when Esperanza and I were heading for Sanny's store, I said, "Maybe Lolo Peping does have loose screws."

Esperanza paused and in a grown-up voice said, "I've been observing people for a long time now, and most act like their screws are loose. What that means is that Lolo Peping is no different from them and is normal."

"Oh," I replied, thoroughly impressed with this logic.

Sanny's sari-sari store was a delightful place with everything anyone could imagine. Sanny kept it well stocked with standard supplies like rice, corn, coarse salt, mongo beans, agar-agar, and spices. She covered the walls with brooms, kites, coconut husks, coconut shells, woven mats, magazines, and periodicals. She also had forbidden cakes—fluffy pink ones that Mama swore would give us stomachache if not cholera. There were lemon drops, rice and corn cakes, salted plum seeds, and little paper and wooden toys that we could buy for a centavo or two.

While I wandered about, Esperanza went straight to the shopkeeper. "A box of Guitar matches, Sanny," Esperanza said.

"What you need matches for? Matches no good for children," Sanny replied. She was Japanese, around twenty-five years old, with a six-month-old baby girl called Sumi. Sanny had difficulty pronouncing some words. She was beautiful, with a lovely oval face and petal-smooth skin.

Without hesitating Esperanza lied, "Mama needs matches."

Outside I asked, "What's that for?"

"You'll find out," she replied.

Along the way, she stopped under a lomboy tree and picked up some leaves. We went straight to the yard, and she gestured for me to be quiet. I checked on the grown-ups having merienda on the verandah and looked back at Esperanza. "What are you doing?" I whispered.

She was rolling a leaf into a small cigar. "I've seen Laydan do this," she said, referring to our old cook, who spoke in a monotone.

When Esperanza finished, she pulled out the matches from her pocket and lit the cigar. My eyes grew big, certain that Papa, Mama,

Lourdes, or their visitor, Max, would notice us. But they were engrossed in their talk—about war as usual—and Esperanza took in a big breath and blew smoke out her nose. I was impressed. "Let me try," I said, grabbing the cigar. The smoke grated my throat making me cough.

"You don't know anything, do you?" Esperanza said, but she had a greenish cast to her skin.

"I'm dizzy," I said.

"I feel like throwing up," Esperanza admitted. She snuffed out the cigar on the earth and, closing our eyes, we sat quietly to catch our breath. We could hear the grown-ups talking.

"So, Max, will Ubec fight to the finish?" Lourdes asked. She was short and fat, with a faint smell of cinnamon. She was younger than Mama, although people often mistook her for being older. Mama was taller and more glamorous. Lourdes said she grew old from the cross she bore. What she meant was her husband, who had left her when Esperanza was only a baby. Actually, Mama said it was a blessing in disguise that he took off with another woman because my aunt became very successful in the catering business she was forced into. My aunt had a good business mind just like my grandmother.

"To the end, Lourdes," Max said, smiling broadly. He had his nose broken twice in America, and it leaned to one cheek. Although he looked fierce, Max had an easy smile and laugh. There were few Filipinos in America when Papa was there, and when he and Max ran into each other, they became friends. Papa returned to the Philippines while Max stayed in America, hoping to make it big as a boxer. He never did and he eventually returned to the Philippines to settle down. When he married Nida, everyone was sure the marriage wouldn't last. Nida wasn't exactly the sweet and passive Filipina that Max had dreamt of back in the States. But as things turned out, Nida and Max were happy together.

"Maybe we should burn the city like the ancient Filipinos did when the Spaniards were attacking. Didn't Chieftain Tupas and his men send the women and children to the hills while they torched the village?" my aunt continued.

"They lost anyway. But I suppose they didn't want to turn over an intact village and port to the Spaniards," Papa said.

"Spaniards, British, Americans—they come to Ubec," Mama said.

She put her cup of chocolate down. "You'd think Ubec was the wealthiest city on earth instead of a sleepy seaside place. What do we have that these foreigners want?"

"Ubec is part of the Philippines, and the Philippines is strategically important," Papa said.

Lourdes waved her right hand, indicating it was all a lot of foolishness, but the men continued the conversation.

"It'll happen," Max said. "Quezon's still hoping the gadam Japs will skip the Philippines, but they're in China, Formosa, Korea. And the Japs aren't real nice. Co-Prosperity for East Asians is their slogan. Co-prosperity my ass—ay, pardon my language," Max said.

"People believe the slogans because Westerners take advantage in Asia. Europeans treated the Chinese like dogs, in China, mind you. Not that the Japanese treated the Chinese better."

"We're ready. MacArthur just has to give the word. We'll be kicking gadam Jap ass if they try to kick us around. Hell, I wasn't a boxer for nothing," Max continued.

"Max, Max, try Lourdes's empanada," Mama said. "All this talk of war. There won't be any war. And if the Japanese did have the nerve to attack, why the Americans will wipe them out in no time at all. The USAFFE's ready; the Armed Forces have modern planes—"

"Angeling, I heard the airplanes are antiques, American rejects; and the Filipinos in the USAFFE look like Boy Scouts in their short pants," Lourdes said.

"Boy Scouts?" Mama asked, incredulously.

"I saw a picture of them, young boys, in short pants."

"Ay, *madre mia*, you mean our future depends on Boy Scouts? Maybe Papa's right after all, to stock up on all that food."

Lourdes nodded.

"Boy Scouts," they cried in unison, and the sisters chuckled as they shook their heads.

# First Casualties

❧

The Royal Theater, one of three movie theaters in Ubec, was second-run, with a weary-looking woman in wooden slippers—the usherette—collecting the orange tickets. People said half the rats in Ubec lived in the theater. Fat rats with long wiry tails scuttled under the seats to fight over spilled soft drinks and discarded snacks. Most of the seats were broken and the roof leaked so that during rainy season, the general admission section flooded. From the loge, one could see the movie reflected upside down on the wet floor.

The Royal had been first-run, with crimson velvet drapes and snappy uniformed ushers. Mama and Lourdes still talked of the premier showing of Vicente Salumbides's film *Besame!* there. But in 1941, the Royal showed two-year-old Hollywood and Tagalog films, and the audience rattled in the theater like bones in a box. Usually, only the loge and balcony were occupied, by lovers and university students cutting classes. Once a year, though, over the Christmas holidays, the Royal presented a live performance by the Chinese Acrobatic Troupe, and the house was full.

This December, Esperanza and I skipped toward the Royal to see the acrobatic troupe. We had twenty-five centavos in our pockets and we stopped by Sanny's sari-sari store for some snacks.

Sanny and her husband moved into Ubec four years ago, and they opened a little store that burned down during their first rainy season in Ubec—lightning struck it down, which was pure bad luck, everyone agreed. The bank wouldn't lend them money to rebuild because they were foreigners and there was no telling when they'd return to Japan, leaving their debt unpaid. Sanny and her husband were in a desperate position until Papa lent them money. "They'll pay," he had said. So Sanny minded the store, while her husband traveled from barrio to barrio, buying and selling. They paid off their debt immediately.

Sanny was finishing feeding her baby, Sumi. We cooed at Sumi, a good-natured little girl with a round face and hair sticking straight up in the air.

"We're going to the Royal, can we take Sumi?" I asked, after we bought some nougats and lemon drops.

Sanny, whose husband was often away, was only too glad to have her hands free. She asked, "What showing? Is it *Daragang Bukid* again?"

"No, *Dalagang Bukid* is gone. The acrobats are here," I said.

"They good," she said as she wiped the baby's face with a clean rag. She handed Sumi to me and we hurried to the theater. Esperanza acted as though she did not care, but I knew she was jealous that I had Sumi.

We sat in the front row of the loge section, with feet raised to avoid the rats, and we waited in giddy anticipation for the show to begin. Sitting on my lap, Sumi sucked her thumb quietly as she looked around.

I pried her mouth open and checked her gums. "Look, Sumi's got three teeth," I said. "Sumi's cute," I continued, stroking the baby's fat cheeks.

"She's a dumb baby," Esperanza replied.

"She's not dumb. She's cute."

People shushed us. Soon the curtains parted, the drums rolled, and a one-eyed man with a raspy voice announced that the show would begin. One by one the performers appeared on stage. Jugglers threw half a dozen balls in the air. Three child acrobats bent backward with their heads peeking between their legs, making them look like four-legged crabs. Exotic Chinese ladies with floor-length braided hair, twisted and contorted their bodies as they balanced glasses full of water on their heads, hands, and feet. Clowns ran in circles, pretending there was a fire.

Later, a woman dressed in a tight red-sequined dress walked to the center of the stage and bowed. The lights dimmed. She strutted to a fake brick wall and faced it, her back to the audience. Quick as a bolt of lightning, a man's arms were around the woman's back. The hands caressed and stroked her, moving up and down, traveling to her buttocks. The audience laughed and Esperanza giggled loudly.

Sumi rubbed her eyes and began squirming. I jiggled my knees to pacify her. "It's not that funny. What's the matter?" I asked Esperanza.

"It's just a trick. Take a look, see it's just her arms. She's wrapped her arms around herself."

True enough, when the woman twirled around, she was indeed all alone. She bowed while the audience clapped and hooted. Some men hooked their fingers into their mouths and whistled. Sumi grew more restless.

"What's wrong with her?" Esperanza asked, pointing her chin at Sumi.

"I don't know."

Sumi whimpered louder.

"Shut her up, people are complaining," Esperanza said.

"I'm trying." I jostled the baby faster, but Sumi began crying.

"Give her to me!" Esperanza grabbed the child and Sumi screamed.

People glared at us. "What's that baby doing here?" an angry woman asked. "Get that brat out of here!"

We started to leave. Near the doorway, the baby howled and

Esperanza pinched her arm. "Why did you do that?" I wailed. "That's mean, and you'll have to confess that."

"She's bad! She's Japanese and Japanese are bad."

Sanny shook her head at the shrieking baby. "I don't know why she cry and cry. No good to have baby cry, neh? Brings bad things."

We quickly left before she noticed the pinch mark on the baby.

After counting the dead once again, Grandfather walked by the dirty kitchen and he sniffed Lourdes's fish rellenos. He stopped right then and there. A deep furrow formed between his eyebrows and he became silent and pensive. During suppertime he spoke to my father:

"Nando, pay attention, the Japanese have bombed Clark Air Base; MacArthur and the USAFFE are racing to Corregidor and Bataan. It is only a matter of time, Manila will fall, and the Japanese will cut off all supplies to MacArthur and the USAFFE until they surrender or die."

Papa, sucking thoughtfully on his pipe, replied, "The Americans won't let that happen, Peping, there are thousands of American soldiers there. The Japanese have already bombed Pearl Harbor, the Americans won't allow them to do any more damage."

"Nando, you are like my own son. I know you have great affection for these Americans, but don't be naive. The Japanese will take over and the Canos won't be able to lift a finger about the matter. And you know why? Because they've deployed most of their forces in Europe, that's why. It'll be a while before they recover in Asia, and when they do they'll need our help. But right now, consider Luzon lost. The Visayas, including Ubec, will go. Mindanao will be the last stronghold against the Japanese. Japan has Northern Asia; America must hang on to the southern part. Nando, pay attention, when the Japanese come to Ubec, they'll go after you."

"I'm a teacher, Peping, not a politician or soldier."

"You're an engineer professor, and trained in America at that. You not only know a lot about the existing roads and bridges, you can help them build new ones," Lolo Peping said.

"If they come, the guerrilla regiment's ready."

"Good. Guerrilla warfare will be the only solution. But be careful of those Canos. The thing with Americans is they watch out for themselves first. Don't believe all that malarkey about brotherhood and equality, always ask if this or that benefits Americans, Filipinos, or both, before you go into it. Keep in mind that the Americans lied to us. A mango doesn't turn into an avocado. They said they'd help us get rid of the Spaniards, that America would honor Philippine independence, and what did the Canos do? They betrayed us! Once we just about beat the Spaniards, they turned against us," Grandfather said.

To further illustrate his distrust of Americans, Lolo Peping told us what happened in the island of Samar at the turn of the century. The Americans, who took over the town, arrested and imprisoned all men over eighteen years old. The prisoners had to work for the American soldiers. Unable to tolerate the repression, the men with the help of the townspeople revolted one Sunday morning. Using machetes, bamboo lances, whatever weapon they could find, they attacked the surprised Americans, killing more than half the company. In reprisal, Brigadier General Jacob H. Smith ordered Major Littleton W. T. Waller to kill all Filipinos, saying: "The more you burn and kill, the better you will please me." Since the rebels had fled to the hills, the Americans methodically tortured and killed the civilians. They burned houses, destroyed crops and livestock until at last they ferreted out the rebels. Then they killed them all.

Grandfather said that during the Philippine-American War, the Americans killed 16,000 Filipino soldiers and 200,000 civilians.

All the talk of war made us late in setting up our nativity set, or *belen* as we called it, but eventually the men dragged an old table into the living room and we spread a green tablecloth over it. The servants brought in buckets of sand. Very carefully we spread the sand over the tablecloth. Mama placed potted plants around the table and Lourdes had the idea to place a large mirror on one part of the table. We covered the edge of the mirror so the portion that showed looked like the lake of our village. We arranged the nativity figures in this setting. Mary and Joseph stared at the empty crib in the center. The three kings were walking toward the manger. The shepherds stood near the lake. We placed the chickens, donkeys, and a cow in the manger, and we scattered the townsfolk here and there.

Lourdes and Mama decided our belen could use some palm trees. The year before we had made palm trees from green and white crepe paper glued to bamboo sticks. Esperanza and I volunteered to buy the crepe paper at Sanny's store.

She smiled when we walked in. "What you two want today?" she asked. Sanny used rice powder on her face and piled her dark hair up on her head. She was really very pretty. Once she put on a Japanese kimono, just to show Esperanza and me how it looked, and she showed us how the robe closed, and how to tie the wide belt. I even got to try on her wooden slippers.

"Crepe paper, Sanny. We're going to make palm trees for our belen," I answered.

"Ah, parm trees," she repeated. She was carrying Sumi, who hid her face from us. "Sumi cry and cry arr night," Sanny said, as she wiped off the baby's drool.

"Give her whiskey," Esperanza advised.

"She'll get drunk," I said.

"Nah, Laydan said whiskey puts crying babies to sleep."

"Raydan say that? Raydan, ord and wise. Ah, maybe I give Sumi sake, neh?" Sanny concluded.

We bought our crepe paper and bamboo sticks, and we hung around for a few minutes to tickle Sumi, who only screamed.

"Brat," Esperanza said, when we left the store.

"She's just a baby. Besides she doesn't feel good."

"Little Japanese brat," Esperanza insisted.


On Christmas Eve, we learned that MacArthur and the USAFFE had retreated to Corregidor and Bataan. While Mama and Lourdes carried on with the cooking and Christmas preparations, they occasionally broke down and wept.

Esperanza dropped a figurine on the glass lake, which only got the grown-ups more excited. We found another piece of glass, replaced the lake, and we spent our time on the verandah, waiting for the procession.

A bit later we saw a trail of people led by an acolyte no bigger than ourselves. The boy was furiously ringing a silver bell. Behind him were the priest and four men carrying a wooden stand with the statue of the infant Jesus in a crib. A dozen people streamed behind. We ran to our mothers and announced, "They're here." They handed us fifty centavos each and we raced to the door. We handed the money to the acolyte, while the priest nodded in acknowledgment. The procession then moved on to the next house. Leaning against the door, we watched the group move away like a slow and lazy snake.

At dusk, when we tuned in to our regular soap opera, *The Triumphs of Love*, we heard instead MacArthur announcing over the crackling radio: ". . . to save the metropolitan area from the ravages of attack . . . Manila is declared an open city . . . In order that no excuse may be given for a possible mistake, the American High Commander, the Commonwealth Government, and all combatant military installations will be withdrawn . . . The Municipal Government will continue to function with its police force, reinforced by constabulary troops . . . Citizens are requested to maintain obedience to constituted authorities and continue the normal processes of business."

People gathered in clusters along the sidewalks to discuss these developments. "Goddamn Japs," they muttered.

The grown-ups sent us to bed at seven so we could rest for the midnight Mass. We lay there for a long time, listening to the women clinging to the hope that the Japanese would ignore Ubec, that Manila was all they wanted, Papa saying as calmly as he could, "When the time comes, we may have to evacuate."

We listened until their voices faded into murmurs and what we heard were the occasional patterings in the crawl space above. Esperanza said there were dwarves living up there. I said they were mice, but she insisted that she had had things disappear and reappear, that the dwarves teased her. We talked about Christmas, our new dresses with ruffles and black tights and black patent shoes, about the different nativity sets we had seen, the most beautiful being the one at nearby Casa Gorordo with Bathsheba bathing near the well and King David staring at her from his palace window. We discussed the pig that had been slaughtered earlier, how Bitong had slit its belly, how Laydan collected its blood in a huge metal basin, how they had shoved the bamboo pole from the pig's behind to its mouth, and how they twirled it over the burning coals.

At last we fell asleep. I dreamt we had a picnic in Talisay. It was after a strong typhoon and Lolo Peping brought Esperanza and me to the seashore. Grandfather was dressed in his old military uniform, complete with sword and an antique pistol. We poked through the kelp searching for something unusual. We looked for dead fish, sea urchins, fat black eels, driftwood of the most fascinating shapes, or perhaps even a dead whale. After walking a great distance, we found tiny red crabs crawling on the sand. We walked on and found ourselves near a cemetery where we spotted a human skull. It sat on the white sand, so perfectly white itself that it was only the light and shadow pattern created by the sunlight streaming through the eyesockets that allowed us to recognize it.

In my dream I exclaimed, "Someone drowned!"

"No, *hija*," Grandfather replied, picking up the skull and turning it in the direction of the cemetery on the hill. "The sea rose and the waves dug this up. Let's go bury the poor man's skull."

The three of us climbed the hill and I stared with fascination at the crosses and tombstones knocked over by the winds and rain. There were exposed coffins and seaweed scattered around like slimy brown garlands. We found a spot under an acacia tree where we dug a hole. We buried the skull, and prayed aloud for the repose of the poor soul.

I was drenched with sweat when Papa awoke us. There was a certain tension in the air that I could not quite pinpoint; it was akin to the strangeness before a typhoon. In church, Esperanza and I fidgeted as we stared at the giant nativity set by the side of the altar. It had lifesize statues and Mary gazed lovingly at the baby Jesus, who was in His crib at last. Joseph stood by holding his staff. The lovely angel dangled from the ceiling. The pieces, the plants, the lights were positioned where they should have been; everything should have been perfect, but something still wasn't right.

The Mass was long, tedious. Father Odell spoke about God the

Father's greatest gift to mankind, His only begotten Child, and he talked about Christmas as the holiest of days, the day when we should all love one another. It took forever to receive Communion because the lines were long, and even the men known to keep mistresses received Holy Communion. But at last it ended and we went home.

The dining table was laid out with the *media noche* banquet—ham, roasted pig, blood soup, fish rellenos, sansrivals, leche flan. While Mama fussed over the table, Papa got the bowl full of candies and coins for the traditional *sabwag*. He instructed Esperanza and me to get ready, then he threw the coins and candies on the floor. We scrambled for them, and my cousin boasted that she had more. Later, while chewing nougats, we hung star lanterns out on the verandah. We were balanced on chairs when suddenly the sky turned bright red like a brilliant sunset. For a moment, we held our breath and stared at the awesome sight. We looked around—there was a fire not too far away. Flames leaped up to the eerie red sky. Dark smoke billowed up. For a long while I stared in dreamlike fascination, even after Esperanza cried, "It's a fire!"

The grown-ups rushed to the verandah. After a quick survey Papa said, "It's coming from the corner." He went out to investigate while Mama alerted the servants in case the wind blew the fire our way. Lourdes ran around packing some necessities in case we had to leave our house.

The fire grew stronger still, and the smoke remained thick and fine ash fell on our faces. I recalled the ill flavor of my dream, and my breathing became shallow while my heart knocked violently.

The firemen arrived and the people gathered on the streets. There was much commotion and shouting—"Sanny's store . . . impossible . . . too hot . . ."

Papa, grimy with soot, slammed the front door and his voice trembled with anger. "Sanny and Sumi are dead!" When he regained his composure he told us that the firemen found an empty kerosene can near the store; someone had started the fire on purpose.

"But why, Nando? Why?" Mama asked.

Shaking his head, he replied, "There's been talk that Sanny's husband is a Japanese spy."

Inside the house, Esperanza skulked about in embarrassed silence. "I didn't mean to pinch her so hard," she finally said. "But she was bad, screaming like that. She was."

I could barely hear her words as I stared at the Jesus in our belen. *He* was in His crib; Sumi wasn't. Then the tears formed and blurred my vision of the nativity set.

# *The Visitor*

◈

*A* woman much younger and prettier than Lourdes visited us one day. Her eyes were red from crying, and she carried a wicker basket filled with clothes.

"I'm Tecla. Excuse my presence," she began, "but you see I am the common-law wife of Mario." Casting glances at Lourdes, she said, "I know you are his church wife, so it is fitting that you know that Mario's out there in Corregidor with MacArthur."

She went on to tell us that the Japanese had occupied Manila and that MacArthur and the USAFFE were running out of supplies. "They're starving," Tecla wailed. "Mario's out there, starving."

My aunt, who was Mario's rightful wife, found herself in the awkward position of having to console her husband's mistress. "Well," she said with great dignity, "don't worry too much about it. He'll get out. The Americans won't abandon them. They'll bring their bombers and more men and drive the Japanese away," Lourdes said.

Tecla cried some more and said Manila was a disaster. The incessant shelling of Corregidor was deafening. Japanese were everywhere; soldiers filled the sidewalks; Japanese had taken over desk jobs at city hall; Japanese teachers were starting to teach children Nippongo.

"*Madre mia*," Mama exclaimed. "That will be the day, when the children speak Nippongo."

The mistress looked at Esperanza. "Mario and I were never blessed with a child," she wailed. "And now he's going to die."

To calm her down, Lourdes gave her some hot chocolate and spoke to her in a soft cajoling tone. Before Tecla left, the two women hugged and pecked each other's cheeks.

Tecla was barely out the door when Mama turned to my aunt and told her she was a fool. Lourdes merely shrugged her shoulders. "I look at it this way, Angeling, that poor woman had to put up with Mario's womanizing and drinking for more years than I did."

Esperanza became morose soon after the woman's visit. My cousin refused to play with me, running outside to the flame tree instead, staring up at the clouds, or playing with the turtle that waded up and down the gutter near the dirty kitchen.

I left her alone, minding my own business, but finally I sat beside her on the huge branch of the flame tree. "It doesn't matter," I said, saying the most consoling words I could come up with.

"I hate him and I hate her," she said. "I hate everything."

"I hate them too."

We sighed.

"Mama cried," she said. "And it's all because of them."

"I hate them," I repeated.

"I'll show you something," she said in a conspiratorial tone. "C'mon."

She climbed down the tree, and passed by the dirty kitchen where my aunt was making four dozen lumpias for the Club Filipino. Esperanza peeped in and whispered, "Mama's busy, we'll be fine." She then led the way to her mother's bedroom.

"Be quiet," Esperanza instructed. "Lock the door after you."

I did.

"Cross your heart and hope to die," she said.

After I drew a cross on my heart with my right finger, she walked to the dresser and pulled it open. I caught a glimpse of my aunt's silk underwear. Esperanza dug under the clothing and pulled out a bundle of letters bound by a green satin ribbon.

"What is it?" I asked.

"Shhh," she said, as she carefully untied the ribbon. She riffled through and selected one envelope. She pulled out a photo which she displayed to me.

I stared at the image of a man and woman standing side by side. It looked like a lot of other old studio pictures, with a fake backdrop of a bridge and stream.

"My father!" she said, triumphantly.

I realized that it was my aunt after all, when she was young. She wore a native dress and beamed happily beside a handsome man who appeared equally joyous.

As quickly as she had whipped the picture out, Esperanza put it away. She stared at herself at the mirror. "I'm ugly. I look just like a sparrow," she said with a sigh. She opened another drawer and pulled out a pair of scissors. "Look," she announced, "pinking shears."

We found scraps of cloth in the remnants pile, and taking turns, made pretty zigzag edges with the scissors.

I had the scissors when Esperanza went to the standing mirror. She stared at her face for a while, then she ordered, "Cut my hair."

I stared at her with my mouth unhinged.

"Cut it!"

I shook my head, horrified at the thought.

"I'll do it then." She grabbed the pinking shears from me and began cutting her bangs. She undid her braids and cut her hair. Long dark locks fell to the wooden floor. Her hair was terribly uneven so she got the regular scissors and tried to straighten her hair.

I swiftly got into the spirit of things and suggested areas that she had missed. When there was very little hair to cut, Esperanza wanted to cut mine, but I ran out of the room. My aunt saw me. "What are you girls up to?'' she shouted. I didn't answer, and a look of horror crossed her face. She quickly traced my steps. I heard a loud scream that echoed all the way to the yard.

Esperanza got the hairbrush—ten times, right across her behind. She screamed like a pig being slaughtered, but acted as though she didn't care after the spanking. My aunt burst into tears every time she saw Esperanza. "Her hair looks gnawed by a rat," she wailed. Mama said Ramon the hairdresser would fix everything tomorrow, and not to worry about a thing.

Deep in trouble, Esperanza and I and stayed out of the grown-ups' way by hanging around the dirty kitchen.

We watched Bitong polishing his boots. Papa had given him his old brown boots, and even though the boots were too big, Bitong stuffed the toes with paper and he cherished the boots with all his heart. Bitong carefully applied the brown wax. He rubbed it in, then he spat on the leather and rubbed some more, and he polished and buffed until his boots shone.

"What're you doing, Bitong?" Esperanza asked.

"What do you think?" Bitong replied. He was nineteen, thin like a string bean.

"Are you going to Slapsy Maxie's later?"

"Too expensive."

"The Big Dance then?" Esperanza continued.

Ignoring her, Bitong held out his boots to admire them. "There now, they're clean."

"Are you going to put them on and pretend you're a cowboy? We saw you yesterday; you had your boots on and you pretended to shoot Momoy."

"I did not," Bitong said, clearly embarrassed.

"Yes, you did. Didn't he, Yvonne? We saw you. You were walking funny, like you wanted to go to the bathroom or something, right near the monkey."

"They're clean," Bitong said.

"You missed a spot, Bitong." Esperanza planted her grimy finger on Bitong's boot, leaving a perfect fingerprint.

Bitong held up his boot to catch the light. "All I see's the dirt you left."

"Right there, right there," Esperanza continued, marking up Bitong's boots some more.

"Stop it, Esper. You're making them dirty," Bitong complained. He gathered his things, hugged his boots to his chest, and left the kitchen.

Esperanza stuck her tongue at him, and she began marching around the rough-hewn table. Round and round she went, increasing her tempo with each round. Laydan finally told her to stop because she was getting dizzy. The cook was frying a slab of liver and it sizzled and blood bubbled up and oozed out. Esperanza and I made a face at the liver.

Laydan said, "Liver-strengthens-the-blood."

"I like my blood the way it is," Esperanza said as she sat on the bench and took out something from her pocket. "Yvonne," she called.

I sat beside her. Esperanza held up a needle so it glinted. "Watch this," she said.

She licked the needle and inserted it into the skin of her left palm. After poking it in and out four times, she tugged at the needle, which strained against her skin. A tiny bit of blood appeared, the sight of which made my stomach curdle. "See how nice my blood looks," she said. "I need to toughen my skin some more so it won't bleed." Yanking out the needle, she handed it to me. I shook my head.

"Scared?" she said, knowing very well that I was.

"It's simple, even the monkey can do it. You lick the needle so its clean, otherwise you'll get cholera, then you start sewing. Just pretend it's our sampler. I can sew my fingers together."

I stared at the needle, mesmerized by the shining metal.

"Try it sometime," she said, putting the needle away.

"Esperanza, you act like the Evil Man of Sakadna sometimes," Laydan said. "You two eat your liver and I'll tell you about my dream."

"No, not your dream again, Laydan. That's boring. Tell us a story instead," Esperanza said.

"If you want a story, you have to listen to the dream. Eat your liver and rice," grumbled Laydan. She was ancient, even older than

Grandfather. She used to be an epic singer, but according to her, the gods and goddesses had punished her, and now she could only speak in a lifeless voice. Laydan had learned quickly from her teacher, Inuk, and she had entertained the notion that she could be as great as he was. For her vanity, the gods took away her gift. But her stories were still good.

We shoved the dreaded pieces of liver around our plates and watched the fire in the wood-burning stove.

Old Laydan said, "I dreamed I was in a forest. I came across a mountain spring, flowing sideways from a cliff. I cupped my hands to collect water and taste it. There's nothing sweeter than spring water. Then a strange thing happened—I found this mouth in my hands. It was wide open, singing the epic about the hero Tuwaang. I was appalled, but the mouth said, 'Laydan, I've waited for you long enough.' "

"What does the dream mean?" I asked.

"It doesn't mean anything. She probably had a stomachache and had a bad dream," Esperanza said.

Laydan paused and stared at the smoke from the wood-burning stove. She was a stocky woman with sparse gray hair anchored into a skimpy knot by a tortoise shell comb. Her neck was thick and fleshy from goiter. Laydan's broad and dark face reminded me of a mask. It had little expression and had the same quality as her flat voice. She said, "Dreams are messages from the gods. My dream feels like a good omen. The deities are telling me that I will come across something important. I will discover something."

"Like gold?" Esperanza said with interest.

"No, child, nothing like that. It means learning something."

"Like what, Laydan?" I asked.

She stopped to think for a moment, then replied, "The great epic singer Inuk often said to me, 'Laydan, become the epic.' I would like to understand his words."

"But how could you become the epic?" I continued.

"I don't know. Perhaps because of my pride, I did not allow myself to become the epic. I was too busy being the epic singer. And perhaps because I could sing a few epics, I thought I was important. I became vain—vanity is a sin."

"Killing is bad. It's worse than vanity or concupiscence," Esperanza said. "Maybe your gods will punish the Japanese for what they're doing."

"Don't talk that way or else the gods will hear you and get angry."

"Tell your story, Laydan. I'm getting bored," Esperanza said.

Laydan held her breath. Her eyes took on a faraway look as she began.

In the beginning, there existed the Sky, the Water, and a magnificent bird. There were no islands and continents then, and the bird had to fly constantly. After flapping his wings and gliding about for a long long time, the bird grew weary. He thought to himself: I need a rock or bit of land to rest on. He spread his wings and flew on and on, searching for a resting place, but found none.

The bird pondered for a long spell, then he flew to the Sky and shouted: "Sky, Water is angry at you and wants to swallow you up." He later swooped over the sparkling Water and said: "Water, Sky wants to destroy you."

On hearing this, the Water bubbled in fury, its powerful waves lashing upward, while the Sky hurled islands and continents at the foaming Water. They battled until the Sky emptied itself of all the soil and rocks. When the Sky stopped, the Water quieted down.

Meanwhile, the bird—who had witnessed all this—smiled. There were now islands and continents, and he immediately flew to a beautiful island. He rested, preening his colorful plumes. Later he spread his powerful wings and hopped onto shore where he saw a long piece of bamboo—two nodes long—floating by. The Water, furious at the troublemaking bird, pushed the bamboo against the bird. The magnificent bird hopped away, but the bamboo struck his legs repeatedly. Growing ill-tempered, the bird pecked violently at the bamboo nodes.

After a while, the bamboo split open. The bird peered inside and found a man sleeping. The man was a fine creature with strong limbs, and the bird became jealous. He thought: I don't like this man; he will be a nuisance. He lifted his head to peck the man, but just then the other bamboo node split open. Out popped a woman with gleaming brown skin and long hair shimmering depths of ebony. As she opened her eyes, she caught sight of the magnificent bird attacking the man. Quickly, she grabbed the bird's colorful tail and pulled with all her might. Crying in pain, the bird flew away, never to return. The woman and man lived on the beautiful island and became the parents of all people.

When Laydan had finished, I clapped my hands; I truly loved her tales. They brought me to places I had never been; they made me see people (and creatures) in a way that I could never see in my ordinary day-to-day life.

Laydan had not moved the whole time she told her story, but now she began tidying up the table and setting pots and pans in order. "Vanity eats at your soul," she said, "and things get turned around. You see things cockeyed. You do things that you would not ordinarily do." She paused, as she considered something. "Yes, maybe vanity can also make you mean, because vanity makes you think that you are always right. Maybe war and killing also come from vanity."

Esperanza hit the table with her fist. "I thought so," she said. "The Japanese *are* mean and vain."

# The Decision

❧

My grandmother, Lola Beatrize, had been married to another man before she became widowed and married Lolo Peping. Her first husband had been a pot-bellied handsome man, a drunkard, and a total disgrace. Once the first husband had been thrown up on the center aisle of their town church during the mayor's daughter's wedding—and it had been the wedding of the year. During a flag ceremony, he had zigzagged to the flagpole and urinated on the pole in front of the entire town. At May fiestas, he invaded people's homes, zeroed in on their alcohol supply, and guzzled their gin, rum, beer, vodka, and whiskey until the hosts or hostesses had to shove him out of their houses. He liked to drink until way past midnight at the corner sari-sari store, and his voice echoed throughout the neighborhood, "Your mother's cunt smells!"

Lola Beatrize, a hardworking businesswoman, a regular churchgoer, with good social standing, pretended as best as she could that her husband's drinking and accompanying disgrace never happened. On one occasion, a distant relative of hers stayed for supper and her husband, drunk as always, moaned, groaned, and thrashed about in the adjoining bedroom. The relative jumped at every God-awful sound, but Lola Beatrize carried on with supper as though nothing were wrong; "Pass the patis, Tiyo," she told the relative, and to the maid, she ordered, "Go get more rice." And to the relative, "How's the tira-tira, Tiyo, it's fresh from the sugar cane refinery."

In a place where most men were fishermen, grandmother's first husband planted sugar cane on land leased from the Spanish friars. Bleary-eyed and dazed, the husband couldn't keep track of the farm, and consequently Lola Beatrize had to supervise the tilling, watering, and cutting of the measly stalks.

She always had a good head for business and in addition to taking care of her husband's farm, she had a part-time business, a little store where she sold lemoncito juice and rice cakes along the isolated trail leading to the field where the Virgin Mary reportedly appeared. Some farmer's children—three of them—had been weeding this field one day when the sun started spinning and throwing off all sorts of colors. Frightened, they huddled together as the sun danced in the sky. The youngest one, a boy of five, heard Mary's voice saying, "Don't be afraid." He glanced around and saw the figure of Mary under an acacia tree. "That praying woman says not to be afraid," he told his sisters. He pointed at the acacia tree, but the sisters saw nothing. "That woman, holding a rosary," he insisted. The girls dragged the boy home and told their parents about the strange happenings. Thinking this was the work of the devil, the parents dispatched the boy to some relatives in another town. The father got other farmers together and they cut down the acacia tree. But the matter didn't end there because the Virgin Mary continued to appear on the exact spot, tree or no tree. However, she only allowed children to see her up close; she quickly disappeared when adults approached her. That's how Lola Beatrize got the idea of expanding her business. She also rented out binoculars to pilgrims, who gladly paid two centavos per three minutes to get a better view of Mary.

Lolo Beatrize declared it was Providence when one Sunday a runaway cart hit her husband head-on so he bounced, hit a boulder, and cracked his skull. His brains spilled out like uncooked white rice, and the flustered owner of the cart tried shoving the mess back into the split head. The owner gave Lola Beatrize three Spanish gold coins as compensation for the loss of her husband. She took it as a bonanza, and right before Christmas at that; her husband had never earned a peso in his entire life.

Her first husband's gruesome death made her realize that relatives of the dearly departed do indeed prefer presentable corpses. She was thus inspired to enter the funeral business, and took it upon herself to learn all she could about preparing the dead, from using the right needles and tubes during embalming, to applying the exact amount of makeup on the face for a "natural" effect.

She was operating a funeral business plus other buy-and-sell ventures when she met and married Lolo Peping. My grandfather, a gentleman and owner of several haciendas, found the funeral business too depressing and talked his wife into getting rid of it. They had the two daughters—Angeling and Lourdes—and by all accounts were happy, until her heart suddenly stopped many years ago, long before I was born.

Lola Beatrize spoke to my grandfather when he visited her grave. He visited her every day, with a can of azucenas flowers and a candle.

"The Rhode Island Red, Peping," she said.

"Pa, how can the dead talk?" Mama said when Lolo Peping reported this incident. But my grandfather was convinced that Lola Beatrize, good businesswoman that she was, was giving him a message from the other life, a gambling tip, so to speak. Lolo Peping announced he would gamble on any Rhode Island Red rooster at the cockpit. Esperanza and I begged to go with him, and our parents said yes, figuring it was a good idea for us to accompany him, should his mind wander.

Along the way, Lolo Peping ran across a friend of his, Butyong Ilaga, or Butyong the Rat, named for his size, not for his character. Butyong the Rat was a regular at the cockpit.

"Let's not talk of war, Butyong. Let's talk gambling. Got any tips?" Lolo Peping said, getting straight to the point.

The little man slapped his thigh happily. "Sure I do."

"Well, are you going to share this information with an old man?"

"Listen to this, Señor Peping, the native rooster is a sure winner."

Grandfather chuckled. "That's not what I heard."

"I'm putting all my money on the native rooster," Butyong the Rat said.

Grandfather laughed.

The cockpit had almost a thousand rowdy people. The handlers, on opposite sides of the rink, stroked their roosters and spoke encouraging words to them. One rooster was a large muscular Rhode Island Red; the other was a little native rooster of multicolored feathers with a dazed expression. Fifty bet-takers, called Kristos, walked around with their arms extended like Christ on the cross, taking bets from the frantic audience. It was four to one on the little rooster, and after Grandfather bet all his money on the Rhode Island Red, he smiled happily. "We're going to win today, girls," he declared as we sat in the front row.

I smiled back, although I started getting nervous when the knife man attached the blades to the cocks' legs and handed the birds to the trainers. The judge blew his whistle and after one last stroke, the trainers released the birds. The Red walked to the middle of the rink aggressively; the little rooster paused and cast a bewildered expression at the spectators before he strutted forward. The Red attacked repeatedly, while the little rooster hopped here and there to avoid it. Lolo Peping cheered lustily. When the Red leaped up in the air, the little bird scurried beneath to avoid the fatal blow of the razor sharp spur. The Red leaped once again, hoping to thrust his spur into the little chicken, but the latter scurried away.

Esperanza nudged me and said, "Lolo Peping's going to win."

The thought of Lolo Peping winning made us giggle, and we stood on the bench to see above the Kristos' heads. Just when we were indeed certain to win, the little rooster moved upward as though he were going to leap. The Red ducked and quickly advanced, intending to dive under the little chicken to safety. But the native rooster didn't complete his jump; and before the viewers and, most important of all, the Red knew what happened, the puny little chicken with the uncertain gaze thrust his metal spur deep into the large rooster.

I winced at the sight of blood and took several deep breaths to check my rising nausea. The game was over. The chicken doctor, needle and thread in hand, rushed to the Rhode Island Red to try and save it, but he soon shook his head at the lifeless bird.

"What happened?" Lolo Peping asked his friend later. By now he had contracted the dazed expression of the winning chicken.

"Simple," Butyong the Rat explained, "the little one beat the shit out of the Stateside chicken. I've seen that little one before, and he always does that trick. He does a little fake, like he's going to jump, and the other rooster always falls for it, then it's all over. The poor loser's fried chicken. That little bird is the best cockfighter that ever lived. This is his fourth fight and they're going to retire him now. What a life, be a stud, get fed like a king. Damn, that was a great fight!"

"I should have known better than to bet on a Stateside chicken," Lolo Peping concluded with a sigh.

In late February, President Quezon left Corregidor, and on March 11, General Douglas MacArthur also left for Australia.

"They have abandoned us. What will we do?" Mama asked. "Corregidor and Bataan are doomed. The Japanese will take over."

Papa said, "I'm making leche flan."

"Flan? Nando, it's no time to cook!" Mama shouted.

"Angeling, I'm going to make the most delicious leche flan in all of Ubec. It will surpass Lourdes's flans."

Mama burst into tears and ran to their bedroom. Unruffled, Papa asked for Esperanza's and my help. It was an important project, he said. He would be expanding his mind.

Before making an important decision, Papa liked to cook. Cooking not only relaxed his mind, it allowed him to "release his creativity." It was a habit he picked up in his college days; instead of cramming during exams, he cooked. He almost always came out ahead of his engineering class. Papa said that he studied diligently throughout the semester and therefore all the information was in his brain. There was no point trying to shove that material in overnight. Cooking loosened up all this knowledge from his mind.

Esperanza and I abandoned our skipping ropes and rummaged through the cupboards for the flan mold, the large yellow enamel mixing bowl, the egg beater, and two wooden spatulas. Papa carefully selected six brown eggs, holding each one up in the sunlight and peering through them before cracking them.

We lined up the ingredients on the kitchen table, and Papa took the mold and poured in one-third cup of sugar. He tilted the mold to show us the bottom, then he mixed the eggs, milk, and remaining sugar in the bowl. When the mixture turned frothy, he asked us to get the bottle of Napoleon brandy. We raced to the cupboard, found the green bottle, and hurried back to the kitchen. Papa measured out a tablespoon, sniffed it, and allowed us to smell the brandy before pouring it into the bowl.

Holding the mold over the fire, he carmelized the sugar, swirling the golden brown liquid so it coated the bottom and sides of the mold. When he finished, he poured in the mixture. He placed the mold inside a doubleboiler and instructed Laydan to lower the heat.

We played chess—Esperanza and I against him—for exactly thirty-five minutes, then he declared that the flan was done. He lifted the mold out of the doubleboiler. Using the end of a sharp knife, he checked it, beaming when the knife pulled out clean. "Perfect!" he exclaimed.

After the mold cooled, he flipped the dessert onto a serving platter. With a teaspoon, he poked some flan from the side and handed it first to Esperanza, then to me. We rolled the flan in our mouths. "Good, Tiyo," Esperanza said. "It's like rainbows," I echoed.

Papa tasted it, closed his eyes for a moment, then announced, "We must go to Mindanao."

We were not the only ones who decided to leave Ubec. People were rushing to the countryside. They carted their belongings to their ancestral homes, away from the city of Ubec where the Japanese would most certainly come.

Lolo Peping refused to leave Ubec. Lola Beatrize, he explained, was buried there, and he would be damned if the Japanese would drive him away from his beloved wife's grave. He had been in jungles, seen more bloodbaths than a normal man had in a lifetime, why couldn't he be left in peace? Lourdes said she doubted if Lolo Peping could take the hardship in Mindanao, that she and Esperanza would stay with grandfather; after all, the Japanese had no reason to hurt them, they would be fine.

When news broke that Bataan and Corregidor had finally fallen, the grown-ups became as jittery as sparrows before a heavy rain. The Japanese, we learned, were herding the skin-and-bones men like cattle toward Capas, Tarlac. The USAFFE had fought for three months, with dwindling supplies, fed only with hope that America would send reinforcements. "We are the battling bastards of Bataan—no papa, no mama, no Uncle Sam," they reportedly said to one another, before they became too weak to fight.

Our things were in the boat. Papa told me to kiss Lolo Peping, Lourdes, and Esperanza. I did so, mechanically like a wind-up toy. I had been feeling a whirlpool in my soul; one minute I was excited at the thought that a group of us—my parents and I, Max and his wife Nida, Laydan, and Bitong—would be going to Mindanao; the next minute, great sadness would overcome me at the thought of leaving our house, my grandfather, aunt, cousin. But the single comforting thought that I and everybody else believed was that the war would not last longer than six months.

"I'll see you in a few months, Angeling, when all this trouble is solved," Lolo Peping said, calling me by my mother's name. His mind was a bit addled that day. "Be a good girl." He planted a kiss on my forehead.

My aunt gave me a big kiss and hug, her cinnamon scent lingering in the air. Esperanza, bitter because she would have to continue going to school while I would be off, begrudgingly gave me three lemon drops. I gave her the gold band from a Tabacalera cigar which she slipped onto her middle finger. We smiled at each other, a bit shyly. What could we say? What was there to say? I felt awkward, different, and afraid. "At least you won't be looking up Mother Ignacia's nostrils," Esperanza said, and we laughed a little.

As we drove away, I watched them until they looked like tiny dolls waving good-bye, then I turned my attention to the burned-out rubble where Sanny's store had stood. I felt anxious, as if I were entering the Royal Theater when it was pitch-black and there was no telling if a giant rat would brush against your feet.

We passed by the old houses on Colon Street and the churches and buildings built of stone from the Spanish times. I had never noticed before how beautiful they looked with the moss and grasses growing in the cracks. Someone had scribbled "I shall return" in charcoal on a wall—MacArthur's words when he left Corregidor. "Pa, look," I said, calling his attention. He read the words and smiled at me. We all stared at the words with an expression of hope.

"It'll soon be over," Mama said, rubbing her big belly.

# The Trip

The waves were sometimes higher than our boat. Because Mama was nauseous, Papa brought us to the deserted uppermost deck for fresh air. A wave splashed overboard, spraying us.

"Too much fresh air," Mama shouted above the wind.

"It's good for you," Papa shouted back.

"I like it," I contributed, feeling the dampness against my face.

"Doesn't this remind you of when Typhoon Sisang ripped off the kitchen roof and water was all over the place? Poor Laydan, she was in a tizzy trying to salvage the pig heads and other strange things she hung all over the place," Mama said.

They laughed at the memory, and they started talking about the old days. Do you remember the Conga number at the Club . . . do you remember when Rosario Aguirre slipped while doing the tango . . . do you remember when we went to Talisay for a picnic and Yvonne swallowed her tooth while eating roasted pig . . . do you remember?

Mama had been nineteen when she met my father, a thirty-two-year-old widower whose first wife had died during childbirth. The baby had also died.

A couple of years after his first wife passed away, Papa happened to see a group of women shooting baskets at the university gym. He noticed one girl who aggressively elbowed her companions for the ball. The girl caught the ball on a rebound, but she twisted her ankle as she fell. The game stopped. The girl screamed. Papa abandoned his briefcase and ran to the girl.

"My leg, my leg," moaned the pretty plump girl.

"Angeling Almario's leg is broken, Professor," one of the girls said.

"No, I'm fine," Angeling insisted, as she tried to stand up, but crumpled.

"What will we do? Her leg's broken. Can you help us, Professor Macaraig?" the girls asked.

Papa picked up the girl, who was in her bloomers and all, and brought her to her house. She had a broken tibia and needed a cast. Bedridden for a month, her only salvation from boredom was Papa's daily visits. By the time her cast was removed, Papa and Mama were engaged.

My parents were still reminiscing when two women stumbled up the deck. The waves had grown worse. The women were pale, quiet, and miserably seasick. When the boat lurched from side to side, one woman threw up. But they were too ill to move away from the mess.

Mama stood up. "Nando, Yvonne, it's time to go."

Downstairs, Papa said, "I hope you don't want to turn back, because we can't. We're committed to joining Fertig's Division."

"Nando, it's wartime. In Ubec, the Japanese might go after you. Can we take that chance? Of course not. There's the baby coming, and there's Yvonne. We'll have to take what comes. Why, in no time at all, this whole thing will be over. It'll be like a vacation. Besides, it's funny. Didn't that awful mess remind you of those American soups, you know those terrible canned things that Laydan abhors? I hope she's feeling better though, poor woman." They laughed, hugging each other. They drew me toward them and we three looked out at the rough sea.

William Cushing, an American guerrilla leader in Mindanao, found a place for us in the mountains. It was a guest cabin of an American logger who had abandoned Mindanao for the safety of Missouri.

Cushing was an enormous man who ate a whole roasted chicken and half the ox tongue that Laydan simmered in a sauce with garlic, vinegar, and native palm wine. Despite his healthy appetite, he had the pale and intent look of a Redemptorist priest.

The grown-ups sat around the fireplace after supper. Cushing poured out palm wine for the grown-ups, and they all settled back in their hammocks and rattan chairs. Mama, unaccustomed to the chilly mountain climate, pulled a blanket over her legs. I sat beside her with my ear pressed against her stomach, listening to the baby's faint heartbeat. I could feel its movements.

"You should make it to Malaybalay in a week's time," Cushing told Papa. "There are no roads, but Isiong will be with you. He's the best guide I've got. He knows all the guerrilleros in the area. Fertig's expecting you and the men. He'll tell you more about it, but Admiral Yoshida has just been appointed the new Chief of Staff. Isoruku Yoshida has no scruples whatsoever. If he needs to, he'll destroy the archipelago for the glory of the Rising Sun. At this point, Nando, it's imperative that the different guerrilla groups unite. Right now, we've got Martin Lewis causing problems in Ubec. MacArthur's orders are clear: coordinate all ground, air, and sea operations; cut all lines of supply; isolate the enemy. So what happens? Lewis goes into this big ego trip."

He paused, looked at Mama, and continued, "I'm not sure if Angeling should continue the trip. In her condition, it might be better if she stays here until the child is born."

"We'll be all right, Bill," Mama said, patting her stomach.

"There's a doctor along your way—Doctor Meñez, good man, that doctor. You probably know him. His wife's a doctor, too; they've got three children. They're God-sent. We were tramping in some swamps and some men came down with malaria. The men were sweating and shivering, and I was sure they wouldn't make it. Well, Doc gave us some quinine. He also set the bones of one of the boys who broke his leg. Dumb kid climbed a coconut tree for some coconuts, but he fell down. He could have lost his leg—hell, he could have died. Good thing Doc Meñez was there.''

''Doc's a good man. He practiced in Ubec for a while. Any news of the survivors of the Death March, Bill?'' Papa asked.

''Just that they were in pretty bad shape. They're lucky they managed to escape. They said the Japanese bayoneted those who couldn't walk; there was hardly any food. And the women, well, the Japanese soldiers raped them. They got an American nurse pregnant, then they blinded her, cut off her arms and tongue, and set her free.''

At this point, Mama put me to bed. She still wanted to protect me from this war that had descended on us. Unable to shake off the image of the nurse, I prayed the way Mother Ignacia had taught us once. She had told us to imagine the Sacred Heart of Jesus and to make the drops of blood from His Heart fall over us, and we would be protected from evil. That night I made the blood of Jesus fall on the unfortunate nurse.

For about a week after we moved into the cabin, the men met daily with other guerrilleros of the area. They nailed the map on the wall and spent numerous hours discussing where the Americans were, where the Japanese were, and where the guerrillero headquarters were. They talked about weather, roads, equipment, money, food, and just about everything. The women were relegated to the outdoor kitchen, and in Mama's case to the bedroom because she was always feeling tired. Nida, who felt sorry for my sick mother, kept her company. I tagged along with Laydan, who seemed to know the area well.

''I was born near here, Yvonne,'' she said. ''Did I ever tell you about the time I was born?''

She had, but I let her talk. At least Laydan did not dwell on the war.

''Big-bellied, my mother accompanied my father to Datu Ambian's fields. There with other workers, they helped clear the land. When work was done, Datu Ambian had seven chickens and five monkeys slaughtered for the thanksgiving feast. The renowned Inuk, the most famous epic singer of that time, was summoned. After the sun sank behind the betel nut grove and the fires were lit, when eating was done and people had settled on the Datu's floor and around his house, Inuk sang, '*Duan lad si Tuwaang . . .*' " Laydan paused as if reliving the memory.

She continued, "My mother said his voice rose and quivered above the palm leaves; his voice sank low to hover over silvery streams. His cadences prickled human hair. Like one bewitched, my mother watched the old epic singer in his beaded clothes and rainbow-colored turban. When labor began, she begged my father not to move her so far that she couldn't hear Inuk. In a nearby worker's makeshift hut, I was born."

"How did you learn the epics, Laydan?" I asked.

"From Inuk himself. When I was twelve, I begged my parents to allow me to travel with Inuk. I cried for days until my mother accompanied me to the singer to inquire if I could be his apprentice. I sang to him the epic fragments which I had learned from a villager. He made a face, saying I had a lot to learn, but he took me in. We traveled from village to village for weddings, funerals, all sorts of celebrations, and Inuk would sing these beautiful songs, about the maiden in the skyworld, and the gentle goddess Meybuyan who watched over the dead babies in the underworld, and other stories. Many songs. Ah, Inuk was wonderful. He would lift his eyebrows just so, and twist his wrist in exactly the right way. He would sing for ten to twelve hours, and his voice—no human being ever had a voice like that."

"Why did you stop singing?"

Laydan's broad and dark face became more stolid. Her fleshy neck quivered. "The deities punished me. I became too proud. I was learning the epics and became too vain. Inuk told me, 'Laydan, become the epic,' but I did not know what he meant."

She would not say more.

The morning we heard that guerrilleros spotted Japanese soldiers in Mindanao was when my scalp felt as though it were on fire. My head was terribly itchy and no matter how fiercely I scratched, the itchiness didn't subside. Mama checked my hair and burst into tears. "Lice! Yvonne has lice. What is happening to us, Nando? We are turning into animals!"

In order to get rid of most of the pearly-white nits, Nida cut my hair. Nida proved to be a good companion. During those past visits to Slapsy Maxie's, she had seemed enormous and formidable, but in fact she was easy to get along with and quite helpful, especially to Mama. To make light of my tragedy, she said, "You have pretty hair, Yvonne."

"Will you cut everything?" I asked, fearful I would look like Esperanza with the butchered hair.

"It'll be short with bangs. It'll be nice on you. Your hair's so thick. Mama had hair like yours till the day she died. Even though she became very thin, her hair always remained thick. If you hold still, I'll show you her hair."

"What hair?"

"Mama's hair. When she died, I cut her hair as a memento."

This was the first time I'd heard of keeping a dead person's hair as a souvenir, and I was getting excited at the thought of seeing and maybe even handling a dead person's hair.

"She had TB," explained Nida when she returned with her mother's hair in her hands. The white hair was long and tied on both ends with black satin ribbon. "Don't you think that's lovely?" she asked, stroking the hair gently. Suddenly she laughed, saying, "Max detests it. He thinks it's scary. He lived for so long in America that he thinks like an American. Americans get scared of things like that. They're frightened of a lot of things—animal innards, blood soup. But this is the confusing thing, they're not scared of eating bloody meat. That's how Max likes his beef, bloody. 'Rare' he calls it, but it looks uncooked to me. Once Max asked me if I wanted to live in America. I thought hard about it. This was after Mama died, so I didn't have family here or anything. I thought and thought, but I told him no. There's a part of me that can take a little bit of difference, but over there everything's different. There's snow, and even the food's strange. Max talks about broccoli sometimes. That was his favorite vegetable. I don't even know what it looks like. And besides, I'd miss stewed fish and kamunggay vegetables.''

Although I laughed with Nida, I was studying her mother's hair-piece. It felt eerie to be near a dead person's mass of white hair. I could feel my spine tingling.

I was still pondering over the dead woman's hair when Laydan and I went to the marketplace to buy kerosene for my hair.

''Nida showed me her mama's hair,'' I said.

''The woman's been dead so long, it must look like a rat's nest.''

''It was white and thick. She died of TB. Nida liked her a lot. She was probably very nice. I'll bet she never screamed at Nida. A person like that with white hair like an angel's, I bet she never yelled.''

Laydan stopped, tilted my chin up, and looked at me. ''Your mother's pregnant and doesn't feel well. She has a difficult time. You'll be all right. The kerosene will kill the nits and lice, and I'll comb them out.''

It was true that Mama looked wilted. Her face had grown thin although her belly hung out in front of her. She was always nauseous and tired, and recently she'd been crying a lot. I was used to seeing her vivacious and social; I could not understand what was happening to her. I wanted her to be as she was—happy and beautiful and energetic. Since the war broke out, everything was different. And Nida was right, a little bit of difference was all right, but a lot was too much.

After buying what we needed from an old man, Laydan said, ''By the way, what has happened to the town called Kumin?''

The old man, toothless with red gums from chewing betel nuts, laughed. ''No more Kumin. All gone. It's now pineapple plantation.''

''Ah, that is too bad. I come from Kumin,'' Laydan said.

''Americans bought all the lands and turned them into logging places or pineapple plantations.''

''By any chance,'' Laydan started, ''have you heard of Inuk?''

The man slapped his lap and spat red juice on the ground. ''Who has not heard of Inuk? There has never been another epic singer like him.''

''What happened to him?'' Laydan asked.

''Saddened by all the change, he went to a hill where he sang for three days and three nights. Then he disappeared, and it is believed that he ascended into the skyworld, just like our great hero, Tuwaang.''

Laydan became very sad at this news.

The horses were swift and we made good time that first day. The next day, the terrain became rougher and the trail disappeared. It was late afternoon when Papa decided that we might as well stop and make camp.

I was picking firewood with Laydan when she suddenly paused and looked around her.

"What's the matter, Laydan?" I asked.

"It's just like my dream," she replied.

She looked around the jungle growth. "Listen," she said. There was a distant sound of gurgling water. Like a sleepwalker she followed the sound, while I trailed behind. Laydan went deeper into the jungle, then she stopped in front of a spring seeping out from the cliff. She cupped her hands and took a sip of the water. Later she began climbing a rock and, alarmed, I ran back to the camp to alert the grown-ups.

I was explaining what happened when we heard one note—perfect, like the tinkle of a raindrop falling into an emerald green pool. It was Laydan. We heard another note, then Laydan began singing about Tuwaang. She sang in flawless pitch and tone. Everyone abandoned their tasks and we made our way back to Laydan. We found her up on the rock singing, and even her face became animated, and her hands gestured in the air. Her voice traveled through the jungle and for the longest time, we stood there mesmerized by her singing.

As she sang I pictured in my head the epic hero, Tuwaang, on his journey to save the maiden who spun the rainbow. The beautiful maiden was fleeing from the evil giant with a fire-shooting wand. After a long battle, Tuwaang defeated the giant. Using his magic betel nut, Tuwaang restored life to the devastated places.

When we recovered from our reverie, it was dark and a nearby bush was completely covered with glittering fireflies. The men wanted to flee because they thought the place was enchanted. Mama shouted at Laydan to come down, but it was as if the old woman were in another world, and we could not reach her.

Back at our camp we could still hear her singing. She sang through the night until dawn. We later found her beside a guava tree, brushing her few remaining teeth with some leaves. ''I saw Inuk,'' she reported, ''riding a cloud shaped like a boat to heaven. I still don't know what Inuk meant when he said, 'Laydan, become the epic.' ''

# Baby Brother

‧✿‧

At two o'clock, Papa selected the spot where we would have lunch. It was near a clear stream with enormous rocks for us to sit on. We were looking for banana leaves, which would serve as our plates, when Papa commented that the area reminded him of the Smythe River in America.

"It was a lot like this, Yvonne," he said, his voice resonant with warmth from the memory. "No orchids like these, no lauan trees; there were pines and enormous redwood trees. There were otters in the river. But it was just as peaceful as this place."

"Like a church?" I enjoyed listening to Papa's stories about America. After high school he had stowed away on a freighter bound for California. And he had gone to engineering school in Indiana, but in the summers he picked fruit and he traveled all over the huge country.

"That's right, a sanctuary." Papa smiled and for a moment we listened to the birds and the river rippling over the white pebbles. We smelled the rich earth and felt the warmth of the sun on our faces.

"It's different there," I said, remembering Nida's comments about America. "There's snow, and the food's different."

"Yes and no," Papa replied. "The trappings are different, the externals, but there are certain things that remain the same everywhere."

"Like what?"

"There are people, and people are the same everywhere."

"But they look different."

"But they're basically the same. They fall in love, or they become afraid—it's all the same there or here. Feelings, relationships are the same everywhere."

I paused for a while, trying to absorb his words, then I said, "Is it like this? I love Lolo Peping and Esperanza, and in America there could be a girl like me who loves her grandfather and cousin?"

Papa chuckled. "Something like that."

We were walking back with the cut leaves, when Papa spotted a log that was partly in the river. He stopped walking and said, "Let's see if there are any."

"Any what?"

He turned over the log. "Just as I thought," he declared, poking at wormlike protrusions clinging to the log's bottom.

"What are they?"

"Dragonfly larvae. They make good bait. I went fishing with an Indian who taught me that. Bloodstone—that's right, Jack Bloodstone was his name. He was a big man with hair braided down his back."

"Did he have feathers in his hair, like a real Indian?"

Papa chuckled. "That's just in the movies, Yvonne. Jack wore ordinary clothes. He knew a lot of things."

"Did you like it there, in America?"

"It's a fine place. I made some good friends there."

"Lolo Peping hates Americans."

"Your grandfather fought the Americans in a war. He knew them as enemy. There are good and bad Americans, just as there are good and bad Filipinos. It's like that everywhere."

"Are there good Japanese?"

He stared at the sky while pondering the question. "That is a difficult question because now the Japanese are our enemies. But yes, despite this war, I believe there are good Japanese. There are bad ones too. It is hard to understand, isn't it? I find it difficult, especially when terrible things are happening.'' He tousled my hair, and we surrendered the banana leaves to the women.

Papa later met with the men, and I headed for the riverbank. As I passed by some decaying leaves I heard rustlings underneath. Using a stick, I flipped open the leaves. There on the damp ground, I found two turtles attacking an enormous slug. Startled, they quickly hid in their shells. I tried to coax them out of their shells, but they had their own ideas. One of the turtles peeked out and stared at me with his beady brown eyes, but the moment I tried to touch him, he snapped back into his shell. However, when the unfortunate slug in front of the turtles writhed, the turtles could not help themselves and they both came out of hiding to peck at the slug. I hunted for slugs and worms and placed these in front of the turtles to rid them of their shyness.

I continued playing with them until Laydan whisked them away and put them in a basket. ''Turtle soup's good for long life,'' she said. As I watched the two creatures struggling to claw their way out of the basket, I pictured Laydan's turtle soup served in the turtle's shell. Even though people swore turtle tasted like chicken, I could never bring myself to eat it. Turtle soup was one of the saddest sights on earth.

Mama was happy that day. During lunch, she said enthusiastically, ''I'm so hungry.''

''You're eating for two, Missus,'' Nida kidded. ''Maybe for three.''

''Not twins,'' Mama said. ''Would you like twins, Yvonne?''

''Yes,'' I replied happily. ''Then Esperanza can carry one, and I can carry the other.''

''They might turn out to be like those Cabarubbias twins,'' Mama continued.

''Not those terrible boys, Missus. I heard that one would dump eggs on the floor while the other poked a screw driver into the electrical socket,'' Nida said.

''Their mother has pure white hair, and she's younger than me,'' Mama replied. ''I might end up with white hair, too.'' She laughed.

"I'll keep one baby," Nida said jokingly. "Max wants a child so badly."

"Have you tried a novena? A pilgrimage always works. How about dancing the sinulog prayer to the Child Jesus? That always works. There was a woman, fifty years old, Nida—fifty, mind you, old enough to be a grandmother—and she danced the sinulog during the feast of the Santo Niño Child Jesus, and in no time at all, she was pregnant. Fifty—can you just imagine?"

"Mama prayed to Santa Clara to have me, Missus. That's why she called me Bienvenida—good news, good news, that was me. I'm just not the religious type. I don't bother God about those things. You know the saying, God takes care of those who take care of themselves, so I watch out for myself."

"How can you say that, Nida? It's only prayer that's keeping me going right now. Do the sinulog, just try it, and before you know it, you and Max will have a child," Mama urged.

"We'll see, Missus," Nida said, and Mama sighed.

We were putting things away when a mountain man on horseback came toward us, his horse thumping a rhythmic beat. He was covered with soot. Sweat trickled down his face making little paths on the black grime.

"Japs back there," he panted as he tried to catch his breath. "Four of them . . . shot my carabao . . . stole my chickens . . . burned everything . . . my hut . . . everything," the man continued.

Isiong, the guide, small and wiry, narrowed his eyes in thought as he asked the man about distance and time. "Señor Nando," he addressed my father, "we better go to Doc's place at once."

We quickly packed and left. Riding in back of Nida, with the vines and bushes whipping my face, I hung on tight. Even though Mama complained of stomach cramps, we rode for three hours straight, stopping only when she finally shouted, "Nando! Nando!"

Papa, who was ahead with Isiong, tugged at the reins to turn his horse around. Nida and I had already jumped off our horse.

"My stomach, and there's water," Mama said. Beads of sweat covered her upper lip.

"Her bag of water broke!" Nida shouted as she led Mama to a

thicket where Mama immediately squatted. I watched her stomach heave as she involuntarily held her breath. "I feel strange, Nida. Nando—my stomach hurts. It must be the coconut meat I ate. I feel like going, but nothing's happening."

Nida shouted, "Nando! The baby!" Laydan got a blanket, and I helped her spread the blanket near my mother.

Isiong and Bitong shifted their rifles from one shoulder to the other and stared questioningly at one another. "Señor Nando," Bitong finally spoke up. "The Japs."

Papa stopped. I saw the veins on his forehead throbbing, squiggling about like little worms. "Damn the Japanese! We are not moving my wife while she is having our baby." Bitong and Isiong lowered their eyes, and Papa hurried to the thicket.

By this time, Mama was lying on the blanket, curled up on her side like a baby. I twirled the end of the blanket and watched her, fearful she would die. She grimaced for a few seconds, then her face relaxed. I was thinking of something to say when she said, "We can't stay—the Japanese."

Kneeling beside her, Papa placed his right hand on her huge stomach that moved as though it had a life of its own. "Everything's fine, Angeling. Take it easy, don't worry about a thing."

Max called out, "Nando?"

"Yes, yes," Papa replied. He looked around and mumbled, "Sun's down . . . moon a crescent . . . jungle thick . . . visibility close to zero." He addressed Max, "We can't move Angeling, so we'll hide nearby, behind that bamboo grove. Have Bitong bring Laydan and Yvonne deeper into the jungle. Isiong should take the horses someplace else in case they make a sound."

Max passed the information to the others.

Papa handed his .45 caliber revolver to Nida. "Nida, if we're quiet, things should be okay, but Nida, if anything should happen, that is, if they get us, use the . . . I don't want them getting hold of her . . . They can be very . . ."

Nida nodded. "I know what to do." Their eyes locked in understanding. The corner of the blanket that I twisted was wet from my hands' sweat. I felt faint. My blood was turning into molasses, thick and slow.

"Go," Mama said. "They'll be here."

Papa wiped off the perspiration on Mama's face. "Do you know that the first time I saw you, you were perspiring? You were the most beautiful woman wearing bloomers in that gym."

Mama smiled wanly. "Go!"

After Papa kissed her, I threw my arms around her neck. "Ma . . ." I said, then paused. I wanted to say something to her, but all I could think of was how scratchy the woolen blanket felt.

"Yvonne," she said softly, "do as they say. It'll be all right, child."

"Ma . . ." I tried again, "Ma, this blanket's itchy."

Laydan pulled me away.

Isiong disappeared into the jungle with the horses. Using a machete, Bitong hacked away a path until the jungle became so thick that his cutting made little difference. We crawled under the bushes and sat on a gigantic root. It was difficult to see the tip of our noses. In the distance, one of our horses snorted, and Bitong cursed under his breath. But after an eerie silence, the jungle came alive with sounds—owls hooting, birds chirping, a wild boar grunting. I sat quietly, wondering why all I said to my mother was that the blanket was itchy. I should have said something else. I could have said, "I love you, Ma." Or, "Ma, you'll be all right." What I really wanted to say was: "Ma, don't die." But you didn't say words like that, otherwise you might tempt Fate. It was calling attention to my mother's condition, making a suggestion that was unthinkable.

After a long while, I heard the crunching of twigs and gravel, the neighing of horses. The guttural sounds of Japanese men cut through the jungle air. Laydan held me tight. As they came closer, my blood rushed to my head. I wondered briefly if I could indeed die and be gone from this earth, disappear—forever, as Mother Ignacia once said.

Then the sounds moved on. I wondered where they went, what they did. Did they carry guns? The memory of that .45 revolver in Nida's hands came to my mind. One Japanese talked for a long time;

the others spoke rapidly in turn; they burst out laughing, and then they left. Laydan remained still, but I had developed the strong urge to giggle.

Once Esperanza had told a joke—my cousin could be really funny sometimes. She could make faces and do all sorts of things with her body to make you laugh. "There was a child," she had said, as she pushed her stomach out, "with worms in her stomach, so that her stomach was very big, just like a pregnant woman. Her mother de-wormed her and warned her not to walk around barefoot again. One day the child saw a pregnant woman and she went up to the pregnant woman. 'I know what you've been doing to get that big stomach,' the child said." At that point of the story, Esperanza had howled with laughter. "Get it? I know what you've been doing—get it? She went around barefoot, get it?" I had laughed with her.

Esperanza's words now began running through my mind, and I struggled to keep from giggling. When I stirred, Laydan pressed my head on her lap and we stayed frozen for a long time, leaving our hiding place only when we heard Nida calling for help.

I found my mother with her head tilted down, rocking something in her arms, and she gave a soft rhythmic moan. She was all right! I was starting to feel relief from the nervousness that possessed me, when I made out the figure of a baby; I clapped my hands excitedly, but Papa held me back. He opened his mouth but there was no sound. He finally shook his head and walked away. I felt like giggling once again, and I had to struggle to be still.

While the women assisted my mother, the men silently dug a hole. Papa stood quietly, studying the sky and the terrain around him. He looked like an old man, with shoulders hunched, looking weary, ex-hausted. He quickly picked up the blue prune-faced infant from Mama and wrapped it in some cloth. It was the same size as my doll in Ubec.

"He should have lived, Nando. There's nothing wrong with him. If not for the cord, he should have made it," she said, in a voice filled with so much sorrow that my heart felt frozen.

After the burial, the men dragged enormous rocks and piled them on the grave as a marker. Papa picked me up and pointed out the North Star. "There it is, and there are the *Tres Marías*." His Adam's apple quivered. "When all this is over, we'll come back and get him to give him a decent burial."

I could barely see the stars. Esperanza's joke began playing through my head, and it required all my will to keep from giggling.

Our fourth-grade classroom had a bulletin board with a picture of purgatory. The picture had flames with souls in their midst staring pleadingly upward. The first time Mother Ignacia put the picture up, she had talked not only about purgatory but also about limbo, that this was the place where unbaptized souls went. That night in the jungle when the silly urge to giggle passed, and while we tried to get some rest, I thought of Mother Ignacia's picture. The difference between purgatory and limbo, according to the old nun, was that purgatory was temporary, while limbo was forever. My baby brother had not been baptized, and I wondered if he was now in limbo, and if limbo had flames like purgatory and hell. "Please dear God, please, don't let him end up in limbo. Please-please-please, I'll be good; I won't laugh and talk in church; I will never lie; I will never be angry at Esperanza again, please dear God, please, not limbo," I prayed repeatedly.

# Doc Meñez

❦

$\mathcal{E}$ven with Mama bleeding a lot, we left for Doc Meñez's house the next morning. I rode behind Papa on the part-Arabian horse named Robino. The men, still jittery, hugged their rifles close to their sides. As the trail grew steeper and narrower, I grew certain that the horses would slip and we would tumble down the ravine; but they were true mountain horses that instinctively knew safe ground. Once, however, the horse carrying the dynamite stepped on a rock that gave way. For a while he teetered precariously, but the animal triumphed and kept his balance. The cold mountain wind whipped my face and I shivered.

"Get my jacket," Papa said. His voice had a metallic quality I had never heard before, and briefly I wondered if he was angry at me.

After slipping it on, I put my arms around him and he tied the dangling sleeves in front of him. I dozed off along the way and would have fallen if not for the sleeves.

I thought I was dreaming when Isiong cried, "There it is."

We made it to Doc Meñez's place! I looked at the two-story house made of wood and nipa. We could stretch, eat; we could use the outhouse; we could rest under the shade of the nearby acacia tree. Doc would check Mama, erase some of yesterday's agony. It was another day, and we were closer to Malaybalay.

At the top of the mountain, Isiong's horse began neighing. Robino stopped, pawed the ground, and planted all hooves to the ground. Papa had to hit him before he hesitantly plodded toward the house.

By the time we arrived, Isiong had jumped off his horse and was now standing by the door. "Doc!" Isiong called, knocking on the front door. No one answered, and the guide knocked harder. Isiong shouted louder, "It's me, Isiong!" When there was still no answer, he turned the doorknob, pushed it open, and peeped in. "*Puta!*" he cursed as he bolted inside.

"Stay here," Papa told me. He got off the horse, went inside Doc's house, but he was soon back out. "Bitong!" he called. "Come quick and don't bring the others."

The rest of us waited under the acacia tree. Mama lay down and put her feet up, her bloody skirt around her. I hated the red-brown stain on her skirt and I turned my attention to a mother sparrow frantically hopping from her nest to a branch. "Ma," I said to my mother, "look at the bird."

"Yvonne," she snapped, "this is no time for birds!"

I stared at her. Her eyes glared back from deep hollows. Mama looked angry or something, and I was not sure if I was to blame.

"She's scared, Ma," I explained.

"Oh, Yvonne," she repeated softly as tears slid down her face.

"She's scared for nothing. It's just too bad for her, because we're not going to hurt her. Look at her, flying back and forth and we're just sitting here, not doing anything. Why is she scared?"

I was still prattling when Bitong returned. He was talking fast, barely coherent. "Japs got them. Hacked to pieces."

After a brief pause Nida asked, "What about Doc?"

"Back there, trying to put them together. *Puta*, second grave in two days." He grabbed a shovel.

"Shit!" Nida said. "Gaddam Japs!" She had been careful with her language in front of my mother, whom she considered a lady, but now Nida's tongue flowed with obscenities. "Mother-fucking-Japanese-fucking-shit!"

The sparrow continued twittering and flying. The feeling that I was watching an old movie at the Royal came to me.

Mama's voice cut through the fog I was in. "Yvonne, pray with me," she ordered, as she pulled out the rosary from her pocket. "In the name of the Father, and of the Son, and of the Holy Ghost . . ." She had a wild expression as she fingered the rosary.

"Hail Mary, full of grace, the Lord is with Thee . . ." we repeated, the words a kind of salve.

Then another commotion erupted. Doc came running toward us with what appeared like a ball in his arms. The men were shouting, trying to catch him. A sense of horror possessed me when I realized Doc was clutching a woman's head.

"Doc, come on, Doc," Max called out as he pursued the doctor. "Gadamit, we have to bury her."

Doc was medium-sized and graceful, and like an agile dancer he ran from side to side, slipping away from Max. Finally Bitong grabbed Doc from behind, then Max punched the doctor, who collapsed like a young sapling. The men took the head away. While the women applied a cold compress to Doc's swelling jaw, I followed the men to the backyard where they had dug a hole. Half-hidden by a flowering kanding-kanding bush, I watched the burial of Doc's family. A terrible chill gripped my bones; I had the sensation of looking at sides of beef. The glistening of the white bones, the redness of the muscle and blood reminded me of the meat hanging at the butcher stalls in Ubec's open market. I thought of the animal innards that Laydan transformed into soups and casseroles. I was shaking uncontrollably by the time I returned to the acacia tree.

Everybody was too busy, too occupied to notice me, and I shivered violently with my teeth chattering. Laydan wrapped a blanket around me.

When we resumed our journey, I rode with Laydan and I said, "Do you think the bird's fine now, Laydan? She was so scared."

"The bird is fine, Yvonne," she answered. "Listen to me, child, do you remember the goddess Meybuyan?"

I stared at her blankly.

"She lives near the underworld river, do you recall? She has breasts all over her body. You see, she is a kind goddess, and she nurses the infants who are too young to cross the river to the land of the souls. I am sure that Meybuyan is taking care of your brother and the doctor's children." Her words were calm and soothing.

From the mountain people and guerrilleros, we were able to piece together the events that led to the massacre of Doc's family.

Doc Meñez had the gift of seeing people's auras. As a little boy, he could see colors flushing around people—pink if they were affectionate, red if they were extremely angry or happy, blue and purple if they felt meditative or religious, golden if they were kind and loving, gray if they were depressed or ailing, green if they were healing, and black if death stalked them.

When he was six, he had observed a woman encased in a coal-black aura. It was the first time Doc had noticed a black aura, and he immediately reported this to his mother. His mother, suspicious that her son's ability was the work of the devil, merely nodded, hoping the boy would quickly forget the matter. "Yes, son, yes," she said, waving her hand in mild annoyance. As the woman with the black aura crossed the street, a carriage came along and hit her, flinging her five meters away. She died instantly from a broken spine and Doc understood what a black aura meant.

This ability helped Doc in his profession because he could look at his patients and, even before scientific diagnosis, could tell which parts of their bodies were ailing. "Ah, it could be your kidney or liver," he would say to those with gray auras emanating from their midriff. When the auras turned green, he knew the patients were better. And those with black auras wouldn't pull through.

The guerrilleros and mountain people confirmed the good things we had heard about Doc Meñez. Doc and his wife, Jesusa Meñez, were graduates of American medical schools who could have made a good living in America, but they chose to return to the Philippines. After working in Ubec City for a while, they settled in the remote area of Mindanao to help the people there. Doc would ride—even walk— miles, taking the entire day if necessary, to treat a child with beri-beri or dengue fever. Often he lacked medicines and could only prescribe native herbs and remedies. But he had what the people called "healing hands," and his touch was sometimes enough to cure some.

The night of the massacre, he had been on another mountain assisting a young woman in labor. It was her first pregnancy and she was as skittish as a wild mare about the matter. Although an experienced midwife lived near her, she begged Doc to deliver her baby. The husband arrived one early morning to inform Doc that the woman had started labor. Doc picked up his black bag and said good-bye to his wife and three children. As he leaped onto his horse, he saw dark auras around his family members. He paused, uncertain about what to do. His wife, who practiced medicine in the makeshift clinic on the first floor of their house, waved at him. And Doc, straddled on his horse with the anxious husband beside him, finally decided it was the slant of the sun's rays that had made him see things.

After traveling for three hours, Doc and the husband found the pregnant woman cheerfully polishing the bamboo-slatted floor. She explained that her contractions had stopped. Doc decided the baby had dropped and was due any time, so he ate some rice and bitter melon while waiting for the labor pains to resume. Late afternoon, when nothing happened, Doc told the woman she probably had false labor. He was about to head home when the woman's bag of water broke. Within the hour her contractions started again. She had hard labor and finally gave birth after midnight. The actual birthing was easy—the baby more or less fell, like an overripe mango—and really, Doc didn't have to be there. But Doc bore no ill feelings as he rode the three hours back home.

The sky was slowly turning mauve, and the front door slammed wildly against the doorframe. Full of misgivings he entered, then he found a bloodied machete glistening on the floor. He turned and saw the body parts of his family. Doc was confused; his mind could not comprehend what the limbs and blood were all about. As the truth sifted into his brain, he grew frantic and ran about collecting the parts and trying to piece them together.

That was how Isiong had found him. Reasoning that the Japanese were after Doc for helping the guerrilleros, Papa ordered the men to pack Doc's things, including his medicines, and lock the house.

# Women Warriors

❧

$\mathscr{I}$ kept wondering about the mother bird in Doc Meñez's yard. For a long time, even after we arrived at our new home, I thought how silly the bird had been to be so afraid of us, when in fact, hurting her and her babies had been the furthest thought from our minds. It made me want to laugh, thinking about it; we were more scared than she had been. She just didn't know it.

Mama cried when she saw the two nipa houses, and she went to the bedroom of one hut and lay down. After making sure Mama was all right, Papa checked the place, saying, "There's a bedroom in each hut, and there's a river nearby. And there's an outhouse. This will have to do. We could have lived closer to headquarters, but this is safer. Here, we're just mountain people."

The two houses were on stilts, with ladders leading to a room divided in two, to resemble a living area and a bedroom. Another door led out from the living area to the backyard. The roofs and walls were made of thatch. Laydan had an outdoor hearth, and the men later built a large outdoor table and benches. They also propped up nipa palm leaves to provide shade over this outdoor eating area.

The grown-ups decided that Papa, Mama, I, along with Laydan and Isiong (until he returned to William Cushing's headquarters), would occupy one hut. Nida, Max, Bitong, and Doc would have the other. It was all temporary anyway; MacArthur would soon return. The men would be at Lieutenant Colonel Fertig's headquarters most of the time and they would be carrying out the orders: to destroy enemy motor vehicles and bridges, tear down telephone lines, burn food dumps, capture enemy ammunition, all summarized as "hit 'em where they ain't."

Late at night, there was a loud thud on the bamboo-slatted floor. Something heavy had fallen and it scurried across the floor. I sat up. My heart knocked against my ribs as I tried to see what was in the room with Laydan and me. It moved, a swift dragging motion, and I made the sign of the cross. My fear of the supernatural came to life, and I imagined that a witch had transformed herself into some creature that was right there in the room, waiting for the chance to eat me. Or maybe the witch had not figured that Mama had lost the baby, and this evil thing with a long sucking tongue wanted to eat the baby. The thing out there moved once more. By this time, a little bit of the dawn's light filtered into the room and I could make out a small furry creature with little bright eyes. It looked back at me. I was certain that it would approach me, when it suddenly scampered across the room and up the wall. It was a rat.

In the morning, Laydan affirmed that it was a coconut rat. There were coconut trees all around us, and where there were coconuts, rats abounded. That was why the coconut trunks had metal sheets wrapped around them, Laydan explained. The smoothness of the metal made it impossible for the rats to climb up the trees.

"I hate rats," I said. "Even at the Royal, I hated them."

"They won't hurt you. If you were a baby, that would be something else. In my village some rats ate a newborn once."

"How? What happened?"

Laydan would not tell me.

"Can't we do something?" I asked, desperately.

"I'll see, but don't make a fuss, because your parents have a lot on their minds. Here, give this bowl of porridge to the doctor," she said.

Doc was curled up in the corner of the hut like a dark rock. His thick hair was matted with red-brown blood. His face was contorted from the torment he felt in his soul; Doc could not even cry. His eyes were closed, crusted over, and flies buzzed over them.

I couldn't help thinking of how he must have felt seeing his family the way he did. The awful memory rose in my mind and I tried brushing it away. I shook him gently, but he didn't move. I put the bowl of porridge down and moved closer. I pried his eyes open and peered into his pupils. They were glassy, like the eyes of a dead fish. "Doc," I whispered, afraid of startling him. His eyes remained devoid of feeling or intelligence. Although he stared straight at me, he did not see me. He pushed me away as though I were one of the pesky flies hovering over him. I finally returned the porridge to Laydan and told her that Doc was still sleeping.

I checked on him periodically, watching his chest rise and fall to make sure he was still breathing. I had this nagging fear that he would suddenly die, right there, without our knowing. That would have been very sad.

When the men began extinguishing the lamps that night, Doc awoke from whatever daydream he had been in and began screaming for his wife and children. He ran out of the hut and crawled around, clawing at the earth. When the men tried to pull him up, he grabbed a machete and waved it at them. They had to tie him to one of the supporting poles of the hut, and he thrashed about all night, howling and shrieking, so that we became fearful the Japanese would hear him.

We found him in the morning, slumped on the ground with blood crusted on his wrists. Nida loosened the manila rope binding Doc. "It's too tight," she grumbled. "How could they do this to him. Now, he's all cut up. Go get some water and a clean rag, Yvonne."

We washed and changed him. While combing out the tangles in his hair, Nida said, "Doc's a good man. He helped Mama and the girls at Slapsy Maxie's." She stroked Doc Meñez's hair. "A sick person likes to be touched. It's love they need most of all." She paused. "I talked to Mama while she was dying and even after she had stopped breathing. The hearing's the last to go. We better let him rest for now."

Doc lay still for a long time, but a little later he began moaning, and Laydan sent me to him with some porridge. He stirred and rubbed his eyes. Doc looked confused as he stared at me. I smiled at him, glad that he was awake. His baffled look lingered. Finally he spoke, "Where's your mother?"

"In the kitchen. It's time to eat," I said, offering him the soup.

He blinked his eyes and gave a wan smile. His voice softened. "I'm glad she's in the kitchen. I am not . . . I don't feel well. Amalia, call your mother, child. Tell her my head hurts and I feel lousy." He flung one arm over his eyes and forehead.

Not knowing what to do, I told the women what happened. Nida volunteered to feed Doc. When she approached Doc, he stared at her. At first he appeared confused, then very swiftly his eyes flashed in anger. Doc swung his bound hands at Nida, knocking down the porridge. "Get out! Where's Jesusa? Jesusa!" he yelled. Nida shrugged her shoulders, picked up the bowl and spoon, and left.

Later she fixed Doc some lunch.

"He'll just go crazy again, Nida, better leave him alone," Max warned.

"He's helped us, Max."

When Nida offered him food, Doc shoved it away. "JE-SU-SA! JE-SU-SA!" he bellowed.

"Doc, listen to me," Nida said matter-of-factly, "your wife and children are dead, Doc. The Japs killed them. We're sorry they died, Doc, but the sooner you accept this, the better off you'll be. It's best to bury the dead and get on with life. I know it's real hard, Doc; I know how you feel."

Doc's dark eyes flicked wildly around the room, latching onto me.

"Amalia, call your mother, right now!" His voice had such a tone of desperation.

"That's Yvonne, Doc. Yvonne Macaraig, the engineer's child. That's not your girl," Nida explained. "Your family's gone, Doc."

Doc covered his ears with his hands and shook his head. He began gnashing his teeth and contorting his body so that we wondered if he was having a seizure. A girl in church had an epileptic seizure once, and Doc looked like her, twisting, shaking, mouth foaming, as though possessed by the devil. I felt bad for him, and I wished I could have pretended to be his daughter to make him feel better. He eventually calmed down and lapsed into a sullen silence. But he refused to eat and talk. This went on for several days, but Nida was persistent in trying to help him. Gradually he allowed her to groom him and spoon-feed him.

One day she offered him palm wine, which lulled him into a stupor. Seeing that his violence had waned, the men freed him and continued giving him palm wine to suppress his rage. Doc, in this drunken state, remained passive, spending most of his time on his mat, asleep or gazing at the flies in the air. One evening, however, he stumbled over to Max and in a garrulous voice shouted, "Hey Max, where'd you pick up your wife?"

Max's crooked nose twitched, but he ignored Doc and continued polishing his rifle.

"Max, you second-rate-mother-fucking-boxer, I'm talking to you. Where'd you find Nida? Her titties are up to there . . ." He straightened out his arms in front of himself. "She's a whore, Max, a mistress of what was his name again? Kong King King, or was it King Kong King?"

Max's expression changed from one of annoyance to that of an angry carabao. His nostrils flared and his shoulders humped upward as he got up from the bench and walked over to Doc Meñez, who was weaving about. With his right hand, Max steadied the doctor as he gave him a powerful left punch.

Nida screamed. "Max, he's suffering."

"He called you a bad name," mumbled Max as he returned to the bench.

"What of it?" Nida shrugged and helped Doc up.

"You act like you're proud of it." Max ran his hand through his hair in a gesture of embarrassment.

Nida faced Max. Her narrow waist accentuated her big bosom and wide hips. Her abundant hair, usually knotted at her nape, was loose that night and it flew wildly around her. I—all of us—could not keep from watching her. Hands to her waist, with her armpit hairs peeking out, she growled, "Listen, Max, I was seventeen when Mama and I moved in with Ong King Kin. It was the only way I could take care of Mama. I told you that when we met. You can say this or that about me, but I'm no hypocrite. I'm not proud of what I did, nor am I ashamed." Turning her attention back to the doctor, she wiped off the blood trickling down his mouth.

Doc staggered up. "I've treated your kind with V.D. so many times."

"Shut up, Doc," Nida ordered, as she shoved him back to the bench.

"Did you hear me, Max? Your wife spread her legs for Kong King King—or whatever that Chinese immigrant's name is. Who knows, there may have been other men."

Max snorted. Papa held him back.

Pushing Nida aside, Doc staggered toward Max and Papa. He became more aggressive, like a wound-up top that you've just released. "Let him go, Nando. Come on, Max . . . Come on, Max . . . Nida's a whore! Come on, Max, hit me . . . are you afraid, Max? Hit me . . . hit me . . . Please, Max, hit me. Please . . ."

Max scratched his head with an uncertainty that made us hold our breath. Then he went to Doc. I thought he'd throw him another left hook, but the boxer put his arms around Doc Meñez and hugged him.

Doc went limp in Max's arms and he whimpered, "They're dead, and it's my fault, Max . . . I should have been there . . . would have killed them . . . ripped them apart . . . the baby . . . not even a year . . . she was toddling, just a little thing . . . 'Pappy' she called me, 'my pappy' . . ." Doc began sobbing.

"Listen, Doc," Max said softly, "it's time to rest." And Max and Nida carried Doc Meñez to his mat.

Doc cried for days and we were sure he would die from starvation, or be so crazy that he would never return to our world. But one morning, he stared at the crucifix over the doorway.

"Our Father," he began, then hesitated. "Our Father . . ." He put his hands to his head and rubbed his temples. "Oh God . . . Lord," he whispered, "I can't even pray. What am I going to do? What have I done to deserve all this? Save me. I know that I am a sinner, but help me, save me, don't abandon me. I have tried to do Your Will, tried to be decent to others. So why me, God? Why my family? Jesusa was a good woman, God. All she wanted was to help the people, that's all she ever wanted. In America, that was all she ever talked about, to learn all she could so she could help the people. And the children—they never harmed anyone. There were never any finer children than those three—Amalia, Junior, and the baby. Why did You have to go and take them like that? If it had been me, it would be one thing, because I have sinned. But not those four, God. Jesusa even had the children helping out in the clinic. Amalia used to cook and give food to the people. You made a mistake, God. But now it's done, and I have to continue living. Help me, God. What can I do to want to continue living? Save me."

In his own words, he prayed for the rest of the day, and during suppertime Doc remained sober and possessed some degree of control over himself. He announced that he had made a promise to God.

"What promise, Doc?" Nida asked.

"I'll have myself crucified, Nida, just like Christ."

The Japanese printed their own currency, but lacking gold backing, the money was essentially worthless. People needed baskets of the "Mickey Mouse money"—as Filipinos mockingly called the new currency—to go shopping. Even though the guerrilla regiment later printed their own U.S.-backed notes, Mama preferred bartering for our needs.

She struck a good deal trading some of our salted dried fish—the same dried fish purchased by Lolo Peping months ago. The mountain people, who valued salt (it prevented goiter, a common problem among the mountaineers), had a high regard for Grandfather's salted dried fish. We got pork ribs, beef bones with marrow, brains, produce, kerosene, *and* six fluffy live chicks. Mama said we'd raise the chicks for eggs.

At first we kept the chicks in a coop, but by the time they matured, they scurried about freely, pecking eternally at the ground, and rushing to Mama when she gave her special chicken call, a rolling chortle. She fed them grain and copras mixture, and that was why they were excellent layers, especially the plain brown one that laid eggs olive green in color. The hens' eggs often times—thanks to Laydan's innovative use of herbs, roots, vegetables, and fruits, all thrown in a potful of water—fed nine, sometimes twenty people, depending on whether other guerrilleros joined us.

Late one morning when the men were away, Mama was squatting on the ground hacking open some coconuts while Nida and Laydan squeezed coconut milk from grated coconut meat. I was chasing the chickens around when I spotted a Japanese soldier riding toward us. I ran, sounding an alarm. Before the women could decide what to do, the soldier was in front of us, waving a piece of paper in his hand and speaking in Japanese.

Briefly I wondered if Mama would cry, but she stayed calm and said, "No understand." She tapped her ear.

"Food. Take," the Japanese said in English. He did not look old enough to shave.

"What food?" Mama said.

"Captain, need food." The man made the eating gesture.

The women stared at one another, then Mama straightened up and, machete still in her right hand, handed him the wicker basket with the six eggs I had found that morning.

The soldier took the basket and said, "Chicken." He waved toward the bushes.

Mama bristled. "No chicken."

"Yes, chicken. Girl play chicken."

"If you want chicken, you can get chicken."

The Japanese stiffened and held his rifle tighter. "Get chicken, now!"

"No," Mama replied evenly.

They glared at each other. Briefly, as though weighing the matter, the man glanced at the coconut trees around us. He looked at Mama once more. His voice softened in compromise. "Call chicken, I catch."

71

Mama had a stubborn expression. With her back straight, her lower jaw thrust forward, she sauntered to the front where the chickens roosted. Two of the chickens peeked out of the bushes, checking to see if Mama had grain in her hands. Seeing only a gleaming machete in her hands, the chickens quickly scurried into hiding.

"Call chicken!"

Mama hesitated.

"Now!" He lifted his rifle.

Mama puckered her lips and gave a chicken call different from her regular call. The man crouched down ready to catch a chicken. His eyes darted here and there. Mama continued with her mock call, but soon the Japanese grew impatient. "Call!"

Mama warbled louder.

This went on for a while and I could tell that the soldier understood that Mama was not cooperating. Angrily, he slung his rifle to his shoulder and tried catching the good egg-layer, but she wisely flew into a thorny brush. After ten minutes, the man waved his rifle at us threateningly. Mama stood there, with feet astride, left hand on her hip, right hand gripping the machete, head thrown back. Under her piercing gaze, the man wavered, then he stomped away without saying another word.

Seeing Mama that way made me think of Bongkatolan, the woman warrior with dark hair reaching her ankles. In battle she wore clothes woven and beaded by the goddesses who loved her. Bamboo shield and sword in her hands, hair whipping in the wind, Bongkatolan equaled the finest men warriors. Once, her brother, Agyu, was captured by the enemy and she fearlessly ran into their midst. Swinging her sword to the left and to the right, Bongkatolan killed a dozen men, thus allowing her brother and herself to escape.

She belonged to the Ilianon tribe, who used to live at the mouth of the Ayuman River until the oppressive Magindanaos drove them away. Bongkatolan and her people fled to the mountains, but the Magindanaos were relentless in their pursuit and only drove them deeper into the mountain range. For a while they were safe, but being river people, they longed for their home at the mouth of the Ayuman River. Hungry and broken in spirit, they returned to their ancestral home only to discover that the Magindanaos had destroyed even their ancestral graves.

Wailing, they prayed to the deities, who wept with pity at their desperation. The gods and goddesses rained golden rice on them, and they promised them a land called Nalandangan which would have everything they desired.

After the Japanese soldier left, Mama threw up and shook violently for a long time. That night, fearful that the soldier would return with others, Nida and Mama slept with .45 revolvers under their pillows. Laydan and I had machetes nearby. When a coconut rat fell a foot away and started scurrying, we all fumbled for our weapons; but it was Laydan who struck it with her machete. Its body exploded and the movement immediately ceased so I knew the rat was dead. I could not bear looking at it or the bloody stains that Laydan cleaned away the next morning.

When Papa returned he said perhaps the Japanese was part of a patrol passing through, and that we were very lucky he didn't kill us.

# *Weeping*

❦

$C$louds "pregnant with rain" hung in the sky. I remembered the rainy days in Ubec when the grown-ups stayed indoors and, too weary to nag, allowed their children to play outside. The boys and girls abandoned their games of sungka, Chinese checkers, and cards and rushed outside with umbrellas over their heads. My cousin Esperanza and I used to dance under the rain, twirling our useless umbrellas around, and soon we kicked off our slippers and squished our toes into the soft mud, feeling the earthworms wiggling about. We rummaged through the kitchen until we found coconut dippers, and we rushed to the rain spout. Using the dippers, we collected rainwater, water so pure, and we took long sips like parched desert creatures; and we smacked our lips because the water was good and clean like nectar from some primeval forest. And Esperanza and I danced and played as if we were in paradise and man had never sinned.

———

Even in the mountains where the only people we saw were grimy guer-rilleros and mountaineers, Mama insisted that we wear starched and pressed clothes. It was wasted energy, I thought, but Mama found it imperative to maintain a semblance of civilized living. This was one link we had with our lives in Ubec, and she would not sever that tie. To break that bond would turn us into mountaineers, or worse, into animals; it would be an acceptance that our lives were per-manently changed. My mother survived on the illusion that every-thing was temporary. MacArthur and the Americans would return. The Philippines would be liberated, and we would resume our lives in Ubec.

And so despite the heavy clouds one morning, Mama insisted on washing our clothes at the river. While she and Nida pounded the clothes with wooden paddles, I played with the tadpoles. There were hundreds, maybe thousands of them, in the shallow part of the river. Some had tails, some had legs; they skittered about delight-fully. I found some rocks and formed a corral, then I captured some tadpoles and placed them inside. I was blocking a gap between two rocks when a guerrillero arrived with a letter for Mama. It was from Lourdes. Mama smiled happily as she dried her hands. As she read the letter, her voice tingled with excitement, but it quickly flooded with sorrow:

"By now you know that the retreating USAFFE bombed Ubec before the Japanese invasion. They destroyed most of the administrative buildings, but they also hit parts of the old section. The entire second floor of our house is damaged, but I suppose we are lucky because the first floor is still habitable. The dirty kitchen is serviceable, and although I have virtually no catering to do, we manage. Due to the shortage of food, medicine, and clothing, prices have become ridiculous—three hundred pesos for a ganta of rice! I had to sell my diamond solitaire ring, the one from Mama, to buy necessities, and I have other pieces that I can sell if necessary. It goes against my grain to do this because I know I am not getting good value . . ."

Mama's voice faltered and faded. As she continued reading silently, a forlorn air enveloped her. Tears welled in her eyes and trickled down her cheeks. Later, she gave a loud gasp and she cupped her hand over her mouth. Now really crying, she dropped the letter and ran away.

Nida picked up the letter. "Yvonne," she said matter-of-factly, "your grandfather died." She put her hand on my head and stroked my hair.

Because her words sounded distant, I asked, "What?"

"Your Lolo Peping is dead."

As her words sank into my brain, I felt like an empty tin can rolling down a street. "Read the letter, Nida. Just read it."

She did:

"Papa is dead. During the bombing raid, he went to Sikatuna Street looking for Mama. A brick hit his head. He was unconscious and I finally took him to Dr. Sato Tachiki, the Japanese head of Ubec General Hospital. Papa stayed there for two months, and he was in a coma the entire time. One morning he sat up, smiled, saying "Beatrize," and then died. The good doctor tried his very best, Angeling. We cannot blame him for Papa's death. Papa was old, and we must try to accept his death. There is little you or I or anyone can do. God's Will will be done— although these days, it is difficult to understand His Will . . ." Nida stopped.

"Is that all?" I asked.

She shook her head.

"Then read it. If you don't, I'll read it."

Nida continued: "Esperanza was badly hurt. She, Lupita, and I were in the dirty kitchen when the bombing occurred. Part of the kitchen roof blew off, pots and pans flying everywhere, the neighbor's house on fire, dogs howling, and on top of all this, Esperanza, who had been fiddling with a kitchen knife, cut her arm. Her blood spurted straight into my face. I managed to rip off a part of my skirt and tie it tightly above the cut—thank God Mother Asuncion taught us about tourniquets. Since the flesh around her wound started swelling, I decided to stitch the gash. Esperanza was very brave throughout the entire ordeal. But just when we thought we were through with the worst of things, Pasing next door came to tell me about Papa. We carried him home. He had a dent on his head where the brick landed, but that was it, so he looked quite handsome when we buried him in his military uniform. You should see the other dead around here, Angeling, without arms and legs. Some of them have had their faces blown off. I can understand why Mama wanted the dead to look presentable.

"The doctor also checked Esperanza and he gave me iodine—you cannot find medicines at the Boticas—warning me to keep her cut clean. He removed the stitches in a few days, and excepting for the scar, Esperanza is fine.

"I think of all of you every day. I like to remember our Friday afternoons together, how we all sat out on the verandah to catch the breeze, how we sipped Laydan's hot chocolates, how delicious the rice and corn cakes were. Although the memory is not as delicious as the reality, it sustains me. Remember how silly we used to get, talking about how the German nuns at boarding school starved us when we were children by feeding us nothing but potatoes? Oh, what I'd give for one of Mother Asuncion's potatoes now. And the girls, do you remember how they used to play with Momoy? And by the way the poor monkey did not survive the bombing. Life was so carefree then, Angeling."

After folding the letter, Nida hugged me. Her enormous breasts against my face smothered me. I felt as though I were suffocating. I pushed her away and went to the river where I cried. When I found some dead tadpoles, I tried to get them upright and swimming once more, but they lay there totally limp. I freed the live tadpoles, and I picked up the dead ones and buried them on the bank. I made a little cross and stuck it in the ground.

As I studied the burial ground, the memory of Laydan making hot chocolate came to me. Using pure solid chocolate tablets, she would melt the chocolate slowly in the blue enamel chocolate pot, and she would whip in pure cream. Lolo Peping loved Laydan's hot chocolate. He used to close his eyes as he sipped the rich frothy drink slowly. "Ahh," he used to say after the first taste.

The clouds thickened and it began raining. The women scurried to get the laundry from the line. The rain fell so thick that in no time at all the place was muddy and the river rose. The clothes were soaking wet, and some of them fell into the mud; it was a bad day to do the laundry in the first place.

Wednesday, market day, I watched the mountain people walking down the trail to the village to sell or trade their produce. Carrying enormous conical baskets on their backs, they strode with a rhythmic bounce in a straight line. It was always like that; mountain people always walked single file, even when they were on a wide stretch of land. Esperanza even had a joke about mountaineers marching single file in the heart of Ubec City. It was dumb, I thought, dumb. They were like ants. No wonder foreigners could come along and push Filipinos around. If people behaved like ants, then they would be trampled upon like ants. I would never behave like an ant, I decided.

I later lay under a guava tree and imagined our house in Ubec as it had been: The old stone well with the little catfish at the bottom; the frangipanis casting the delicate scent of the pink and white flowers; the enormous flame tree dripping with carmine flowers; the second-story verandah with the bougainvillea vine crawling up and providing shade. Were they still there? I thought of Lolo Peping and the time we went to the cockfight. I tried to rearrange the events of that day, making the Rhode Island Red cock win, and picturing Lolo Peping's ecstatic face. "We won, girls! Beatrize was right, after all," he would have said. It would have been really something to talk about, to wonder about while we had our merienda on the verandah. The news would have been all over Ubec. And other people, over their own cups of chocolate or citrus drinks, would have pondered on Lola Beatrize's affection for Lolo Peping, affection so great that it transcended even death.

I imagined Lolo Peping meeting Lola Beatrize in heaven. What would they say to each other? Would they find themselves older? Or would they appear as they had when they first met and fell in love?

On Lolo Peping's bureau there had been a black and white wedding photo of him and Lola Beatrize. Lola Beatrize appeared thin and serious. Even with her elaborate Maria Clara outfit (with the wide sleeves, loose blouse, and floor-length skirt) she exuded a practical air. Her hair was sleeked back in a tight bun held in place by a pearl-encrusted comb.

Her smile seemed cautious—she had been married to a drunkard who caused her enough premature purgatorial anguish as to allow her to go straight to heaven upon death. In the photo Lolo Peping appeared romantic; his eyes sparkled in the photo—you could actually see the sparkle as white dots in his dark pupils.

I knew that Lolo Peping loved Lola Beatrize, because many years after her death, he continued visiting her grave every morning. After laying down a bouquet of flowers and lighting a candle, he conversed with her as though she were right there. At home, he meticulously preserved her things as if any minute now, she would enter the door and brighten his existence once more. I thought to myself that if Lolo Peping and Lola Beatrize met once again in the after life, he could ask for nothing more. This would be heaven for him.

In this way I tempered my sadness.

Laydan found me under the guava tree. "We have been looking for you," she said.

"I've just been here," I replied. I didn't feel like talking to her or to anyone.

"You better come and eat," she said, "we have turtle soup."

My mouth hung wide open—she was talking about one of the turtles I had found near the river on our way up to Malaybalay. I stared at her and burst out crying. "Turtle soup! You killed my turtle! I hate you, Laydan! I hate you! You're a—a killer." I pummeled her with my fists. I tried to scratch her face. I wept over the cauldron with the dead turtle, its shell intact, although its flesh floated about in shredded bits. My tears would not stop. I felt sorry for the defenseless turtle. I looked at Laydan with her broad dark face, her ridiculous fleshy neck, her eyes that displayed deep hurt. She looked stupid, like some ignorant peasant. I hated her.

# The Prisoner

୧ଙ୬ଙ୬

The guerrilleros were building a floating bridge to transport men and equipment. Papa and his men were on an outrigger making their way upriver when they spotted three Japanese soldiers on a boat, patrolling the river. The guerrilleros hurriedly paddled behind a nipa grove where the overhanging palm leaves gave them good coverage. It was a moonless night and they waited in absolute silence with their rifles cocked. The patrol boat slowed down and Papa thought they had been discovered and shooting would erupt, but the patrol boat sped away.

Papa and his men waited for a long while before they continued upriver. There they learned that the other guerrilleros had a squirmish with the same three Japanese. The guerrilleros killed two Japanese soldiers trying to escape, and they captured one. It fell in Papa's hands to keep the prisoner and turn him over to Lieutenant Colonel Fertig for a military trial.

"Why didn't you kill him?" Mama hissed when she saw the prisoner.

"He's a prisoner of war."

"Where are you going to keep him? He'll hack us to death like the Meñez family. And what if others show up, like the one who wanted my chickens?"

"I'll handle it," Papa said.

"If he tries anything, anything at all, Nando, I will personally cut him up into pieces."

Papa told the men to bind the man's wrists and legs, and to tie him to one of the stilts of our hut. There he lay like a sack of rice near the ladder. He was around forty years old with a serious face and gentle eyes. With great difficulty, he managed to sit up and lean against the pole. The men took turns watching him. When the Japanese as much as groaned, the guard kicked him and pointed a rifle at him. Doc's eyes glittered flashes of scarlet when he saw the soldier, and the grown-ups had to watch Doc.

When Papa checked the soldier later that afternoon, he shook his head and grew angry at his men because the prisoner had dirtied himself. Handing the men a set of his own clothing, Papa told them to clean up the prisoner, change him, and not to let the incident happen again.

"Thank you, Sir," the prisoner said in English.

Surprised, Papa nodded at the prisoner.

The next day while Papa drilled me with my times table, the prisoner called out, "You are a teacher, Sir? I am a teacher also—English."

Papa hesitated. "I—I teach engineering."

The prisoner looked at me and his stoic face softened. "I also have a daughter. She is eleven. Akemi loves pine trees. She says they sing when the wind blows. And rivers—ah, how she loves rivers. I hear a river rushing nearby."

This bit of information made me feel sorry for him and I said, "There are tadpoles in there. I play with them, but sometimes they die."

"Death is sad, but it is also honorable, neh?" His face settled into

*81*

a melancholy expression. He became quiet and pensive, remaining that way the whole day. He refused to eat lunch and supper.

Lying on my mat that night, listening to the coconut rats scampering on the rafters, I imagined the Japanese girl Akemi in a kimono with cherry blossoms. She was lovely, like a young Sanny. Did she use rice powder on her face and pile her hair up on her head? What was she thinking of? I wondered. Perhaps she too wanted this war to end, so her father could cross the ocean and return home. I pressed my ear against the mat trying to figure out what the prisoner was doing, what he was thinking, but all I heard were the crickets and I fell asleep.

The next morning, the men left for Fertig's headquarters with the prisoner. Still annoyed with Laydan over the turtle soup, I stayed away from her, practicing my reading instead on an elementary book that mentioned snowflakes and oranges. I wondered what they really looked like—snowflakes and oranges. Papa said snow was like powdered sugar, and oranges looked like large mandarins. When he went to school in America, he had to wear heavy coats to protect himself from the cold, and in the summer while picking apples and oranges, he had to cover his head from the fierce sun. I wrapped a bandanna around my head, covering my ears, pretending there was snow all around. I searched for eggs and picked kangkong leaves in this way. Later I helped Mama and Nida dig for roots—they were very meticulous about this because some roots were poisonous.

We did not expect the men back that day, but in the afternoon, they appeared like somber statues. They got off their horses and plodded about in silence. Without speaking, Papa went directly to the river. He removed his shirt and pants and shoes and, in his undershorts, got into the water.

Mama broke into a run when she saw Papa swimming in the river. "Nando! What are you doing? It's cold, you'll catch pneumonia."

Papa waded to the bank and they fell into each other's arms. "I'm a teacher, Angeling," he said with great sadness. "I'm not good at all this."

"I know, Nando, I know."

"He tried to escape—I had no choice. I had to do it. What could I do?"

"You had no choice, Nando, none whatsoever."

"If only he had not tried to run away."

"He's enemy, Nando, forget it. They would have killed him anyway."

"What makes me happy is seeing my students' eyes flood with understanding. That is what I understand. I don't understand fighting and hurting and killing. I've killed a man, Angeling."

"Forget it, Nando. It's the war."

"I'm tired, Angeling. I'm weary of this war; I'm weary of waiting for the Americans who have been promising us help. I'm sick of this death that surrounds us. We kill; they kill. I'm tired."

"You have to forget and move on, Nando. We have no choice."

"I know that, Angeling. My intellect, this brain knows all that. It's my liver and my spleen; it's my insides that revolt against all this. I enjoyed it, Angeling. I enjoyed squeezing the trigger, and I enjoyed seeing his blood drain to the earth. All I could think of was our boy buried out there. And I hated how I enjoyed it."

Papa cried on Mama's shoulders for a long time.

# Old Flame

꧁❈꧂

$\mathcal{U}$pon learning that the former governor of Ubec, Gil Alvarez, would be at our mountain hideout, Mama and Nida fell into a desperation over food. Mama reluctantly agreed to have one of her chickens slaughtered; Nida picked bananas and scoured the bushes for more eggs. Papa called me and said, "Yvonne, your hair's falling into your eyes. Go get my bag."

He pulled out scissors and a comb from a black leather bag that reminded me of Doc Meñez's bag. Papa got a piece of cloth, threw this around my neck, wet the comb, and ran it through my hair.

"I'm not Ramon, but I'll do the job. Don't move so I don't hurt you."

I sat still, waiting for the cold feel of metallic scissors against my skin. He cut my bangs and trimmed the back.

"It's the coconut-shell style. It's short so we won't have to cut it all the time. Any more lice problems?"

"No, Laydan washes my hair every day with gugo."

"That's good . . ." He paused and chuckled. "I just had a vision of your mother fussing when we had dinners at home. Remember how she used to check the Wedgwood china and the sterling service before the guests arrived?"

Mama, dressed in a trailing gown made of fabric like gauze, would meticulously rub off the slightest smudge on the silver. She used to hold up the crystal one by one to make sure they were spotless and sparkling.

Papa and I looked at the dirt ground under our feet, the chickens scratching about, old Laydan gutting the unlucky chicken. Mama was putting coals into the metal iron so she could remove the wrinkles from her cotton dress with the hibiscus print—the prettiest one she had with us.

Imitating Mama's voice I said, "The governor is coming to dinner, be sure and wear your best barong tagalog, Nando."

"The governor? Well, certainly, Angeling," Papa replied.

We laughed and Mama asked what was so funny.

"Nothing, Angeling," Papa said, "just a little joke between Yvonne and me."

Nida talked Mama into applying the scarlet juice from native berries to her lips and cheeks. Mama had initially protested, saying in tactful terms that she didn't want to look like one of the girls at Slapsy Maxie's. Nida assured her the chic women in the world were reddening their lips and cheeks—didn't Betty Grable, Greta Garbo, Ingrid Bergman, and the other Hollywood actresses? Mama couldn't argue about the truth of what Nida had said, and she rubbed on just a little bit of the berries so she appeared as though she were blushing and it wasn't wartime. Nida also used some of the scarlet juice on her face.

"Is it true, Missus, that Gil's kiss could make a girl faint?" Nida asked when Papa was not around.

Mama waved her hand in the air. "Foolishness," she said, and she turned her attention to Laydan, nagging her about the chicken getting overdone, and did she remember to stick lemon grass in it, lemon grass has the best flavor, and what about the rice, did she pick out the tiny pebbles from the grains? Laydan, who had been looking tired, glided about, ignoring the fuss over the governor.

At the sound of approaching horses, Mama peered in the broken mirror to check her hair and face. She barely finished combing her hair when Gil Alvarez showed up.

Gil Alvarez was a tall, muscular man without fingernails. He had an incessant tick under his left eye, and he was also partially deaf. After greeting him with a peck on the cheek, Mama excused herself on the pretext of checking the rice. I caught her holding the rice pot's lid in midair and crying softly.

Alvarez, one of two Philippine entries to the 1928 Olympics held in Amsterdam, won two silver medals for the platform and springboard diving events. Athletic, handsome, and intelligent, he had been Ubec's heartthrob. Alvarez had been in love with Mama, and she with him. They planned to get married, live by the seashore, and have eight children—four girls and four boys. Their firstborn would be called Cristobal or Cristina, depending on the sex of the child. But while Alvarez was away training, Mama broke her tibia at the gym, met Papa, and married him. It was Fate, plain and simple, but Gil moped around after the wedding, then on the rebound married Pilar Cuneta, a former Miss Philippines. The girls in Ubec mourned his marriage; one reportedly jumped off the Cathedral's bell tower.

Gil Alvarez successfully entered Ubec's political field when he was only twenty-nine. Since he was governor of Ubec when the enemy invaded the island, the Japanese asked him to join their puppet government. Alvarez declined; the Japanese promptly went to his home. They raped and shot Pilar Cuneta-Alvarez before bayoneting four of his five children. The oldest boy, named Cristobal, survived the massacre by hiding behind sacks of rice and brown sugar. The Japanese arrested Alvarez and threw him in a prison camp, where they plucked off his fingernails and applied coarse salt onto the open wounds. They also held a water hose against his ears, destroying his left eardrum. Some guerrilleros, with the help of girls from the defunct Slapsy Maxie's—who diverted the guards' attention—rescued Gil Alvarez.

Traveling by submarine, Alvarez went to Port Moresby in New Guinea to meet MacArthur, who asked him to head the guerrilla movement in Ubec Island. To fund his activities, MacArthur gave him gold bullion and told him to recruit more guerrilleros for Ubec. He urged

Gil to coordinate activities with Lieutenant Colonel Fertig, head of the guerrillas in Mindanao, as well as the troublesome Martin Lewis, who had (without MacArthur's blessing) installed himself as guerrilla leader in Ubec.

Having just met with Lieutenant Colonel Fertig, Alvarez was at our hideout to talk to Papa.

"Prof," he said (Papa had been his calculus teacher at the university), "we need engineers desperately. Can you join us?"

Papa asked, "What happened to Solon, Mangubat, and Roberto?"

"All dead, Prof. The Japanese arrested and killed them within a week after their arrival in Ubec."

Papa tsked, remembering his colleagues. "What about the Americans? Don't they have engineers?"

"Yes, Prof, but they're at a loss. They don't know the geography, the weather. They don't even understand why the men refuse to cut down old trees. They're horrified at the number of leeches, lice, chiggers, and mosquitoes—"

Max interrupted, "Pardon my language, Governor, but the gadam Americans can't even bring themselves to wipe their asses with coconut husks."

Papa chuckled. He had been trained in Valparaiso University in Indiana, and he knew what Americans were like. He comprehended their finicky nature, their love of precision, and at the same time he knew about the Filipino *mañana* habit. He understood both worlds. He was familiar with Ubec's terrain; he could smell an approaching typhoon; he knew the availability of local materials to fix the docks, roads, bridges, hospitals, airfields. He knew he would be a great asset to the guerrilla movement in Ubec.

Papa turned to Mama, who had now stopped crying and joined us at the table. "What do you think, Angeling?"

"Nando, you know the blood of Tupas flows through my veins. If Ubec needs us, then we must help Ubec."

To further entice Papa, Alvarez said, "Prof, you'll have everything you need—a real house in Taytayan, which is under guerrilla control. It's safer there than here. You'll have trucks, jeeps, bulldozers, cement, steel pipes. We have everything, Prof, down to acetylene, burlap bags, bitumen, and dynamite. And I just picked up some gold from MacArthur to buy whatever we need. MacArthur has just liberated Buna. It was a brilliant campaign—the Americans had three axes, one taking the Ko-koda Trail, another taking the Owens Stanleys east of Moresby, and the third along the north coast of Papua. By the time the Americans con-verged in the Buna-Salamaua-Gona area, the Japanese were committing hara-kiri left and right. MacArthur's planning the Philippine offensive. It won't be long now, just a hop, skip, and jump and he'll be here.''

"Gil, you knew before you came here what my answer would be,'' Papa replied.

Gil Alvarez stretched his hand across the table and shook Papa's hand. He was so happy, his face twitched even more. He turned to Mama. "Angeling, you married a good man.''

Blushing, Mama cleared the table.

The moon was high and its silver rays fell on the palm leaves and filtered down to where we were. Laydan was soaking the next day's mongo beans, and the other women washed and stacked the plates. The fire in the hearth had turned into mesmerizing embers.

Gil Alvarez congratulated Laydan for the delicious supper. Aside from roasted chicken, she had stewed pig snouts—where she got them, we didn't know, for pigs were a precious commodity and people weren't slaughtering their hogs.

Sucking on his pipe, Papa told Alvarez about the ten-meter con-crete bridge they recently blew up. The men dug pits two meters deep at both sides of the north and south abutments. In each of the four holes, they placed 150 pounds of dynamite and attached a cap and a fuse a meter long. He instructed the detachment at the bridge to fire the charges, that he had two minutes before the fuses burned through to the blasting caps. The man panicked, lit the fuse too soon, and some tanks were left on the other side of the bridge, under the mercy of the advancing Japanese.

Doc talked about the men who had blackwater fever and yaws (they would die); the lucky ones who only had hookworms and ringworms. He told us about the American soldier he treated recently—nineteen years old, with orange hair and sunburnt skin peeling off his nose. The soldier had been in the swamps and found leeches on his legs. He didn't know that salt or heat would have loosened the leeches' hold. While prying them off with his knife, he accidentally cut his leg. The wound became infected and developed into a fullblown tropical ulcer. But Doc said that excepting for a deep gouge in his leg, he'd probably make it.

A little later Papa said, "Yvonne, tell Governor Alvarez what Mama did when the Japanese soldier came."

"Oh, Yvonne, don't," Mama said, pretending to be embarrassed.

"Go ahead, Yvonne," Papa insisted.

"Yes, Yvonne, tell me what your Mama did," Alvarez said.

I stood up and told the story, gesturing to show where the man had stood, making guttural sounds to show how the Japanese soldier had made his demands, standing defiantly as Mama had done, with the machete in her hand.

"Mama was just like Bongkatolan the Woman Warrior," I said.

I twirled around, waving an imaginary sword in my hand. I completed my turn with my feet astride, the way Mama had stood, the way Bongkatolan might have stood; and for a fraction of a lifetime, I *was* Mama, I *was* Bongkatolan.

Alvarez looked at Mama with admiration. Maybe it was the moonlight, but despite the tick in his face, I noticed his handsome cheekbones, his strong jaws. He had a gentle way about him. "Knowing you, Angeling, you would have gotten yourself killed over a chicken," he said.

"Gil, it's not the chicken, you of all people must know that. I just hate how they come here, in our own country, and push us around."

"You sound exactly like my grandmother, Nay Isa."

They laughed, then Mama said, "Ah, Gil, tell Yvonne about your grandmother."

"Yvonne, do you remember my grandmother? She was the little white-haired woman who used to occupy the first pew of the church, on the right side, right in front of the bleeding Christ."

I nodded. "She only had one foot."

"That's the one. Nay Isa fought during the Philippine-American War. She rode a horse well; she was a sharpshooter. A very spirited woman. On her death bed, she was still telling the doctor and priest what to do. General Perfecto Poblador made her commander of a bolo (machete) battallion. Riding her horse, leading her bolomen, she won three battles against the Americans with their fancy Mausers and Krag-Jorgensen rifles. She caught a bullet in her left foot and they had to amputate it. Even with one foot, she wanted to continue fighting, but she kept falling off the horse. To make her stop fighting, General Poblador put her in charge of a military hospital in the mountains to take care of the wounded and comfort the dying. Once, Nay Isa heard that Poblador and his men had lost their Filipino flag, so she stitched one up and crossed enemy territory—on one foot, mind you—to personally deliver the flag to the general."

"Your grandmother was really something, Gil. No wonder they called her the Bisayan Joan of Arc. I don't think I can compete with Nay Isa," Mama said.

"I'll put my gold on you, Angeling. Prof," Alvarez said, "any way I can recruit Angeling into the movement? She'd straighten out Martin Lewis, and she'd scare all the Japanese out of here."

They laughed.

# Death of an Epic Singer

༄

$\mathcal{M}$y anger toward Laydan had dissipated into a feeling of shame. I was embarrassed at my display of temper. I was never one to do things like that; it had always been Esperanza, and I did not know what to do. For days I did not talk to Laydan, but at last I went to her in the kitchen. "Laydan . . ." I started to say, then I didn't know what to tell her. I stood there watching her with doleful eyes. She continued with her work, as though nothing had ever happened between us.

"This is how you cook it, Yvonne," Laydan said. "Drain the mongo beans, because the water gets scummy. Rinse them, throw them in the pot. Then add coconut milk, dried fish, and you can add garlic. Adjust the taste later. Don't put in too much salt, because the fish is already salty."

After balancing the pot on the clay kiln and adjusting the burning wood underneath, she asked, "Tell me, Yvonne, what happened when the governor was here?'' Her dark eyes shone with curiosity, like those of a child.

"What do you mean, Laydan?''

"When you told your story about your mama, what happened?''

I knew what she meant. "I was Mama and Bongkatolan for a little while.''

"You saw them in your head and you copied their movements?''

"No, I *was* them.''

"I see,'' she said, and became somber.

Ever since her experience at the cliff when she saw Inuk riding the cloud, Laydan seemed to drift from us. It was a gradual happening undetected by most. She cooked, did the chores, and she was in no way confused the way Lolo Peping used to get, but she had an absentmindedness that I alone detected. It was as if she did not care for this world. She became more and more preoccupied with the past and rambled about it a lot. She was talking when we walked to the river to get water.

"Yvonne, did I tell you when I first saw Inuk? I was six, at a funeral celebration of Datu Ambian's first wife. A comet with a long trailing tail hung in the sky; and I sat on the mat entranced, from sunset until dawn, listening, observing him. Even then, I tried to imprint in my memory the notes and phrases. He was wonderful, Yvonne, eloquent and graceful. That night, he ended his song by pointing at the comet. 'Tuwaang ascended into the skyworld on a skyboat like that star,' he said. I stared at the heavens and saw gods and goddesses, giants and beautiful maidens, and I knew I wanted to be an epic singer like Inuk.''

As we lifted the jugs to our heads, she became sad. "I knew ten songs, ten songs, Yvonne—considered a feat, for the songs are long and very difficult—and Inuk told me I would sing in his place at Datu Ambian's second wedding. It would be a grand feast and I conjured up notions of fame and honor—I would be known as Laydan the most renowned bard of her generation; datus from all over Mindanao would look for me. But on the day of the wedding, I awoke with a rusty throat, and after rinsing my mouth with saltwater, discovered that I could not say a single word. Not a word, Yvonne. I left, Yvonne; I did not have the face to show him what had happened to me.''

Laydan was still talking when, on top of the hill, we happened to see a woman across the river. She was clothed in some strange material that billowed around her and she was studying us. Since she did not look like a mountain person, I wondered about her presence. Laydan put her water jug down and stared at her. The woman gave a slight nod, and the old cook nodded in return.

"Who is she?" I asked later.

"I'm not sure."

"She knows you."

"Yes," she said, and refused to discuss the matter any further.

A few days before we were supposed to leave our mountain hideout, Laydan could not get up from her mat. Mama called Doc Meñez, who didn't have to use his stethoscope on Laydan—he could see a black aura around her.

"You and I know what's going on, Doc," she said, "let's not waste time. Call Yvonne."

I went to her.

"Yvonne," she said, "go to my things and find the beaded vest."

I went through her bundle of clothes and I handed the vest to her. It was a hand-beaded piece that required numerous hours of work.

She ran her fingers lightly over the beadwork. "It's yours, child. It belonged to Inuk."

"What do you mean, Laydan?" I said, feeling a painful weight in my chest.

She wagged a finger at me. "Don't cry. Here, help me sit by the window. Let us watch the clouds. Maybe we'll see Inuk sailing by."

She breathed rapidly for a few minutes, then she calmed down. We peered upward for a long time.

"Laydan, don't die," I finally said.

She snorted a laugh. "You know how old I am, Yvonne? When the Americans were our enemies, I was already old." She paused. "That is very old. It is a gift to be that old, but the time arrives when it's a burden. It's confusing, Yvonne. When the American soldier ate here, the one with white eyelashes, I had to tell myself that he was no longer our enemy, and that I should not splash the hot soup into his face. Like your Lolo Peping, the memory of what Americans have done to us still grips my mind. Now I have to train myself that Japanese are now the enemy. In forty years the Japanese may be our friends. It is very confusing to be old.''

"Don't leave me, Laydan. I need you.''

"Don't be foolish, Yvonne. You don't need me. I said that about Inuk, but as you can see, I managed to become quite old without him. That Inuk—he makes me angry, when I think about it. 'Become the epic, become the epic,' he said. I thought it was something you could learn. If he had told me from the start it was a gift, I wouldn't have wasted all these years trying to understand him. Well, at least the deities have forgiven me.''

"They could not be so cruel, Laydan.''

She seemed pleased with what I said. "Did you see her face?'' she suddenly asked.

"Who?''

"Her—across the river?''

I shook my head.

"It is good that Meybuyan came for me; she really is kind. My neck is getting tired. We're not going to see him. Help me back to the mat, I need to rest. It will be good to rest.''

She closed her eyes and her breathing became more difficult. I was about to call Mama and Doc Meñez when she spoke. "Yvonne, I know you won't forget them.''

"I will always remember your stories, Laydan,'' I replied.

Doc attended to Laydan, but two hours later she died.

We buried her under a lovely orchid tree with ferns sprouting all around. I asked Bitong to carve a small boat out of wood, which I placed on top of her grave. I slipped on Inuk's vest and wept. After a while, I remembered Laydan's chiding me not to cry, and I tried to stop. In my heart I whispered to her that I loved her, but I knew that she already knew that. I told her how sorry I was for all the bad things I had done to her, but I also knew that she knew that too. Then I thought that what Laydan would have really wanted me to do was to tell one of her stories. To ease my grief and to honor Laydan I told the story about her beloved epic hero, Tuwaang, and the Maiden of the Buhong Sky.

The Giant of Pangamanon was a horrible creature who stomped about the skyworld burning castles and vegetation with his fire-shooting wand. Passing through the Buhong Sky, he was about to burn down the castle there when he happened to see a beautiful maiden spinning rainbows. The Giant crouched behind the trees and watched her delicate fingers fly over the golden spindle. He observed the graceful twist of her neck, her lovely face, and he fancied himself in love with her.

Impetuously, he roared out to the Maiden of the Buhong Sky that he wanted to take her away and marry her. The Maiden, knowing of the Giant's wickedness, quickly made herself invisible and fled.

The Giant became angry and he destroyed the entire Buhong Sky so nothing was left but a layer of ash and burning embers. Then he stomped through the different layers of the skyworld to find the Maiden.

The destruction of the Buhong Sky and the subsequent flight of the Maiden, left the world dingy, gray, and rainbowless. A dreariness and hopelessness possessed the heavens and earth. Growing weary at the sense of desperation, the deities conferred. They were furious at the Giant, but since they were not supposed to interfere directly, they decided to seek the help of the mortal most beloved to them, Tuwaang.

The deities prepared gifts for Tuwaang—a magic betel nut, a magic skein of gold, and special clothes woven and beaded by the goddesses. They dispatched the wind with their gifts to Kuaman Mountain, where Tuwaang lived.

Meanwhile, the Maiden of the Buhong Sky had taken refuge on earth. She astonished Lord Batooy and his people when one day she appeared clothed in spun fragments of the rainbow. She was weeping and before Lord Batooy could decide what to do, she made herself invisible and hid in the castle. They could not find her, but they heard her eerie sobbing echoing day and night.

In Kuaman, Tuwaang prepared for battle. While putting on the clothes from the goddesses, he remembered his mother pointing to the sky after a rain to show him the arching rainbow. It is a promise, she said, from the Maiden of the Buhong Sky that the rain will always stop and things will get better. She has spun the rainbow with love, and so long as the rainbow appears in the sky, the sun will shine after a rainfall.

Tuwaang tucked the betel nut and skein of gold in his bag and armed himself. He then picked up his magic shield—a gift from the deities in the past—that allowed him to ride on lightning. In no time at all, he was in Lord Batooy's kingdom, where a faint smell of smoldering ash greeted him. Lord Batooy explained that there were numerous forest fires in his kingdom.

"The Giant is coming this way," Tuwaang said. "Warn the people and tell your warriors to be ready. The Maiden is in grave danger. Where is she?"

"We cannot find her," Lord Batooy said. "We only hear her crying."

Tuwaang listened to the weeping that rebounded from wall to wall. "I mean you no harm," he called out. "The deities have sent me to help you."

The Maiden of the Buhong Sky made herself partially visible so she appeared like transparent parchment. "I am afraid," she whispered. She sighed and wiped away her tears. "The Buhong Sky was once filled with starlight and moonrays from which I spun rainbows. But the Giant has destroyed everything. I have no place to go. I am all alone."

She had barely finished talking when a large commotion erupted outside. Enveloped in flames, the Giant burned people, houses, farms, and livestock as he strode toward Lord Batooy's castle.

The Maiden quickly vanished while Tuwaang raced toward the Giant. With his wand, the Giant shot flames at Tuwaang, but the clothes made by the goddesses protected him. The Giant then threw his spear at his enemy, but Tuwaang swiftly stepped aside so the spear whizzed past him. When the Giant drew his sword, Tuwaang was ready with his own sword. They battled until their weapons broke into pieces. Frothing at the mouth from anger, the Giant was ready to use his bare hands when Tuwaang took the magic skein of gold from his bag and threw this at the Giant. The skein wrapped itself around the Giant, trapping him in an enormous cocoon, and Tuwaang slew him.

When the clouds of smoke had settled, Tuwaang and the Maiden surveyed Lord Batooy's devastated kingdom.

"Everything is burned," the Maiden said. "What will we do?"

"Don't lose faith," Tuwaang replied as he took the magic betel nut from his bag. He sliced it into pieces and rubbed betel juice on the dead, who miraculously came back to life. He squeezed the juice onto the ground, trees, and bushes so life returned to Lord Batooy's kingdom.

Afterward, Tuwaang and the Maiden rode a bolt of lightning to the Buhong Sky where Tuwaang also used the juice of the betel nut to restore life to the Maiden's kingdom.

"Now I can spin rainbows," the Maiden said as she surveyed her land, which was emerald-green and vibrant once more.

The sky soon lost its grayness and the deities were pleased that the Maiden resumed spinning her vivid rainbows. They smiled happily at the arching colors, the symbol that the sun will shine after a rainfall.

Before I started telling the story, the people around me had been weeping. It was not just Laydan's death that they cried about; there were many reasons for us to shed tears. But when I finished, I could feel that some peace or hope had settled in them. Perhaps they were thinking that one day soon our sun would shine over us. I myself was surprised that I remembered all of Laydan's story; I did not forget a single line. I could not sing it, as Inuk must have, but I said all of it, and I told it well. Laydan would have been proud of me.

# The Move

$\mathcal{M}$ama wanted to bring the chickens,
but Papa convinced her that it was impractical to carry squawking chickens over mountain trails, through a jungle, across the sea, all the way
to Taytayan. She reluctantly agreed to have three chickens slaughtered,
but she insisted on bringing the brown hen that laid olive green eggs
and the scrawny red hen that laid twice a day.

I watched sadly as Bitong beheaded the chickens one by one. There
was a lot of commotion as the headless chickens raced around for a few
seconds, blood spurting out of their necks before they collapsed. After
dunking them in a cauldron of boiling water, Mama and Nida plucked
their feathers. They gutted the chickens, cut them in pieces, which they
cooked in vinegar, salt, and spices—this would provide our meals during
the trip.

We were about to leave when I remembered the turtle living near
the hearth. It was the same turtle that I had found months ago as we

made our way to our mountain hideout; it was the survivor of the turtle soup incident that had made me furious at Laydan. Tigas was the turtle's name, and Laydan had punched a hole in its shell (by hammering a nail through). She had tied one end of a rope to the turtle and tied the other end to a supporting leg of the hearth. Tigas lived in this way, and although Laydan kept a basin of water near him, and she fed him rice, bananas, scraps of meat, and whatever else was available, the turtle remained wild and wanted only to go to the river. With his neck stretched out, legs frantically pushing the earth, he tugged and pulled at the rope.

I found Tigas in the same desperate posture. When I picked him up, he quickly hid in his shell. A little later he peeked out. I rubbed the rough skin on his head and put him down. He began straining at his rope once more. I got a knife and cut the rope's knot, freeing him. The sudden lack of pressure startled him, and he stared up at me, blinked several times, then he headed for the river as fast as he could.

"The idea," Papa lectured as we rode, "is that the Guerrilla Regiment slows down Japanese invasion. Direct combat means high death toll. To avoid that, guerrilla tactics include ambushing and destruction of roads and bridges that would otherwise make it easy for the Japanese to invade."

"Is that why the USAFFE bombed Ubec?" I asked.

"Yes, Yvonne," Papa replied. "For a long time the Japanese did not have telephones, water, and electricity. They've had to rebuild wharves, airfields, roads. All this takes time, effort, materials."

"Oh, it's like what Chieftain Tupas did when he burned Ubec before the Spaniards landed?"

"Yes, *hija*. But you see, the people are the ones who suffer the most. It is unfortunate that your Lolo Peping is dead. War is like that."

Doc Meñez, who had also agreed to join the guerrilla movement, wanted to burn his house so the Japanese would not use it for shelter. As we approached it, he became agitated; he had not seen his home since the massacre. His shoulders tensed and his breathing became rapid, and Max was ready to pin him down if necessary. Doc's face clouded: his eyebrows formed deep lines in his forehead; and his hands shook as he walked through the rooms. He kicked the leaves and dust on the floor and he stood staring at the horrible dark bloodstains for several minutes. He then announced that he wanted to see his family's gravesite. Outside, he studied the forlorn mound, covered with a layer of soft moss. A bush dripping with rainbow-colored flowers grew in the center of the grave and Doc wept and prayed for his family.

The men set the house on fire. It took a while for the fire to catch, but by the time we started down the mountain, the house was burning fiercely.

When we passed some orchids hanging on trees, Mama insisted that we pick some for my dead brother's grave. Grasses and weeds had overrun the place, and the pile of rocks marking my brother's grave was barely visible. My parents cleared the area around the grave. Papa dragged more rocks and added these to the existing pile. Mama arranged the orchid sprays and we said prayers for the dead. Then, muttering under her breath, she vowed to return to pick up his bones for a proper burial.

The men would take the submarine to Taytayan with Gil Alvarez. Because of limited space, Mama, Nida, and I would have to take the boat. Gil Alvarez assured us that an old man would take us to the boat, and another guide would meet us in Ubec and take us to Taytayan. As long as we looked and behaved like ordinary peasants, any Japanese inspecting the dock or boat should leave us alone.

It was nighttime when we boarded the boat. Mama, who had been complaining about the weight of her wicker basket, peeked in and was horrified to find a brick-sized bar of gold bullion, which should have gone with the men in the submarine. By this time the old man who had brought us to the boat was gone. Mama considered tossing the gold overboard, but Nida insisted that it was too valuable. They finally decided to let me carry the wicker basket—who would suspect a ten-year-old girl of carrying gold for the guerrilla movement?—and Mama carried the two chickens instead.

After we placed our baskets under three cots, I checked the rope tying the chickens' legs together to make sure it wasn't hurting them. I found a flier on the floor. It said:

## HANDSOME REWARD WILL BE YOURS

1. if you capture an American parachutist and deliver him to the Japanese forces;
2. if you report any knowledge of spies in American service;
3. if you inform promptly of any movement of American troops, whether land, sea, or air forces.

THE JAPANESE FORCES IN THE PHILIPPINES

Mama's face turned ugly. "Look at this, Nida. Now they want to make spies out of us." She crumpled the paper and threw it overboard.

We settled down, ready for the lengthy trip, and I was almost asleep when a loud commotion erupted on our deck. A fat Japanese soldier was randomly inspecting bags despite the passengers' protests. He grabbed a boy of around fifteen and began shouting. I could not understand his words, but I understood the tone—"Is he a guerrillero? Is he a guerrillero?" He shoved the boy to a kneeling position and pointed his gun to the boy's head. My mother reached into her pocket for her rosary, her lips already mouthing the Hail Mary. The boy's mother was frantic—"NO, NO, NO guerrillero, he's just a boy!" The soldier stopped—I thought he would pull the trigger—but he pushed the boy away and continued with his inspection. The people watched sullenly as he shook out clothing, dumped things on the floor, poked shopping baskets with his bayonet. He even asked a woman to lift up her skirt to check if she hid anything underneath.

I thought to myself that when he checked our baskets and found the gold bullion, he would shoot me, no, all of us. BANG!—the sound of a gun is sharp and clear; it rattles your insides, dislocates your soul from your body. I had heard the sound many times, when the men shot in the air for fun, or when they hunted a monkey or a wild boar. Most of the time, blood and death accompanied that dreadful sound. This Japanese soldier would not hesitate, not for a second, killing a person.

His eyes said so; they glinted with power and total disregard for us. Nida and Mama fixed their attention on the wicker basket under my cot. When the soldier moved closer to our cots, Mama closed her eyes as though she would swoon. The insides of my stomach curdled. I could not help myself—I bent over and began throwing up.

The Japanese looked at me as I gagged and spewed my supper on the floor. I tried to keep control over myself. I wiped my mouth, took a deep breath, but I retched once again. Dimly, I overheard the Japanese say something with a contemptuous tone, then he kicked a cot and approached us.

Mama's lips moved rapidly in silent prayer. Nida's eyes lit up as she ran her tongue over her lips. Right before my eyes, she seemed to undergo a transformation as she thrust out her chest and slowly walked to the soldier.

Smiling widely with one arm akimbo she greeted the soldier in Japanese. *"Konbanwa."* Her voice was soft and low.

The soldier, with a military intensity that seemed to burst out of his crisp brown uniform, paused to stare at Nida. His gaze rested on her breasts, and Nida took a deep breath and undulated slightly. She continued talking to the soldier in pidgin Japanese. Laughing coquettishly, she toyed with the soldier's eyeglasses and whispered in his ear. For a few heartbeats, the man appeared flustered. Nida hooked her arm under his, and they walked off to the cabin section.

That night, everybody on deck was silent. We heard only the sounds of the chickens, goats, and pigs that the people brought on board. We lay on our cots, feigning sleep, when in fact we felt jumpy. I was restless and wanted to turn, but I dared not. My throat tickled, but I held my cough. I wished I had thrown up on the soldier's shiny boots. I was filled with a desire to kick the Japanese overboard. I wanted to see him struggle in the deep and dark waters, then sink from the sheer weight of his boots and gun and bullets. I wished I were a giant, like the Giant of Pangamanon in Laydan's stories, so I could step on him, and I would watch his guts spill out. I hated him, and I hated the cold fear that filled me, that overcame all of us so that all we could do was pretend we were asleep. Even though we were not walking single file, we had turned into ants, passive creatures who lay there helplessly.

When she joined us in the morning, Nida seemed embarrassed. To break the silence she said, "They're probably in Taytayan by now, Missus. Submarines move fast."

"Nida," Mama said as she reached out and touched her arm, "we've been through a lot together. Do me a favor and stop calling me 'missus.' Call me Angeling."

Nida smiled and said, "All right, Angeling."

For the rest of the trip, the soldier would occasionally walk by our cots, wink, and flash a smile at Nida. Before we disembarked, he gave her two packs of Camel cigarettes which Nida promptly handed to an old man when the soldier left.

# Part Two

*1943—1944*

# Fears

Shortly after we arrived at Tay-tayan, Nida developed a craving for sour green mangoes. She ate three of them at one sitting, with salted shrimp fry, so that watching her made my mouth pucker.

"Nida, you've always disliked green mangoes," Mama chided her once. They were in the kitchen, picking out the little pebbles from the rice. Grade A rice was impossible to get, and Mama said it was only through God's grace that we were able to buy low-grade rice. Otherwise, she said, we would be eating corn meal and roots, even starve like some of those who remained in the cities where food was more scarce.

Nida straightened up and placed her hand on the small of her back. She looked haggard with a greenish pallor. "I don't know why, but they taste so delicious now," she replied. Nida, once full of energy, dragged about listlessly. Her hair, which used to stream about in raven-black abundance, hung in a limp ponytail.

Mama took a breath as though she were about to say something, but she remained quiet.

We said very little then. We had all sunk into a lethargy, a sense of hopelessness that the war would never end, that we would never resume the lives we had. Taytayan was under guerrilla jurisdiction, which meant it was safer, but we seemed to be more afraid than we had been in Malaybalay. Perhaps it was because we had more time to think, to remember what had been before the war, and to imagine the terrible possibilities that could happen to us because of the war. Maybe it was because we *had seen* some of the terrible possibilities in Mindanao, and we were no longer ignorant. It was as if we had eaten from the tree of knowledge and now, although wiser, we had lost an innocence.

The men were often at guerrilla headquarters up in the mountains, and we lived in constant dread that they would die or be maimed, that the town would be attacked by the Japanese while they were gone. We were tense, ready at all times, uncertain at all times. When the men returned, dirty and tired, on horseback or in army jeeps, we counted them like the chickens that we clucked into the coop at dusk. And if some men were missing, the first question was always—are they alive?

One morning Nida vomited, and I thought she would die, that she had caught some strange disease from the guerrilleros. Mama ministered to her, muttering as she often did that we had turned into animals, and why did God abandon us, what evil had we done to deserve this purgatory. I ran off to find rags for cleaning, and when I returned they were huddled together, whispering. They paused when they saw me.

Even though she had lost weight and developed an edgy personality, Mama was still a beautiful woman. She had lost the round face of her youth and her high cheekbones and expressive eyes made her look like a Madonna in an old church. Her dark eyes now flashed with anxiety as she said, "Go and play, Yvonne."

Obviously something was wrong, and when the grown-ups were that way, I would feel a restlessness rise inside me, a fluttery feeling that made me wish I were some bird that could soar up into the sky and glide around that blueness, unencumbered, free.

But I was not a bird. I could not fly, and so I went to the sea, where it was calm and peaceful—perhaps I would absorb some of that tranquility. I floated on my back and thought of Nida, wondering what was wrong with her, worrying that we would lose her.

As the waves rocked me to and fro, my mind wandered here and there with the motion. I finally focused on our boat trip from Mindanao to Taytayan. I had been afraid of the fat Japanese on the boat, and I hated him because of the fear he made me feel. I hated all the Japanese, who seemed to have dropped out of the sky to change our lives. Our existence had been orderly and pleasant, with Tiya Lourdes, Esperanza, Lolo Peping, and all of us in the big house in Colon Street. But now Lolo Peping was dead, and we were in someone else's dark and airless house in an unfamiliar town. We weren't even sure if Tiya Lourdes and Esperanza were still alive. We were hiding, keeping a few steps ahead of the Japanese, the men trying to slow down their takeover of the Islands, the women trying to maintain some kind of civilized lifestyle. Maybe Mama was right, we were turning into animals.

I submerged myself in the cool water, then I swam farther out and floated on my back. For a while the hot sun stung my eyes and I shut them tight. Bit by bit I opened my eyes. It was a March summer day, and the sky was blue with white cottony clouds. I wondered if the great bard Inuk or my beloved Laydan was up there. I bobbed up and down on the sea, studying the clouds for a long time, hoping to catch a glimpse of Laydan or the person she loved. For a while I felt comforted until I heard the distant laughter of some children. I suddenly envied them for the joy they could muster even with fear surrounding their lives.

I dove into the sea, and I looked at the colorful corrals and the schools of fish darting about, until my chest ached and I had to burst up for air. After catching my breath, I closed my eyes and floated. Perhaps this is what it feels like to be dead, I said to myself. The gentle waves felt like a hammock; the saltwater carressed and licked my body and face. An occasional wave splashed my face, the saltwater entering my nose. Sputtering and snorting, I thought, now surely I will drown. I swam farther out to sea, floated once more, felt fear flooding my body as the waves fell over me. I thought of the small body of my dead brother. I remembered Doc Meñez's family all hacked up, and Laydan dying in front of me. There were others—Sumi, Sanny, and Lolo Peping—they were all dead. When I was small, I had heard numerous stories about dead people. There was the one who was buried alive, and when the people dug up the coffin, they found his fingernails clawing at the casket lid. That thought made me shiver—it would be better to die in the sea. There would be no body to bury, no flesh for squirmy worms to feast on.

I had lost all sense of time when I heard my mother's voice from the shore. "Yvonne, you're too far out!" She was waving frantically. "Yvonne, come here right now!" I closed my eyes, pretending I didn't see her. She shouted louder, "Yvonne! Come here!"

I opened one eye and saw her wading into the sea. I did not move. Fully clothed, my mother began swimming toward me. I waited until she was near, then I lifted my head and shouted, "Mama!"

Startled, she sputtered. "Yvonne, stop that foolishness! Get back to shore!"

Because I did not budge, she reached over and hit my arm. Hurt and surprised, I swam back with her.

"What do you think you're doing," she shouted. "You could have drowned. That water's deep, and there are whirlpools. You know whirlpools pull you down."

She continued scolding as we walked home: "What is wrong with you? Look at me when I'm talking to you. You got me wet, now I'll have to change all over again. That's just more laundry for me. I never had to do laundry in my entire life until this . . . this . . . war. I've done nothing but wash and wash—look at my hands, look at the cuts and sores. Oh, just look at how horrible they look; I used to have such nice hands. What do you think you were doing? Answer me."

I remained quiet.

She stopped walking, grabbed my arm and shouted, "Answer me!"

"I don't know."

"What do you mean, you don't know. You almost killed yourself, swimming alone in the deep where you could drown. Why nobody'd have known you drowned. It was a good thing I went after you."

"You told me to go play."

"Don't answer back!" Then she swatted my bottom with her hand.

The sudden sting made me jump and I started crying.

Her voice softened. "Stop crying."

I could not stop. The humiliation of being hit like a small child made my tears fall. I stood there with my head hanging down, sniveling.

"Oh, Yvonne, I didn't mean to spank you." She looked at me apologetically, then she tilted my face to hers and wiped away the tears. "I was afraid you'd drown, Yvonne. That's all, I was afraid. I didn't mean to spank you. It's so hard to try and keep things normal, to go on living. Everything's so difficult. I was afraid I'd lose you too. All I could think of when I saw you out there was your baby brother. He's dead, all alone in that miserable place. I can't lose you too." She was weeping as she hugged me.

In thanksgiving for my safety, she lit some candles in front of Our Lady at the old stone church. Her eyes were closed, her lips moving in prayer. It was quiet in church. The smell of melted wax had a soothing effect, like menthol rubbed onto your chest. It reminded me of the days before the war when we went to church and saw our friends and talked to and about them after Mass or novena. I used to pray then—the Our Father, the Hail Mary, the Apostle's Creed, I knew all the prayers. I used to stare at the burning heart of the Sacred Heart of Jesus and feel compassion and love. But this afternoon, I could not pray. Even though the scent of melted wax had rubbed the edge off my restlessness, I could still feel fear and a deep sadness over a loss that I could not even pinpoint, could not give words to.

On the way home Mama talked about my dead brother. "I still think of him, Yvonne. There isn't a day that passes that I don't think of him. He would have lived if we had been near a hospital instead of in the outbacks someplace. He had no chance, poor child. And then we had to abandon him. Some nights I think of how alone he must feel in that jungle with just the wild animals running around. I know he's in heaven, but I can imagine him out there. Someday, we'll get him and give him a proper burial."

Mama's words reminded me of our family crypt back in the city, and I said, "We'll bury him near Lola Beatrize, so she'll watch over him." Our mausoleum was four-tiered; and the dead were buried above ground. There were niches for every member of the family, a thought which I used to find gruesome but which now seemed reassuring. It was a kind of home.

"Yes, near your Lolo Peping."

I paused, "Ma, even though Lolo Peping's dead, I see him in my head, counting the stars and mumbling about the dead like he used to. He feels alive, Ma. I miss him."

She kissed me on the forehead and hugged me. "Oh, Yvonne, it's also been hard for you, hasn't it? It's been purgatory for everybody. I don't know how long we can last; I don't know if I can take this much longer. It's one thing after another—now it's Nida."

"Ma, will Nida die?"

"Oh, no, Yvonne, she'll be all right. Don't worry about those things. Ah . . . it's probably from those green mangoes . . . ah . . . her stomach's upset," Mama replied.

Back home, we found Nida cutting string beans. She had washed her face and put her hair up in a bun. Nida looked better, although she was still puffy with rings under her eyes.

"It's a good thing I went after Yvonne, Nida, she almost drowned," Mama said, trying to sound cheerful.

Nida smiled at me wanly, then she resumed her work. Her shoulders were scrunched together; she appeared tired and beaten.

"How do you feel?" Mama whispered.

Nida shrugged.

"What are you going to do, Nida?" Mama asked.

Their eyes locked and they remained quiet for a long while. I also kept quiet, sensing something would happen. Nida shook her head, and Mama reached out to clasp her arm. Together they sighed.

"Wait, what about Doc—of course, Doc can help you. Talk to him when he's here," Mama said.

Nida threw a tinny laugh. Like a shadow of her old exuberant self, she stood, arms akimbo, chin thrust forward. "Doc doesn't do things like that. Isn't that just like life? Max and I wanted a child so badly, then something like this happens." She sighed and continued. "I want a child, but not this. I hate this child! Every time I looked at the baby's face, I would just remember that—that—savage. Oh, Angeling, he was a pig. He was all over me. The smell of him made me want to throw up. But it was all I could do to save us."

Now I understood the whispering and Nida's constant lethargy.

"Max would never know," Mama continued.

"But I know."

"It may still come," Mama said. "Sometimes I'm late. Especially with all this. There was a time in Mindanao when it didn't come for two months. I thought I was 'that way.' I should have been happy, but I was upset. Nando and I want another one, but what if it dies—like the other one? And times are so bad—the men away, the food so expensive. They say it's worse in the cities. People are actually eating rats. Maybe you're late because of poor diet. Poor diet can do that."

"I'm always on time."

Mama said, "Say a novena, Nida."

"I'm not religious; never was. I don't know why not because I saw Mama pray day in and day out. She had this small room with all sorts of statues and holy pictures, and there was always a lighted candle in front of her altar. I watched her turn as thin as a toothpick from TB, and she kept praying and praying. Her prayers were never answered. Maybe that's why I don't believe in prayers. Me? I just rely on myself. I've never waited around for someone else to fix things for me. I took care of Mama and myself. When Ong King Kin was around, well, I took care of him too. I took care of Max, the bar, the girls there. I have always just minded my own business. I only finished fourth grade, but one day shortly before Mama died, I had this idea that God was made up by people who need someone to blame for what happens to them. I'm this way because of something I did, and I'll handle it."

"Oh, Nida, don't talk that way. God listens. He is good. This is your cross. We all have our own crosses to carry. Even Jesus Himself went through trials. It will all work out; trust in God. Pray to Him. Talk to Doc; Doc can help you. Doctors know how to—they know what to do."

"Not Doc. He used to help our girls at the bar, but never in that way."

"Talk to him anyway, Nida, and see what he can do."

Nida sighed. "We'll see."

They stopped talking and I walked away thinking how complicated the business of having babies was after all; and women, it seemed, carried this burden alone.

# Bitong

꧁꧂

$\mathcal{D}$oc Meñez returned from the mountains with Bitong, our handyman turned guerrillero, who had accidentally cut off his toe with a machete. A gunshot distracted Bitong, that was why he made that mistake. Right after the accident, Bitong had wept, not so much from the pain but from worry that he would never be able to wear his shiny leather boots again, the ones my father had given him a long time ago and which Bitong cherished above all his worldly possessions. Up in the mountains, Doc had attached the toe to the foot, but the big toe wasn't doing well and Doc brought him to our house for a "leech treatment."

"Leeches are dirty, Doc," I said as I followed him to the swampy nipa field loaded with the blood-sucking slimy creatures. The thought of them made the hair on my arms prickle.

"Yvonne, leeches are one of God's finest creations. Have you noticed how polite leeches are?"

I stopped and stared at Doc, thinking he had lost his mind again. He removed his shoes and rolled up his pants. Patting my head, he continued, "A leech doesn't hurt you when he's feeding. If you leave him alone, he'll get the blood he needs, then he closes up the wound, so you don't bleed or catch infections. My wife and I knew a midwife in Mindanao who knew all about leeches. We used to ask her questions all the time. She was old and knew a lot of things. Isn't that amazing? The older you get, the more things you know. She was learned; she knew more than my professors in the States. This midwife used leeches for all kinds of cures. She even used them to get rid of migraines."

"What's migraines?"

"A big headache."

"Well, ah, Bitong doesn't have a headache, Doc."

"Yes, but he has a big toe with no circulation. Leeches stimulate circulation. You'll see."

Doc Meñez caught six leeches. There wasn't much to it. He stepped into the watery area and stepped out and the leeches were bloating up on his legs. I bent down to peel them off, but Doc told me not to. We just waited until they were full of Doc's blood and fell off.

Back home, Doc checked Bitong's toe, which had turned a sickly bruised color, then Doc applied one of the leeches onto the big toe. "He's sucking! And Bitong you have a nice green aura," Doc yelled happily, all to our bewilderment.

Unimpressed, Bitong continued crying, all the time whining with regret over the times he hadn't worn his boots to keep them looking new. "I should have just worn them," he repeated. "They were my first real shoes, so I didn't want them scuffed, but I should have just worn them."

I felt sorry for Bitong. He had been ten when he joined our household. His mother had brought him from their small barrio to our house in Colon. "He's puny, *señora*, but he doesn't eat much, and he works hard," his mother had told Mama.

When his mother left, Bitong had not cried. He confessed once that he had only felt relief because during the eight-hour bus trip, his mother had fretted that my mother might not take him in. Bitong had six younger brothers and sisters and his mother was at her wit's end trying to keep them all fed and clothed.

His mother used to visit him once or twice a year, but the demands of the other children grew excessive and she stopped visiting altogether, by which time Bitong considered our household his. He enjoyed the movies at the Royal, especially the cowboys-and-Indians ones, and he loved the leather boots that Papa had given him one Christmas, and which he now hugged tightly as if letting go would sever the thread of life itself.

Doc kept a vigil on Bitong's toe, and he happily noted that the toe was turning pink, meaning blood was flowing, which in turn meant Bitong might not lose the toe after all. Since his move to Taytayan, Doc seemed happier. Perhaps being away from Mindanao, where his family had been massacred, dulled that painful memory. Doc devoted himself to healing the guerrilleros and townspeople. He shared their joy at their recovery, and he felt great sadness when they passed away.

To celebrate the good news about Bitong's toe, Doc and I hunted for seashells at the beach. We were searching for the big ones with the soft-bodied animals (which you steamed and poked out with a safety pin), when Nida showed up. While I poked around a tide pool, Doc and Nida wandered away to talk. I could not hear them, but I could see Nida crying while Doc talked. I saw Doc wipe her tears from her cheeks. Later, Nida walked away, and Doc joined me although he became withdrawn.

The first chance Mama had, she asked Nida about what Doc had to say.

"He talked about an American who stepped on a mine and lost both legs. He didn't want to die, and the American struggled hard to stay alive. Doc said he fought hard for three days, but he finally died. Doc says he can't take life away. That's what he said, 'I can't take life away, Nida.' Just like that. He talked about his dead wife and children once more, and what a miracle life is." Nida shrugged her shoulders as though she could not fathom Doc's words.

———

Just when we thought Bitong's toe would be all right, the toe suddenly turned blue-black and Doc talked about amputating it. Bitong wept and asked to see the town's faith healer. Without taking offense at Bitong's request, Doc personally supervised Bitong's trip to the faith healer's house. That was another good thing about Doc Meñez; he always kept an open mind, and was never threatened by others.

We found Mang Viray, a grasshopper of a man with gold backing in his front teeth, in his one-room nipa hut. He was with Marta, the town's seamstress, who suffered from an incessant toothache. Marta had chewed on cloves, said novenas, promised the Virgin Mary all sorts of good deeds if only the miserable toothache would pass. It never did, and as a last resort, she asked Mang Viray to remove the tooth.

After Mang Viray said a prayer to the Child Jesus (his spirit guide), he shoved his big thumb against the woman's ailing tooth, and out it fell. It was quite amazing, and there was hardly any blood. Mang Viray told the seamstress to rinse her mouth with salted water, then she left.

The faith healer turned his attention to Bitong, who was whimpering about his big toe. "I don't want to lose it; I don't want to," he whined.

"Well, boy, I don't want you to lose it either, so let's take a look. Hmmm—I see that Doctor Meñez here has stitched this together, but you might as well have attached a potato to this foot, Doctor. This toe looks bad. I don't know what they taught you at those fancy medical schools, but all I have to do is look. I may be old, but I have two fine eyes—why, frankly, Doctor, it'd take a blind man or a fool not to see that this toe's withering away."

Bitong howled louder and Mang Viray said, "Go ahead and cry, boy. Crying won't heal the toe, but it'll make your soul feel better. When you're through, I can try and drain some of the poison from your body. But I warn you, the toe looks bad, so don't expect too much."

When Bitong calmed down, the faith healer flicked his long fingernail on Bitong's stomach, making a two-inch cut. He placed a copper coin on the cut, then he lay a cotton ball soaked in alcohol on the coin. Mang Viray took a match and lit the cotton, which flared up. He quickly placed a small glass container over the burning cotton. The cotton burned for a while, but it quickly fizzled down. Right before our eyes, Bitong's flesh bulged into the glass container. Blood oozed out of the little cut and clotted into an ugly purple mass. With his eyes rolled upward and the gold backing of his front teeth flashing, Mang Viray said another prayer to the Child Jesus, then he quickly yanked away the glass container. He removed the coin, cotton, and blood clot. With a dramatic flair, he cleaned the wound with alcohol and showed everybody the blood clot, which he explained was poison from Bitong's system. But later, after studying Bitong's toe, he shook his head and said there was more poison, and that he could do nothing else. "Sorry boy, but the toe will have to go," he said sadly.

After hearing the same prognosis from two medical experts, Bitong resigned himself to his fate.

"You could still wear your boots," I said to make him feel better. "You just have to wait until the foot heals."

"People walk funny without the big toe," he sadly replied. "They lose their balance."

"I didn't know that. That would be too bad. But I'm glad you're alive, Bitong."

He sighed and was quiet for a very long time, then he said, "The noise scared me. When I heard the gunshot, I jerked. But if I hadn't pulled back, I'd have lost the other toe as well. It could have been two toes. Last month an American blew off his legs. He was setting the dynamite and it blew off. Both legs. And there was another American whose, whose . . . ah, manhood, was blown off. He died. I'd rather die too than run around without my organ." He sighed. "A toe isn't the worst thing that can happen, but when it's your toe, it's still sad," he concluded.

Surprisingly, Doc became more discouraged than Bitong after Bitong lost his big toe. Doc had been rather ebullient since our move to Taytayan, but now he said, "I'm feeling crazy again." Shaking his head, he continued, "This whole war business makes me lose my sense of equilibrium. People dying, limbs lost, it's too much for a normal man."

He became morose, and just when we thought he'd sink into the state he'd been in after his family's death, he announced that he wanted to be crucified. It would fulfill the promise he had made in Mindanao.

"When, Doc?" I asked as I helped him sort out his medicines.

"Good Friday," he replied.


Despite the exciting news about Doc, the women continued their secretive ways. I found them in the outdoor kitchen, arguing as they fried pork skin called chicharon.

"I saw her, Angeling," Nida said.

"Who?" Mama asked as she stirred the pieces of pork skin swimming in hot oil.

"The midwife."

"Not that woman, Nida. She looks like a witch. You haven't, have you?" Mama paused, wiped the sweat off her face, and looked at Nida.

"No, I just wanted to talk to her," Nida said.

"What did she say?"

"She has remedies."

"What sort of remedies? Those papayas and massages are no good, Nida. I've heard about them."

"I'm not going to have the child."

"It's dangerous, Nida. And sinful. Besides, women die from those things."

"Sometimes death is better."

"Oh, Nida how can you say that, after all we've been through. It would still be yours, Nida, and you would learn to love it. Before you do anything, think about it carefully, Nida."

I stared at the pork skin, bobbing up and down in the oil. Nida really doesn't want that baby, I thought. What a pity, because she and Max had always wanted a child. The memory of the fat, hateful Japanese soldier on the boat nauseated me. Nida did what she did at the boat and got pregnant, and even though she had wanted to be pregnant, she didn't want this child. It was too bad. I remembered the colorful bargirls at Slapsy Maxie's. Everyone in Ubec knew that some of the girls had tow-headed bastards—who their fathers were, one could only speculate. If good people went to heaven and bad ones didn't (as Mother Ignacia had taught me), then these girls would never go to heaven. Well, Nida was just like those girls. And yet I liked Nida. She had been kind to her tubercular mother; she had saved us from the Japanese in the boat. She did a bad thing to do good. I pondered this for a long time until in the end I had to say that Mother Ignacia was wrong, and that ideas like badness and goodness were far more complicated than she taught me to believe.

# Deathless Man

❦

$\mathcal{T}$he jackfruit tree in the backyard was occupied by an enchanted black giant who sometimes made himself visible on moonlit nights. He would sit on the same branch that I was on, and he would smoke a giant cigar. The townspeople swore they had seen him. Even the town's two old maids, called the Virgins, said they had seen him relieving himself one night, which only made the townsfolk wonder what the Virgins actually looked at.

The black giant hadn't always lived in the jackfruit tree. He used to stay in the house we occupied. Townsfolk said that a long time ago, a wealthy childless couple lived in the house. They adopted a child whom they loved tremendously, but the child, for all the pampering he received, turned out to be a cold, self-centered person—a bad egg, townspeople said. When he grew up, this bad egg up and left for the excitement of Ubec City. The couple was left alone in the house. Unable to maintain the huge house as they grew older, they locked up portions of the place, confining themselves to the wing with the kitchen. The black giant then moved into the sealed portion of the house.

When the couple died, some relatives with numerous children moved into the house, and the giant, unaccustomed to all the racket, moved out of the house and into the jackfruit tree. When these noisy children grew up, they also moved to the city, leaving the house under the care of an old man. The guerrilleros requisitioned the house from this old man, who didn't mind moving in with relatives while we used the house.

I always asked the black giant's permission to sit on his branch, because you never monkeyed around with enchanted beings. They could do things to you, if they got angry at you. Once a man annoyed the enchanted spirits at a bamboo grove, and he ended up way up on the very tip of the bamboos. An enchanted spirit also got a young girl pregnant and she gave birth to a baby with webbed feet.

Mumbling another, "Excuse me," I reclined and leaned my head against a branch and looked up at the sky. That afternoon, as I watched the clouds sailing by, I thought of the epic singers Laydan and Inuk, the fact that they were dead and would never tell their tales again. I remembered Laydan as she lay dying, telling me not to forget the stories. Her stories—how could any person forget Laydan's wonderful stories? Her stories were part of my soul; they sustained my spirit.

That afternoon, Nida and her problem made me imagine she was the Maiden of Monawon under the evil clutches of the Deathless Man. Laydan's long and beautiful story was about how Tuwaang saved the Maiden.

The great hero of Kuaman, Tuwaang, set off to rescue the Maiden of Monawon, who had been tricked into betrothal with the Deathless Man. After donning the clothes made by the goddesses, he armed himself and picked up his magic shield, which allowed him to ride on lightning. He later found himself on a grassy resting place where he heard the melodious crowing of a rooster. The rooster hopped toward Tuwaang and said:

"Lord Tuwaang, the deities have sent me to accompany you on your journey. They give you these three golden musical instruments—

gong, flute, and guitar—which you must add to the Maiden's dowry. They have instructed me to tell you these words, 'It is contained in the flute.' I do not know what they mean, but the deities said that when the time is ripe, you will understand.''

Carrying the three items for the Maiden's dowry, Tuwaang and the rooster left for the Land of Monawon. They had barely arrived in the great hall of Monawon when the earth trembled and a roaring sound filled the room. The Deathless Man with one hundred of his fiercest warriors strode into the room. Pale and odorous, he studied the guests and upon seeing Tuwaang, ordered the host to get rid of Tuwaang.

Before the flustered host could reply, Tuwaang stood up and said, ''He who asks our host to commit such a discourtesy is committing a far graver offense.''

The guests murmured nervously. Deathless Man's eyes glinted as his hand slid toward his dagger. His companions pleaded, ''Do not fight here, not at your betrothal celebration.'' To the host they suggested, ''We'd better proceed with the engagement ritual.''

The Lord of Monawon quickly ordered the dowry items for presentation. It was the custom in those days for the prospective groom to match the dowry, thus fulfilling the engagement contract. Only then could the marriage come to pass.

The servants dragged out sacks of rice, bolts of cloth, inscribed brassware, gold and silver coins, jewelry, and other items which they valued. One by one the Deathless Man matched the dowry items until the golden gong, flute, and guitar were presented. He stared hard at the items, and finally spoke. ''I cannot redeem these items, but nonetheless the Maiden will be mine.''

''But Lord,'' protested the host, ''that would break our ancient law. You must match all the dowry items.''

The Deathless Man bellowed, ''I have said that the Maiden will be mine!''

Tuwaang approached the host and the Deathless Man. ''Deathless Man,'' he said, ''you are unable to match the golden gong, flute, and guitar, and the betrothal is broken. The Maiden is free!''

Shaking from anger, the Deathless Man was about to strike Tuwaang when the Maiden of Monawon appeared at the doorway. "Do not fight," she spoke. "I have with me my magic betel box, which will decide if I should marry the Deathless Man or not."

The box rose slowly and floated from person to person. It paused in front of each guest and betel chew flew out of the box into people's mouths. When the box reached the Deathless Man, it paused without offering him betel chew. The Maiden then declared, "The box says I should not marry Deathless Man."

At this, the evil man lost his temper and he flung his stool. He and his companions left the feast and outside they began slaying the warriors of Monawon.

On hearing the clash of metal and the screaming of the wounded, Tuwaang and the rooster rushed outside to join the battle. The rooster used his daggerlike spurs to kill the enemies, while Tuwaang used his sword to slice the enemies like mushrooms. Soon, Tuwaang and the evil man stood face to face. The earth shook and thunder rolled as both men grappled with each other. Tuwaang threw the Deathless Man to the ground with such force that the earth split open and the evil man fell into the underworld.

Since Deathless Man lived in the underworld, he quickly surfaced to resume battle. To taunt Tuwaang, who was growing weary, the Deathless Man said, "Surrender, Tuwaang. You can never kill me. My soul is hidden where no one will ever find it. And as long as my soul is safe, I will never die."

The smell of death hung over them as the Deathless Man grabbed Tuwaang and flung him into the underworld. Tuwaang found himself near the Underworld River, where the gentle goddess Meybuyan lived.

The goddess, who was tending the tiny dead infants too young to cross the river, asked Tuwaang, "Are you ready to cross the river to the Land of the Souls?"

"No, kind goddess," Tuwaang replied. "The Deathless Man threw me down here. I wish to return to earth."

"I know about the wickedness of the Deathless Man," the goddess said. "Come, I will show you the path that leads back to earth." Then she added, "Remember the words of the deities."

"What words?" Tuwaang asked.

The gentle goddess stared at him, smiled, and said, "Just remember."

As Tuwaang scampered up the trail, he recalled the message from the deities—"It is contained in the flute."

He hurried into the house, got the flute, and rushed outside. "I know your secret, Deathless Man. I know your soul is in this flute. Go. Leave the people of Monawon in peace, or I will destroy you!"

"Never!" the Deathless Man replied as he lunged toward the flute in Tuwaang's hands. But Tuwaang was too swift for him. Jumping back, Tuwaang lifted the flute over his head and smashed it to the ground. The evil one shook and shuddered like a dying hog, then he became still.

It was over, finally, the Battle of Monawon, and the wounded were brought to their homes, and the battleground cleared. And the Maiden of Monawon was free at last from the clutches of the Deathless Man.

# Doc's Crucifixion

$\mathcal{P}$apa had his professorial voice when he told Doc Meñez it was not a good time to be crucified. "Wait until the war's over. The Americans will soon be here. We just received a report that General Kenney's planes destroyed some Japanese destroyers from Rabaul Harbor to New Guinea. Air and sea lanes in the Southwest Pacific belong to the Allies," Papa said.

"It's God's will, Nando, and I might as well get it done while there's a lull," replied Doc.

"The Japanese are getting more aggressive, Doc, and there's no telling when the men will need you. Besides, you might damage your hands from the nails."

"Nando, after what happened to my family I went to hell. All of you thought I had lost my mind, and I suppose I appeared to have lost my senses, but I was in hell, Nando. Personally, I would rather have died, but God didn't will it that way. I was alive but burning in hell, and I prayed for salvation. He showed me what to do, Nando, how to pull myself out of that hell. I prayed about this; I have no choice. If the nails go through the metacarpal area in just the right way, there should be no damage."

Papa sighed, remembering Doc as he had been in Mindanao after the massacre of his family. "Doc, if you insist on getting crucified, don't get yourself nailed. You're a doctor and the wounded need you. You can't do much if you're maimed yourself."

Doc considered Papa's words, and he went to church and prayed. Finally, he agreed to have himself tied to the cross. He immediately began making arrangements for his crucifixion. I accompanied him to Elpidio, the town's carpenter, whom we found fuming and kicking a wooden coffin.

"What's the matter, friend?" Doc asked.

"It's a long story, Doc, but someone just canceled an order for a coffin."

"How did that happen, friend?" Doc said. "Dead people don't return coffins."

"It's this way, Doc," Elpidio explained. "The seamstress Marta's husband ate too many crabs last night and had diarrhea and stomach cramps. Thinking he was dying, Marta called me to measure him so I could make a coffin—the cheapest, she said. I said it would cost her four hundred pesos, and right there, in front of her dying husband, she says, 'That's too much, how about two hundred pesos.' Well, Doc, I may be poor, but I've got dignity. I wasn't about to haggle with that poor man listening, so I said yes——"

"A dying person's sense of hearing is the last to go," I added, remembering what Nida once said about her mother.

"That's right, girlie," Elpidio said, and he continued, "Then as I was leaving, I suggested she call the faith healer. No offense meant, Doc, but around here, people prefer Mang Viray."

"It's all right, it's all right," Doc said, waving his hand in the air. "What did he do?" asked Doc, interested in learning something new.

"I wasn't there, I was busy making the fucking coffin. But what I heard is he drew out all his poison."

Doc perked up. "Did it work?"

"Did it work, you ask me? I'm telling you, Marta's husband got well. Healthier than he'd been in a long time. Marta came running over to cancel her order for a coffin. 'Excuse me,' I told her, 'but the coffin's done.' Would you believe it, she refused to pay? Marta's tougher than flint; she kept whining, 'This is clearly God's will. Would you argue against God's will?' On and on she went until I got fed up listening to her." He kicked the side of the coffin.

"Well, friend," Doc said, "don't worry about it, because I've got a job for you. I need a life-size cross in wood. I'll have myself crucified this Good Friday."

"*Susmaryosep!*" exclaimed the carpenter. "I've never seen a real crucifixion. I've just heard about these fanatics in Luzon who have themselves hanged every year. Two hundred pesos, Doc, gold or guerrilla notes, none of that fucking Japanese Mickey Mouse money."

"All right, friend."

I was feeding the chickens when the Virgins, Meding and Petra Santiago—second cousins of Gil Alvarez, the ones who had seen the enchanted black giant relieving himself—stopped by our house one morning. Meding, the older one, called out, "Yvonne, is Doctor Meñez in?" They must have just come from church because they smelled of incense and had their black veils around their shoulders.

After kissing their hands to show respect, I led them to Doc, who was boiling guava leaves for medicine.

"Meding, Petra, what can I do for you?" Doc beamed as he wiped his hands on a piece of cloth.

Charmed, the Virgins smiled demurely. "Getting old, Doctor, but praise God and the saints, we're doing well," Meding replied. The dry skin on her face crinkled like old leather. She glanced at her sister; they stared at each other for a moment, then I caught the younger one give a slight nod. Meding took a deep breath and continued as if delivering a memorized speech: "Doctor Meñez, we heard about your plans, and we know it's an imposition, but my sister and I have come to request that you walk down Gumamela instead of DeLeon. We'd like to see you carrying the cross, Doctor Meñez. Please."

The sisters were remnants of the Santiago family, and people related that they had once owned the entire town of Taytayan plus surrounding areas. Mama said their name brought to mind Spanish land grants and sugar cane haciendas. Actually, the sisters were not as rich as they once had been because their father had squandered most of the Santiago fortune on women and liquor. But the sisters still lived comfortably in the oldest house on the other side of town.

They were in their sixties and deeply religious like their mother, who died when they were mere children. Never married, the sisters were called the Virgins for obvious reasons. Meding, the older one, had had a solitary suitor when she was twenty, but when their good-for-nothing father died one dawn in his mistress's house, Meding broke off with the man and vowed to take care of the sickly Petra. Aside from contracting typhus, which had made her lose most of her hair, Petra also had asthma and eczema. The townsfolk swore she had never attracted a single man in her life.

Even with the war going on and with Gil Alvarez's son Cristobal living with them, they continued their regimented life, getting up at five every day, praying, bathing, making their beds, and later Petra attended to the garden while Meding supervised their servant. After breakfast, and with Cristobal usually at their heels, they hailed a horse-drawn carriage, did their marketing, and then stopped by San Antonio church to light a candle. Petra would pay one of the women to dance a prayer to the Child Jesus, while Meding (a devotee to our Lady of Carmel) said the rosary in front of the statue of our Lady.

They spent their afternoons washing rags, cutting bandages, and sorting out produce for the guerrilleros. Late in the afternoon, they had their merienda on the verandah with a view of Petra's squashes, tomatoes, cucumbers, string beans, and the single row of calla lilies, the only luxury she allowed herself this wartime. Usually visitors stopped by, because the sisters were friendly. The sisters would offer them cassava cakes and inquire about war developments or local gossip. When the sun set and the sawing of the crickets echoed throughout the yard, they had supper. Later, they put Cristobal Alvarez to bed, tucking him in like a six-year-old, instead of the eleven-year-old he was. Meding said additional prayers to our Lady of Carmel while Petra ironed clean rags for the hospital. At eleven they said their evening prayers and retired.

As she now eyed Doc, Petra coughed, ran her hand through her skimpy hair, and echoed her sister's appeal. "Please, Doctor Meñez, we'd like you to carry the cross by our house."

Embarrassed, Doc said, "Excuse me, Meding and Petra, but that's terribly out of the way. I'll be going the opposite way."

The two sisters fanned themselves in an agitated manner. "Doctor, we know it's a detour, but we are two old ladies who cannot possibly stand on DeLeon Avenue under this summer sun to see you. If you walk down Gumamela Avenue, we can at least see you from our balcony."

Doc considered the one-kilometer detour.

Meding fluttered her right hand over her chest. "I'm an old woman, Doctor Meñez, with a weak heart."

Doc sighed and threw his hands up in the air. "All right."

That was one thing with Doc Meñez, he was always willing to accommodate other people. I admired this generosity, but at the same time, I felt that Doc went too much out of his way to help others. That was what had happened when his family was massacred; he had been out helping a pregnant woman. But I suppose, even if Doc had stayed at home, there was no telling if he could have fought off the Japanese. Chances are, he would have been hacked up like the rest of them. So altogether, his kindness toward others saved him. As the people said, Fate pretty much determined things.

Summer and Lent went together, and you knew it was summer by the way the breeze turned warm, so warm it took your breath away. Even though it was wartime, it was a colorful kind of hot, with mounds of fruit of riotous colors displayed on rickety wooden stalls in the outdoor market. It was a rainbow sort of hot that not even the war could destroy—flowers displaying petals of magenta, yellow, tangerine, and chartreuse. It was the sort of hot that made ladies expose luscious brown shoulders and knees as they sighed, "*Susmaryosep!*"—Jesus-Maria-Jose; and they shimmered under the rippling sun.

When Holy Thursday came around, the entire town knew about

Doc's plans. A community spirit overcame the people and even the stingy seamstress, Marta (the one who returned the coffin to Elpidio, the carpenter) surprised us all when she donated costumes for the participants of this real Passion play. She sewed a brown sackcloth robe for Doc, and another brown robe for Max, who would play Simon. There were two Roman soldiers who would help with the crucifixion. The residents of Gumamela Avenue decorated their street with sampaguita flowers, woven palm trees, and freshly cut banana trees with enormous bunches of bananas. Even the shy Good Shepherd Sisters dragged benches against the high wall surrounding their convent to catch a glimpse of Doc as he walked by carrying his cross.

For a while, war was forgotten, and a fiesta spirit overtook Taytayan. Even my parents, who had been convinced a crucifixion was a fanatical idea, wavered and I overheard Mama say, "He blames himself for what happened to his family, and he wants forgiveness."

Papa nodded in agreement. "I guess, Angeling, we all have sins that we could use forgiveness for."

Good Friday, I woke up at dawn, excited over Doc's crucifixion. I had never witnessed such a spectacle. I looked at the silver crucifix above the doorway and tried to imagine Doc looking like Christ. When light filtered into the room, I hurried to the kitchen where I found Doc having his breakfast. "Yvonne, I had the loveliest dream," he announced. "It was about Jesusa and the children."

"Did your wife say something, Doc? Laydan said dreams talk to us," I said.

"Well, Yvonne, I don't remember all the details, but I do recall the flavor of the dream. There she stood with the three children, and they were smiling and waving at me. They had the most wonderful golden auras. If this dream talked to me, it would have been something good, Yvonne."

We continued chatting until we heard the noise of people outside. Townsfolk were congregating around our house and along Gumamela Avenue, to see Doc carry his cross. His cross was outside; everything was ready, and after donning the brown sackcloth, Doc excitedly picked up his cross and propped it on his right shoulder. With Max beside him and the rest of us trailing behind, Doc began dragging his cross.

It was a warm day and perspiration dripped down Doc's face. At first he kidded, "What kind of wood is this? It would have been nice if this were made of balsa." Max and Nida took turns wiping his face, and twice I broke off from the procession to ask for a glass of juice or water for Doc from the people, who generously obliged.

At the end of Gumamela Avenue, the Virgins, with Cristobal shrinking behind them, stood on their balcony, grinning and waving at Doc and the crowd. Doc nodded a greeting, then he made a U-turn to return to DeLeon Avenue. It was at this point that his breathing grew shallow. He stumbled once, but Max took the cross from him to allow Doc to catch his breath. After a few seconds, they marched on, past the Good Shepherd Sisters, who peeked over their high wall.

By the time we reached Mount Buntis, Doc was grimacing in pain. Salty sweat rolled into his eyes, blinding him at times. I had never seen Doc look so tired and I was getting worried. When he fell at the summit, Nida wanted to call the whole thing off, but the people booed and several threw pebbles at Doc. "Hey, I risked my life walking through enemy territory just to see him. If he wants to be crucified, let him be crucified. It's his promise to God anyhow."

"He's right," Doc whispered, "it is my promise. Let's continue. I'm okay."

"Doc, you don't look too good," Max said.

"I'll be fine, Max."

He lay on the wooden cross and Max tied his hands and feet to it. When Max and two other men propped up the cross, Doc groaned, but he nodded his head to indicate everything was all right. We stood staring at him bound to that enormous wooden cross. It was a rather remarkable sight, with the hot summer sky above him. I thought to myself that surely whatever Doc owed God, whatever sins he had committed, whatever it was that he needed salvation for, was now being paid for. Doc was magnificent on that cross.

He was up there for a full seven minutes before Mama noticed that he had stopped breathing. "Look at him, look at him, he's not moving," Mama shouted. Because she was rather high-strung, the men didn't take her seriously. But when Doc remained still even as a bee buzzed in front of his nose, I said, "Mama's right." Papa studied Doc and ordered the men to quickly bring the cross down. Mang Viray, the faith healer, hurriedly checked Doc's pulse. He furrowed his brows as he ran his fingers over Doc's wrist, temple, and neck. Then he confirmed my mother's observation. "He's dead," he said simply.

The people gasped in disbelief at Mang Viray's words, making me confident that the faith healer had made a mistake. Mama made the sign of the cross while Nida pulled at the ropes around Doc's hands. The people were pushing, shoving, but I kept my ground near Doc. I observed Doc's chest to see if it rose and fell, but it did not move at all. As people milled about not knowing what to do, I ran to Doc and pounded on his chest. That was one thing with dead people, they did not move. If Doc's chest would only move—if it would only go up and down . . .

"Yvonne, stop it!" Mama said. "Nando, Nando, do something."

Papa pulled me away. "It's no use," he said as he held me close to him. I could smell my Papa's sweat, feel his warmth. "We'll take him home," he called out to the men.

My arms were wrapped around my father. I discovered that if my eyes were closed, I could blot out the world around me. It was all a silly mistake; Doc was fine. He was just tired from the walk. It was all because of the silly Virgins, asking him to make that detour.

Papa picked me up and started carrying me home. I felt tired, and I could hear my father's voice echo in my head as he told people to clear the path for Doc's body.

Later he put me down, and hand in hand we walked ahead of the men carrying Doc's body on their shoulders.

"He's all right, isn't he?" I insisted.

"Child, Doc's gone."

"Where?" I looked back at Doc's body with his arms dangling like pendulums. The hot summer air felt oppressive.

"He's dead, child," Papa said.

"But there's no blood." That was the other thing with dead people; they usually had blood on them. There was no blood; surely he was still alive.

"It is good that he fulfilled his promise," Papa continued in a soft voice. "A man is only worth his word."

Farther down the road, Elpidio, the carpenter with the extra coffin, practically danced around us while dropping broad hints about his available coffin. Unable to hold himself back, he finally approached my father and said he'd sell the extra coffin to us for a hundred pesos, a steal he insisted. It was too much, even for my patient father, and he snapped, "We'll discuss it later on."

The idea of this man trying to get rid of the ill-starred coffin made me feel like giggling. There he was, a grown-up, behaving that way. It was rather funny, and I could feel myself on the verge of a giggling fit. Holding myself back, I remarked, "Pa, he's embarrassing himself."

"He's poor, child. Poverty makes people do all sorts of demeaning things." Papa's voice had softened; he had already forgiven the ridiculous carpenter.

Later, I could barely look at Doc lying on his cot, totally limp and lifeless. I saw Doc crazed; I saw him pull himself together and use his talents to ease other people's purgatory. He was a good man, and something inside of me felt like it was cracking. Doc was gone, I told myself over and over to comprehend this reality. Another one dead. We were all dying, one by one. We were gnats that lived for a moment, then fluttered down dead to the brown earth. Still, he did fulfill his promise to God, and what was it that Papa said?—a man is only as good as his word. Doc's word was always good.

The women wept shamelessly as they removed his brown sackcloth. Mama kept repeating he shouldn't have done it, that it was a foolish thing to do, that she had been against the idea in the first place. Nida, who had special affection for Doc, was too overcome with sorrow to speak.

"We had better wash him before he turns stiff," Mama said.

Stiff—I had forgotten that a person turned rigid upon death. Once Laydan told me of how some mountain people handled their dead. They tied their dead onto a chair near the entrance of their house. There the person stayed for three, four days. Meanwhile the corpse slowly bloated up, and sometimes quite suddenly the fattened thighs forced the legs apart so it seemed the corpse moved. Then body fluids oozed out of the openings—eyes, nose, mouth, ears—at which time people plugged up these openings with cloth. And meanwhile, the stench increased. All this happened to the dead man strapped to this chair by the doorway; he was a kind of a spirit guard so nothing evil slipped into the home. Then eventually, when the body was no longer recognizable, the people buried the corpse. Later, much later, they dug him up, cleaned his bones, and placed these in an enormous jar.

Was Doc really turning stiff? I chased away the mental image of his bloating corpse. I studied his body; he appeared as though he were merely sleeping. The women had composed themselves, and they had a basin with water, a washcloth, and some soap, and they began cleaning Doc. I was pondering the scene of the two women washing Doc, and feeling the melancholia of the moment, when the women suddenly screamed, dropping the basin with a gigantic clatter. I looked at Doc's naked body and saw that he was developing an enormous erection. As they stared at Doc's organ that had miraculously stirred to life, the women continued screaming, but they recovered and quickly threw a sheet over him before the men arrived. Doc heaved a big sigh, then he sat up and calmly said, "I'm so hungry. Could I have some bitter melon and rice?"

Doc was alive! Suddenly the air turned light and clean, and sparkling sunshine streamed into the room. My soul within me expanded.

While shoveling the food into his mouth, Doc described what had happened. It was like a dream, he said. He was carrying his cross up a steep hill. The cross was heavy and, growing tired, he wished he could get to the top where he wanted to be. Sweating profusely, with constricted chest, he climbed on. Near the peak, he found a stream blocking his path. He was deciding whether he'd wade across, when a woman called him from across the stream. It was his wife, with their three children skipping around her. They appeared lovely with golden auras, like angels without wings. Doc started to cross the stream, but his wife shook her head. "Go back, it's not time yet." It was at that moment when Doc sat up.

I observed Doc eating with a tremendous appetite. He was perspiring from his frenzy to satisfy his hunger. I dished out more food, and he smiled at me. Yes, Doc was alive! And I grinned back at him.

———

Even as Nida's belly grew, no one discussed her condition. She had gotten rid of her pallid look and her daily nausea, and she had a lovely flush on her cheeks and a rounded belly. Everyone knew she carried life in her, everyone, that is, except her husband, Max. Max had slowed down; the war had been unkind to the aging boxer. Once he had been a young warrior, but now he was too old for the fighting, the discomfort, the nerve-wracking uncertainty, the pain and illnesses surrounding him. He himself had contracted malaria, and even though Doc gave him quinine, Max never recovered and was prone to shivering and sweating. Once a hefty man, he became gaunt. Once strong with an easy laugh, he became morose and talked often of his mortality. It was not that Max was afraid to die, because death he said was a brief matter. It is easier to die than to live, he often said. What concerned Max was that one day he would die and leave nothing of himself behind. "There is a cycle in nature," he pointed out once. "Look at the trees, see how they drop seeds that grow into other trees, look at the animals and observe how they reproduce. They continue to live, but I, when I die, I will be gone forever." He was referring to the fact that he and Nida had never had children. Now, with Nida being the way she was, things became rather awkward, and so we all kept quiet, leaving it up to Nida to tell Max—or to Nature, for surely one day soon, the size of her stomach would reveal it all.

One night after Doc's crucifixion, Nida gathered the nerve to talk to Max. "Max," she blurted out over supper with everybody listening, "I'm pregnant."

Max blinked his eyes, like a startled turtle. His nose that leaned to his cheek flared.

Nida continued, "It's not yours, Max. The father's not anyone you know. All I can say is that I'm this way because I had to do what I had to do."

The silence in the dining room was broken only by the sawing of the crickets outside.

Doc, who had acquired a special status from his resurrection, came to Nida's rescue. He cleared his throat and with a scholarly voice said, "It's a fine child, Max. Nida has a fine pink aura surrounding her. A fine child."

"I wanted to get rid of it. I already made arrangements with the midwife, but I couldn't do it, Max. When it moved inside of me, I knew it had its own life. It moved, Max, inside of me, and I couldn't kill it." Nida placed both hands on her protruding stomach. Her lower jaw jutted out with determination.

Max remained quiet. He was staring at Nida with an expression that was difficult to decipher. I wasn't sure if he was going to hit her, or if he was going to weep. Very slowly he got up and walked toward Nida. He put his arms around her, gritted his teeth, and began crying.

"I'll dish out more rice," Mama said, as she hurriedly left the dining table.

"Well, now, I have some work to do," Papa said, also leaving the table. "Go get the map, Yvonne."

Everyone trickled away, leaving Max and Nida alone. In the next room, our ears were cocked, but all we heard was Max's sobbing.

The next day, before the men returned to the mountains, I saw Max and Nida under the enchanted jackfruit tree. Max had his right ear against Nida's stomach, while Nida stroked his head. Max was happy. I had to shake my head in wonder at how Life poked fun at Max. He went to America to be a famous boxer, and he drove a cab and never found fame. He returned to the Philippines to marry the sweet and passive Filipina woman of his dreams, and he fell in love with Nida, a woman with a past. Max and Nida were childless, and now Life presented them with a Japanese soldier's bastard. And they accepted what Life offered them, welcomed it, with mind-boggling joy. Max kissed Nida and lingered beside her for as long as he could before he finally left.

# The Alvarezes

*Papa* was often away and on his brief visits home, I wanted to be near him. Even at home he was busy planning, meeting with other men, but sometimes he had the time to play sungka, a shell game. We used to play it in Ubec and I missed those moments. He had taught me moves so I could stay in the game for a long time. The winner then played against Esperanza, although she was too fidgity to stay still for a game like that.

Papa and Gil Alvarez were talking while I played nearby, hoping they'd finish so maybe Papa and I could play. It soon became apparent that Papa wouldn't have the time to play with me. They were talking very seriously and Gil was upset; I could tell from the twitching of his face as he spoke: "I don't know what to do, Prof, Martin Lewis refuses to cooperate. Since he went underground, he's set up his own head-quarters, and he won't talk or negotiate."

Papa, sucking on his pipe, replied, "Hasn't MacArthur talked to him?"

"He said he would. Based on our talks, I assume he's radioed Lewis. MacArthur made it clear that I'm in charge of Ubec's guerrilla movement. He wants Lewis and his men to join our forces. We should be on the offensive now, but Lewis divides the movement. We can't get very much done. One destroys a bridge; the other wants to rebuild. It reminds me of a snake with two heads, wanting to go different ways."

"I see your point, Gil. But I think it's a matter of communication. Once Lewis understands that MacArthur wants only one unit in Ubec, everything will be fine."

Gil Alvarez sighed, his face twitching violently as he did. "To tell you the truth, Prof, I've been feeling discouraged recently. This war is dragging on and on. We thought it'd be over in six months; it's been one and a half years. The Americans assured us that the war would be over soon, that they'd have their forces out here. All they did was retreat. Then I learned that the Americans themselves suppressed reports about Japanese atrocities."

"Why would Americans do such a thing, Gil?"

"Because they want to continue sending their forces to Europe instead of here."

"Rumors, Gil, rumors. Americans are honorable people. They wouldn't do a thing like that. I lived with them for four years and I know what kind of people they are," Papa continued.

Gil Alvarez was quiet for a while. "You know, Prof, I grew up in a family that hated Americans. My grandmother, to her dying day, never forgave the Americans for what they did to Filipinos. My family considered Americans no better than rats. I defied my family, Prof, when I opened my mind to American ways. I believed in democracy, in their educational system. I was one of the first to discard our native barong shirts for American-tailored suits, even though I sweltered in them. Pilar, may she rest in peace, filled our house with Stateside products. Everything was Made in America. We watched Hollywood movies and read *Life Magazine*. But now, Prof, I'm beginning to think the way my grandmother, Nay Isay, used to."

"Gil, do you now hate Americans as she did?" Papa asked.

"Not exactly, Prof. I've just realized that for all the American clothes and American canned goods, and all the American magazines and books I have crammed into my head, I am not an American. I am a Filipino, Prof. The books that my children studied in school, the ones mentioning snow and apples, are destructive—we do not have snow and apples in the Philippines. We Filipinos have lost ourselves by saturating our brains with all this snow and apples and with American ideas.''

"All that may be true, Gil, but that doesn't make Americans bad,'' Papa insisted.

"The Spaniards were imperialists and Americans are cut from the same cloth. I don't blame them, because it is only natural for them to want to enrich and empower their country; but the fact remains that they're using us, Prof. They came to the Philippines, used our resources and our manpower—Nay Isay bluntly called it rape. And Americans dazzled us, with talk of equality, when if you get right down to it, to an American, only Americans are equal.

"When Pilar and I traveled in California, I saw a sign in front of a restaurant that said: NO FILIPINOS OR DOGS ALLOWED. We quickly turned our heads, pretending we didn't see the sign. We must have felt so bad that neither of us mentioned that sign. I quietly reasoned that the Filipinos referred to were the uneducated pickers, that Pilar and I belonged to another social stratum and were excluded from the discrimination. We went about in our American clothes and spent hundreds of dollars on American products. She bought an entire box full of American marmalade. I forgot about that sign for a long time, but it came to my mind recently. Americans don't consider Filipinos their equals, Prof. At best they treat Filipinos like second-rate citizens. Come to think of it, this Commonwealth Government sets us up as second-rate, so maybe in the long run, it's our fault, for allowing them to call the shots. I'm tired of their calling the shots, Prof, and I'm going ahead with or without American aid. It wasn't our war in the first place. The Americans and the Japanese made the Philippines their battleground. Still, it's my homeland the Japanese invaded. It's my people who are dying, and I've got to do something about it. I can't sit around waiting for Americans to be ready to fight the Japanese.''

Papa, always pro-American, furrowed his brows in concern. He sucked on his pipe for a few seconds, then spoke. "Gil, I'm not a politician. You'll have to follow your instinct; you have always made wise decisions. It is true that Filipinos must handle their own problems, but keep in mind that Americans are our allies. So many of them have died alongside Filipinos. For all the differences, death has a way of making brothers of all of us."

It was well known that Gil Alvarez came from a family of patriots. Aside from his single-footed grandmother, Nay Isay, his grandfather Tal Alvarez was also a hero. At the turn of the century, he had fought side by side with the great hero Emilio Aguinaldo against the Americans. Tal Alvarez had been one of the sixty-one men who held the strategic Tirad Pass while Aguinaldo and some three hundred remaining soldiers retreated to the north of Luzon. The older Alvarez was one of only eight men who survived the Tirad Pass holdout.

Papa explained the situation to me once. Tirad Pass was an extremely narrow trail and men who climbed the thirteen-hundred-meter-high pass could only walk one at a time through the trail. To the left was a deep gorge, and to the right was a precipitous mountain rising about four hundred meters above the trail. A stone barricade across the trail made the climb more difficult.

To further slow down the Americans in their pursuit of Emilio Aguinaldo, sixty-one Filipino soldiers volunteered to fight to their death at Tirad Pass. They were bidding for time—two or three hours would give Aguinaldo and his men that much more time to disappear into the jungles of Northern Luzon.

Using their guns and hurling rocks, the Filipino soldiers were successful in slowing down the Canos. Seeing it was an impossible situation, the American Major March ordered a platoon to climb a nearby ridge with a vantage point. It took the Americans two hours to climb the ridge, but once there, it only took them half an hour to shoot the defending Filipinos one by one with their Krag-Jorgensen rifles. In the end the Americans captured wounded soldiers, including Gil's grandfather.

Gil's grandfather survived and years later, when Gil was ten, Tal

Alvarez took him to see the famous Revolutionary general, Emilio Aguinaldo.

"Tal, is this boy like you and Isay?" Aguinaldo had asked.

Tal had replied, "I hope so, General."

"Your grandson certainly has broad shoulders. What a handsome boy, he reminds me of General Del Pilar. Do you remember how elegant Del Pilar looked with his silver spurs and leather boots? Dozens of girls were in love with him. Why there was a girl in every barrio. Del Pilar did his part in populating the archipelago, did he not, Tal? Perhaps you'll be general someday, Gil?"

"Well, Sir, General, I'd like to be president so I can help the people," Gil replied, and the men laughed.

Indeed, the idea of wanting to help the Filipino people stayed with Gil Alvarez, and when World War II seemed imminent, Alvarez became captivated by the Japanese slogan of "Asia for the Asiatics." Alvarez pondered a United Asia, freed from the manipulations of Western nations, a powerful Asia that could stand on equal footing with the other powers of the world. The idea glistened in his mind and very briefly Gil Alvarez considered collaborating with the Japanese government. But when General Morita barged into his house (the general's men brandishing weapons and making it very clear that Asia would not be for the Asiatics, but solely for the Land of the Rising Sun), and when the general unceremoniously shoved forward a piece of paper for Alvarez to sign, Gil could not touch the damnable piece of paper. He turned Morita down, believing he alone would suffer the consequences. He did not expect Morita's men to return that night to rape and kill his wife and bayonet four of his five children.

I disliked Cristobal Alvarez, but Mama told me to watch him, so I tried to get him to play sungka. He insisted on fooling around under the enchanted jackfruit tree. There he started eating mud and he howled in laughter at my horrified reaction. Cris was tall and handsome like his father, but his character was not like Gil's at all. Mama, who had a strong opinion about Cris's mother, said he inherited his mother's slow mind and mediocrity.

"You'll get hookworms and tapeworms," I warned.

He opened his grimy mouth wide and shoved another clod into his mouth.

Nauseated, I turned away. "I'm telling your father," I threatened, heading for the house, but when I saw Papa and Gil still talking, I went to Mama instead. She sent me right back out. "We promised to keep an eye on him. Go watch him, Yvonne. Hurry, hurry, he's going off some place."

I begrudgingly followed him as he made his way to the cemetery. Before the war, Cristobal used to be an altar boy, the best-looking of them all, so that even older girls giggled when he was nearby. His mother, Pilar Cuneta-Alvarez, former Miss Philippines, had been full of hoity-toity ways which Cristobal copied. Some girls called him sophisticated; some referred to him as arrogant; my cousin Esperanza said he was stuck up. That was in the past, of course, when Cris didn't even want mud on his Stateside leather shoes. Since the Japanese killed his mother and four brothers and sisters, he started eating mud.

Gil Alvarez's tick under his eye only got worse when he heard about Cristobal's oddness, while the Virgins, who took care of Cris, had grand attacks over those mud-eating episodes. And so I kept quiet about the matter; I figured if he got worms, that was punishment enough. There was no need getting his father and aunts upset.

Past the cemetery gate, I lost him and I was deciding whether I'd turn back when he suddenly jumped out from behind a crypt.

"Don't do that!" I yelled.

"Scared you, scared you," he cried, singsong.

"Don't be immature!" I said, knowing I was wasting my saliva.

"Why are you following me?" He had a dark, resentful expression.

"I'm not following you. Why would I follow you? I came to visit the dead."

"You don't have relatives here," he said, glancing around at the mausoleums and graveyard.

"I'm visiting your great-grandmother, the one with one foot."

"She's my great-grandmother, not yours. Why would you visit Nay Isay?"

"Because."

"Because, what?"

"Because I like her. I used to see her in Ubec, and your father told us about how brave she was."

The dark look vanished and his eyes sparkled with interest. "What did Papa say about Nay Isay?"

"That she used to ride a horse when she led her battalion against the Americans. They didn't have guns, only machetes, but she won many battles. I wish she were alive, then she'd get rid of the Japanese."

"She'd cut off their heads. Do you really like her? She was Papa's grandmother, you know."

"I already said I like her. Now, where's her grave?"

Cris led me to their family mausoleum, and we stared thoughtfully at his great-grandmother's marker, which had the carving of a weeping woman near a cross. The crypts belonging to his mother and four siblings were nearby.

I said, "We don't have flowers. We better get some."

"What for?" he asked.

"Because people give flowers to the dead."

"But what for? Dead people don't know if there are flowers or not."

"You give flowers not for them, but for yourself. It makes you feel better," I finally replied.

"Oh," Cris said, pondering my words.

He followed me to the cemetery walls, which were covered with *cadena de amor* vines. We broke off some branches with the pink and white flowers, then we placed them in front of Nay Isay's grave. I also lay some in front of the markers of his mother and brothers and sisters, although Cris did not.

"Aren't you going to give them flowers?" I asked.

He looked down at his feet and curled his toes upward.

"Well?" I insisted.

He glared at me with a scornful expression. "They're not dead. You think they're dead, don't you, like everybody else? But they're not. They're in Iloilo visiting my grandparents. I don't know when they'll be back."

He sounded so convincing that for a brief moment I believed that his mother and brothers and sisters really were alive. But Gil himself had told us of the massacre, and I was sure that Cris had made up this lie. Did he really think he was fooling me? Or was he fooling himself? Yes, that was it—he was trying to convince himself that they were still alive. It occurred to me that most of the time Cris behaved the way he did because of what had happened to his family. In a way he was like Doc Meñez when Doc went crazy. War did things like that to people, and you just had to wait it out, the way we did with Doc. Doc had to find his own salvation; Cris would have to find his. It was like that. You had to find your own way or else you didn't make it.

I did not know what to do or say. I stood there fiddling with the stems of the flowers when he suddenly said, "How come I don't feel better?" His voice sounded hollow. "You said giving flowers makes you feel better."

I saw sorrow lurking behind that petulant expression, and I felt kinder toward him. "It takes a while to feel better, Cris. It's like a cut. You have to make new skin." I held up my left hand. "See that scar. I was scaling a fish and the knife slipped and I cut it right there. But see, it's all healed. There's just a tiny little line."

"Oh," he remarked, staring thoughtfully at my cut. "You mean it's like that inside?"

"Yes, it is," I said. "Maybe she's riding a horse in the skyworld. Or she could be in the underworld."

"Who?"

"Your great-grandmother. She's dead in this life, but not in the next. Laydan used to tell me all sorts of things. Maybe Nay Isay is with Laydan, and the goddess Meybuyan is taking care of them."

Cris scratched his head. "I don't know what you're talking about."

"Laydan used to say that there's the skyworld, the earth, and the underworld. When you die, you go to the underworld, where the good goddess Meybuyan watches the Underworld River. But if you are really special, you go to the skyworld."

"What makes you special?"

"Laydan said you're special when you are loved by the gods and goddesses, like the great bard Inuk, who went straight to heaven on a skyboat.'' I twirled around, gesturing at the sky, remembering Laydan and the numerous times she spoke of Inuk, her beloved, remembering the time in Mindanao when she saw Inuk sailing by on a cloud.

Cris laughed. ''You're talking nonsense.''

''Nonsense? Nonsense?'' I said. ''Everything is nonsense.'' I too laughed and continued twirling until I became dizzy from the sensation of the world whirling around me. I stumbled down, still laughing, and Cris sat down beside me. ''Tell me more,'' he said, ''about these things.'' For the first time, Cris got rid of his arrogant stance.

''Laydan was our cook, don't you remember her? She had a little bun at the back of her head, and she spoke in a monotone, and she had a broad, dark face. She took care of my cousin and me. Laydan grew up in Kumin; she was an epic singer, but the gods and goddesses punished her and she only spoke in a flat voice.''

''I remember her now. She was old and smelled bad.''

I became angry. ''No, she did not! She was old, but she didn't smell. Laydan was . . . was . . . beautiful.''

Cris began laughing as he got up to leave. ''Old and smelly,'' he repeated.

I knew Cris was being obnoxious because of his hurting inside; but I couldn't help myself and I burst into tears. Laydan was beautiful. Her face was not pretty or anything like that. It was her soul that was beautiful, and this beauty spilled out and touched everything around her once you knew her. I missed her; I missed Ubec, our life before the war. I missed the fun times we had in the living room. Papa, Esperanza, and I used to play sungka or chess. Mama used to play the piano. Tiya Lourdes would bring out her pastries for merienda. Lolo Peping would be out by the flame tree, which he and my grandmother had planted years and years ago. It came to me that even if the war ended and we returned home, things would not be the same.

# *Men from the Sky*

꧁꧂

$\mathcal{E}$very night after supper, Mama gathered us in front of the Sacred Heart altar to say the rosary. To give the electric generator a rest, we retired early. In bed alone, I liked to think of Laydan's stories, and I would run them through my head one by one, picturing Laydan as she looked when she told them to me. I missed Laydan, her stories, her constancy, her soothing presence. Her absence made me feel askew, like a blind person without his guide. All my life there had been Laydan. When Esperanza and I were small, Laydan had changed our diapers; she had taught us to eat crisp green onions and sautéed garlic. I could see her cooking in the dirty kitchen or bargaining at the rowdy open market, or applying some pultice to Esperanza's cut or bruise. She had always been there for me to observe, to follow around.

And so in the silence of my imagination, I brought Laydan and her stories back to life. But I was careful to keep all these secret. These imaginings were the one thing that no one could ever take away from me, and I guarded them jealously. The Japanese could storm into our house and kill everybody, including me—there was nothing definite in our lives, life was riddled with uncertainties—but Laydan's beautiful stories, and her memory, would always be with me. No one, not the cruelest Japanese, could ever take them away, ever destroy them.

Doc's crucifixion jogged us out of our lethargy. He had faced Death on purpose and with such bravery that Death lost some of its awfulness. We had choices—to live in fear and dread, or to try and do something about the situation. From Doc's crucifixion, Nida had found the strength to tell Max about her child. Many others were jolted into action too.

To try and improve the food situation, Mama and Nida threw all their guerrilla notes together, and they bought a sassy black sow which they kept outdoors. They borrowed a neighbor's boar—a mean animal, partly wild with tusks—and they promised one-fourth of the litter to the boar's owners. When the sow had two sets of litters, they decided to buy their own boar and another female so the boar would keep both sows pregnant. Mama and Nida often talked about their boar and sows, and the wonderful deals they made bartering the little black piglets for food and necessities.

The men developed more aggressive plans. Up in the mountains, they continued with their guerrilla warfare, hoping to slow down the Japanese, who lashed out at the civilians for hardships the guerrilleros caused. On several occasions, the Japanese razed entire towns as revenge. The guerrilleros would be stunned at such vengeance; then the hatred that welled up would only spur them on to fight even more aggressively.

Papa was busy on a project. A gorge, forty meters across and twelve meters deep, blocked the guerrilleros' way, and he had to build a bridge. He spent long hours in the kitchen cooking so his mind would expand and he would solve his problem.

One windy night, while the leaves of the enchanted jackfruit tree rustled, Laydan came to me in my dream. I was flying in my dream, but later

I began to lose altitude. I was struggling to stay up when Laydan suddenly appeared beside me. She held my hand and together we flew upward. Happy to see her once again, I cried. "I thought you'd abandoned me, Laydan," I said.

"I would never leave you, Yvonne. That's why I'm here."

Then Laydan disappeared, and I was no longer flying. I thought she was on a cloud, so I climbed a tree to get closer to the cloud. Standing on the topmost branch I reached out to try and poke the cloud. But it only sailed away, and as it moved, the cloud began tipping to its side. To my surprise, three men slipped from the cloud and fell to the earth. I scrambled down from the tree and rushed to the spot where the men had fallen. Instead of finding the men, I found an enormous puddle of blood, bright red and starting to congeal. In my dream I was not scared. Instead, I realized that Laydan was warning me about something.

I didn't tell my mother about my dream, fearing she would divine all sorts of meanings—that the devil was involved, or that I was losing my sanity. I considered telling my father, but he was immersed in his gorge project. In the end I kept my dream, like my imaginings, a secret.

It was the rainy season and dense clouds filled the sky. In the afternoon the clouds became darker, and at night the drops fell, first as soft pattering, then in continuous sheets drumming so hard that people pulled their pillows over their ears.

In the morning the rain became heavier and lightning zigzagged across the sky. When Gil Alvarez showed up with two cans of American corned beef for us, he said lightning had struck a tree on Mount Buntis (which means Pregnant Mount).

"It's a strange typhoon," he said, sipping the hot chocolate that Mama handed him.

"How's Cris, Gil?" Mama asked.

"He doesn't say much. What do you think, Yvonne? Go ahead, you can tell me what you think."

He looked worried; the tick under his eye was doing double-time. I wanted to mention Cris's peculiarities, but all I said was, "He'll get worms if he continues eating dirt."

Gil Alvarez sighed, and Mama said, "He's mourning, Gil. Just be patient, he'll get over it in time and with prayers."

"It's difficult, Angeling," he said.

Papa appeared in the kitchen with a map in his hands. "I still don't know what we're going to do about that gorge, Gil. Here, take a look at this." He laid the map out on the kitchen table and pointed out the area with the gorge. "See here, it's forty meters across and twelve meters deep . . ."

Papa and Gil Alvarez were talking when the sound of an engine rose above the rain and wind. As we slid open the capiz-shell window to look outside, the rain whipped in. The enormous jackfruit tree in the yard strained against the wind. Through the gray sheets I saw an airplane. "B-16!" I yelled, excited that an American plane was nearby.

Alvarez stared. "No, Kawanishe flying boat—Japanese!"

He and Papa grabbed guns and ran out into the rain. The other men followed. The airplane struggled against the wind. Before it began spiraling down into the dark foaming sea, I knew what would happen. I watched the guerrilleros ride outriggers, paddling quickly toward the plane. The waves were high and at times it seemed the sea had swallowed all of them, but the waves would recede and I could see the dark outriggers dotting the sea. The plane was partially afloat. Our men dove into the water to get the men from the sinking plane.

They came to shore with two Japanese soldiers. Flinging away the banana leaves which they had used to keep their heads dry, the people picked up stones and began hurling them at the captives. "Kill them! *Puta!* Murderers—kill them!" they shouted. One of the soldiers was afraid, but the other was stoic, proud, arrogant—he would accept his fate. A woman whose four sons were killed by the Japanese flung herself at the arrogant one and she spat at him and scratched his face so streaks of blood lined his cheek. Two guerrilleros had to pull her away. Gil Alvarez had to appoint special guards to escort the prisoners to headquarters.

There had been a third Japanese soldier in the plane who had drowned and had gone unnoticed. When the storm subsided, some children found his corpse in a nearby cove. Soon all the children learned about the body, and the boys immediately searched for sticks while the girls broke off branches with flowers. It was a strange procession we made, a dozen children heading for the cove, waving sticks and flowers. At the moment, we were not sad; we had all seen dead people. We were curious because there was something fascinating about dead people. It was one thing if you knew the person, because it wasn't just that person that passed away, a whole part of yourself tied up with that person also died. If you knew the dead person, you felt sad, and even if you didn't feel unhappy, you pretended to be. But if the dead person was a stranger to you, that was another thing. It was as if that dead stranger was linked to some mystery that you'd like to understand.

The children in front broke into a run when they spotted the body. At first all I saw was a large muddy lump on the shore, drifting peacefully back and forth with the waves. Then the rotten smell hit me, and I felt both a repulsion and an attraction. The corpse was puffy, inhuman. As I stared, it seemed to me that he moved, but I soon realized that it was just the insects crawling in and out of a large hole in the right side of his stomach. The older boys began poking him, chanting, "Jap-Jap, gad-dam Jap." Every time they thrust their sticks into the spongy corpse, a gust of foul odor rose and filled our nostrils. At last we girls told the boys to go away. We shoved them away, threatening to tell their mothers. After waving the ends of their sticks (with maggots and rotten flesh clinging to them) in front of our faces, they ran off, then we tore off the petals from our flowers. We strew these over the dead man so that he appeared buried under a carpet of petals. We chanted prayers for the dead and having said that, we grew somber and left.

Sitting on the branch of the jackfruit tree later, I thought: The dead man was our enemy. The Japanese killed many people. The horrible stories of what they did to prisoners reached our ears daily. They tortured people, shoved steel blades into eyes, punctured eardrums, skinned babies in front of parents. Recently the Japanese went to Barrio Talisay and randomly selected six men whom they beheaded to avenge the death of a Japanese soldier killed nearby. We heard this report from a woman whose husband and eighteen-year-old son had unfortunately attracted the attention of the Japanese. The enemy not only killed them, they beheaded them as well. The Japanese had changed our lives not just for that moment but for always. The Japanese were our enemy. The smelly corpse was my enemy. But, I started thinking, maybe he had a family far away; maybe he had a daughter like me. The Japanese whom Papa had killed in Mindanao had a daughter named Akemi who loved pine trees and rivers. Maybe the dead man at the beach also had a daughter who was worried about her father, who waited for his return, just as I anxiously waited for my Papa's return when he was away. But now, her father would never return. He was reduced to a pile of rotten, mangled flesh. Her father was that putrid mass that we had played with. I hated the enemy and yet as I sat on that branch, I could not help feeling sad for the dead man. You can hate someone with all your might and yet you couldn't help thinking.

I turned my mind to Laydan's story about Lam-ang the Unusual Man. At birth, Lam-ang was full-grown. It was said that before his umbilical cord had dried, he avenged his father's murder by the dreaded tattooed headhunters. He killed them, twenty-five headhunters in all, after which he buried his father's remains.

Tender of age, Lam-ang battled with the crocodile that terrorized the bathers and laundrywomen in his town's river. Lam-ang fearlessly grappled with the mean crocodile, snapped it in two, then hurled the pieces far, far away.

When he grew older, Lam-ang fell in love with Ines Kannoyan, a woman of good breeding from another town. Ines loved Lam-ang in return, but her parents were possessive of their only daughter. "Our beloved daughter had golden toys," they said. "Can you afford the dowry? You must provide a gold clothesline, enough gold to pave the path, solid gold figures of two roosters, four hens, and two lobsters to decorate the front yard."

"I am the son of Juan and Namongan, whose wealth can equal yours," Lam-ang proudly replied as he presented the dowry, assuring the parents that he would provide Ines with everything she wanted.

Lam-ang and Ines were married, and shortly after, Ines carried Lam-ang's child. She developed a craving for all sorts of foods—green tamarinds, guavas, seashells, snails, seaweeds—all of which Lam-ang gave to her.

When Ines hankered for a fish called rarang, Lam-ang did not hesitate diving into the rough sea. It happened that while he searched the deep waters, an enormous monster fish swam toward him, opened its mouth, and with a single gulp swallowed him.

The townspeople gave Lam-ang up for dead, but his mother, insisting Lam-ang was unusual, instructed the people to look for Lam-ang's remains. "Gather these on the beach," she ordered.

Everyone scoured the beaches and the bottom of the sea until they found all of Lam-ang's bones. Then Lam-ang's mother covered the bones with her apron. Later, she pulled away her apron and there on the beach lay Lam-ang, sleeping peacefully. "I dreamt," he said, "that an enormous fish ate me. I am glad it was only a dream."

Lam-ang's wife, his mother, and the townspeople cheered with joy. After helping Lam-ang up, they returned to their homes, convinced that Lam-ang was indeed a most unusual human being.

Still working on the problem of the gorge, Papa was fixing fish rellenos. He took the fish, scaled them, and removed the gills and entrails through the head. He washed and drained the insides. One by one, he pressed the fish bodies to separate the flesh from the bones. Then he detached the spinal bone and slowly pulled this out. Next he pressed out the flesh through the head, starting from the tail. After removing the small bones, he chopped onions, pimiento, and pickles, which he mixed with the fish flesh, salt, pepper, and seasoning. He stuffed the mixture into the cavities of the fish.

"Timber trestle," he muttered to himself, while he worked. "No, the gorge is too deep. A Bailey? That's it, a Bailey would work—no, not enough time."

He was frying the stuffed fish when Gil Alvarez rushed into the kitchen. Out of breath, Alvarez said, "Prof, we just heard over the radio—one of the prisoners is Admiral Yoshida."

Papa almost knocked the frying pan over. "Isoruku Yoshida? I don't believe it! Gil, I don't know what to say, Yoshida's Chief of Staff."

Papa's eyes grew large and he shook his head from left to right. He looked concerned.

"Who's he, Pa?" I asked, becoming afraid.

"Isoruku Yoshida's an important man, Yvonne. The Japanese will want him back. They'll do anything to get him back."

# Martin Lewis

❧

$\mathcal{P}$eople didn't pay much attention to my eleventh birthday because the American Martin Lewis was going to have supper at our house. For months he had avoided Gil Alvarez, but he finally arranged a meeting because Admiral Isoruku Yoshida was our captive.

Mama and I heard Mass in the morning. I could tell she was in one of her edgy moods, because she kept sighing and throwing me annoyed looks when I as much as coughed. When Mass ended, we left the church. She walked so fast I could barely keep up. She headed for the open market but midway, right in the middle of the sidewalk, she suddenly stopped. I looked at her, wondering what was wrong. Tears welled in her eyes, and I thought she was hurt. She started weeping uncontrollably. "Fish—only fish," she wailed in a cracked, pained voice.

I had no idea what she meant, and all I could do was move her away from the curious passersby.

"Fish! Fish, rice! Fish and rice! We're having company and we only have fish and rice." She sobbed louder and mumbled, ". . . hams, rellenos, lechon, turkey . . . everything, now fish and rice." She continued crying.

I figured she was upset that Martin Lewis was coming for supper and we could not serve an elegant meal as we used to in Ubec. To try and make her feel better I suggested, "We still have mongo beans, Ma."

She straightened up. "Mongo, fish, rice, they're all the same. Maybe, maybe, we'll have to sacrifice one of the chickens."

I stared at her with a shocked expression. "We can't do that. They're our hens; they're like—like relatives. They—they lay eggs, and we need eggs," I said.

She took a deep breath. "I don't like the idea either. But fish and rice—I can't stand the thought of serving just fish and rice to visitors. Martin Lewis, of all people—he's used to a life of luxury. Why, he and Alicia Urtula had Beluga caviar for dinner. We will lose face serving him fish and rice."

"But Ma, we brought the chickens from Mindanao. We didn't carry them all the way here just to serve them as chicken soup. Besides, he's a monster. He's killed people. Everyone knows he killed his wife. He doesn't deserve chicken, not one of our chickens. Why do we have to serve him chicken?"

"Because, Yvonne, that is what proper Ubecans do. Wartime or not, we always feed visitors. Even if Satan himself entered our house, we must extend our hospitality." She sighed and looked at me. "Now don't start with one of your moods. It's just a chicken. Besides, it's your birthday."

"But I don't want chicken for my birthday. I like fish and rice. I really like mongo beans. They're my favorite with coconut milk. Laydan showed me how to cook them and everything."

"Yvonne, stop it, please. I can't take any more."

"But please, Ma, don't hurt the chicken. Please!"

"We'll think about it, all right? Now be quiet. If you make me nervous, I'll make a mistake with the change. That Iya Pusang last week cheated me—she gave me eighty centavos instead of ninety centavos.

You have to be so careful nowadays. People are desperate," she muttered as she headed straight to the coconut vendor.

Taytayan's marketplace was smaller than the open market in Ubec. It smelled and it was dirty, but the colorful sights of goods and food for sale and the lively vendors and bustling customers gave it a festive air. I brushed aside my thoughts about the chicken as we passed by the vendors selling fresh flowers for the dead. There were stalls with rainbow-colored buri mats and baskets. The meat vendor displayed slabs of pork beside the pig's head. Children selling garlic, onions, tomatoes, and other seasonings scampered about with their circular wicker baskets perfectly balanced on their heads.

Seven or eight people surrounded the coconut vendor, who was gesticulating wildly. I heard her say, ". . . both arms, poor boy, and only nine, can you imagine. And the poor mother, a widow at that. That boy helped her with everything. But I suppose he'll learn to use his feet. I saw a man without hands use his feet to eat. He could make rice balls with his toes . . ."

Apparently earlier that day a boy had lost his arms when he was sorting coconuts. Japanese spies had planted incendiary devices in some coconuts. When the boy picked up a rigged coconut, it blew his arms off.

Mama was so upset by this news, she skipped buying coconuts for fear we'd hack open a coconut only to have it blow up in our faces. "We'll just have kangkong leaves instead of mongo beans," she announced.

I was relieved that she didn't mention anything about the chicken again, and I stayed in the kitchen to make sure the situation remained that way.

While slicing ginger for the fish, she told Nida about the boy who lost his arms. "Can you just imagine, Nida, both arms," she said.

"Those gaddam Japs will do anything," said Nida. She was big now, her stomach jutting out in front of her like a gigantic ball.

"Nando says that the guerrilleros may have to give Yoshida back to the Japanese Armed Forces to stop this revenge."

"That dirty Jap should die."

"That's what Martin Lewis thinks. Nando said that's why he's coming over, to discuss Yoshida. Lewis wants him dead."

"Ha—I never thought I'd see the day when that mother-fucker and I would think alike. Just thinking of Lewis makes me want to vomit. I'm no saint, you know that, and I'm not one to be casting stones, but he is evil. He killed that man, you know, the father of that young girl. He became angry when the father told him he couldn't take the girl to the city."

"That's just gossip," Mama remarked.

"People's tongues don't wag over nothing. Simeon, the bartender at Slapsy Maxie's, knew a girl who was involved with Lewis. He brought her to the city, in his house. She was only seventeen. He had seen her in some barrio fiesta; she was queen or princess or something. Lewis told her mother she would be trained as a radio announcer of DYUB. The ignorant woman was so impressed, she sent her daughter off with her blessings. They say he is a good lover. Alicia, being a widow and all, was overwhelmed. The first time they did it she had three—"

Mama interrupted Nida, gesturing toward me and saying, "Ah, Nida, the child. Yvonne, go set the table."

I left, knowing they would continue talking about matters that were not supposed to reach my ears. I didn't care because I knew about Martin Lewis. Everybody did. Martin Lewis inspired a lot of stories, the gist of them being that he belonged to the lowest caliber of mankind. The stories were numerous and varied, with more twists and turns than a month of the radio soap opera *The Triumphs of Love*.

Martin Lewis owned DYUB. People said his program *The Triumphs of Love* was the very first radio soap opera in Ubec. In the beginning, people pooh-poohed the program as a newfangled American idea, but it caught on like the plague itself. *The Triumphs of Love* was the most popular radio show in Ubec. Its convoluted plot dealing with love, hate, infidelity, and other melodramatic themes was so popular that many Ubecans cut short their afternoon merienda sessions to listen to it. It was so popular, nine out of ten households in Ubec used Lava soap, the sponsor of *The Triumphs of Love*.

There were so many stories about Martin Lewis that it was difficult to sift fact and fiction. The most fantastic version reported that he had been picked up in San Francisco by the fabulous Manila widow, Alicia Urtula. One summer, so the story goes, as she strolled up Nob Hill, the aging beauty saw the most gorgeous man of twenty-four. The vision of him reminded Alicia of ripe wheat fields, lush and tall, with heads of grain swaying in some slow breeze, a sight which she and her beer-tycoon husband had seen in North Dakota years ago during their honeymoon tour of America. Alicia, forty-nine years of age and still wearing gray to reflect her nine-month-old widowhood, caught her breath and stumbled. She hit the lamppost, her purse flew open, and Alicia almost fell. Flustered at her infantile distraction, the elegant woman rubbed her forehead where a goose egg started to protrude. Shaking her head to compose herself, Alicia snapped her purse shut, pulled up her coatcollar, and proceeded with her walk.

The matter of Martin Lewis would have ended right then and there if only Lewis had pocketed the silver pen that had slipped out of her purse. People said that under normal circumstances, Martin Lewis would have done just that; but this time Lewis, having noticed the sidewise glance cast by Alicia, and more significantly, having caught sight of Alicia's five-carat diamond ring and three-strand choker of exquisite South Sea pearls, very swiftly decided that in this particular case, honesty might in the long run be the better policy. And so Martin Lewis gallantly returned the silver pen to the still-beautiful-though-slightly-sagging and wealthy foreigner. He struck up a conversation with the lonely widow, who welcomed Martin Lewis into her Nob Hill flat. She eventually allowed him into her four-poster bed, that infamous bed on which Alicia Urtula, who was reared by the Benedictine nuns and who had never stood naked in front of her husband, had three successive lustful orgasms in twenty-two minutes flat, thanks to Martin Lewis's youth and virility.

Some people said the multiple orgasms did it, some blamed infatuation, but whatever the reason, Alicia brought Lewis to Manila and kept him in her mansion like some pampered golden lapdog. She even bought him a radio station so he would have something to do—after all, a woman of such high social standing as herself couldn't very well run around with someone who looked and acted like a gigolo.

Then Alicia made the fatal mistake of marrying her American ward. Once the knot was tied, Martin Lewis changed from the subservient pet to a demon who took great pleasure in physically abusing his wife. In the beginning, to save face, Alicia hushed up the matter, and she stayed home so no one would see the multicolored bruises on her face. The physical abuse and Alicia's seclusion grew in direct proportion with each other until Martin Lewis broke her jaw, deforming her face once and for all, and henceforth, Alicia never left home. She died one night soon after the accident and the rumor spread that Martin Lewis smothered her with a pillow.

Manilans despised Martin Lewis so much that he was forced to move to Ubec, where he bought the radio station DYUB. By this time, Martin Lewis was no longer the slim muscular golden boy he had been when Alicia picked him up. He had grown corpulent like a fat albino pig, and had developed a fondness for young girls. He often attended barrio fiestas to pick out young beauty queens—seventeen-year-old girls wearing lipstick, high heels, and long gowns for the first time—and talk the girls' parents into letting him take them with him to Ubec to "train them to be radio announcers." The only kind of announcing they did was the moaning and groaning executed on Lewis's circular bed. When he grew tired of them, he dispatched them back to their barrio with fifty pesos in their purses—hymen fee, Lewis called it.

All that was bad enough, but just before the war broke out, Lewis had taken a fancy to a young girl at some barrio fiesta. The girl was pure as spring water, just like a saint, which only increased Lewis's lust for her. The American talked to the father about training the daughter to be a radio announcer. But the father turned Lewis down, saying his daughter was only sixteen, that she had been queen of the barrio fiesta for the sake of the fundraising Padre Luis, and no, she was not allowed to leave home. No one had ever turned Martin Lewis down before because his radio station was famous, and simple barrio folk were only too grateful to have their daughter become an announcer at DYUB. Lewis grew angry, and he sent two of his bodyguards to beat up the father, only they didn't just beat him, they cracked his skull. The towns-people, led by the distraught mother and daughter, protested, and carried the corpse with the split head all the way to Ubec's city hall where they presented it to the mayor. The mayor ordered an investigation, but then war broke out and the matter evaporated in the midst of more pressing issues. Martin Lewis himself went underground to form his own guerrilla movement, despite MacArthur's command for him to join Gil Alvarez's forces.

At the last minute, Mama couldn't tolerate the idea of not having meat for supper and she decided to sacrifice the scrawny red hen, who used to be a good layer but who had become too old and barren. I cried when the men chased the squawking hen around the yard. She frantically scrambled under a bush, and for a while I felt relieved, thinking she would live. But the men caught her. She flapped her wings in desperation and her feathers scattered all over the place. When Nida, knife in one hand, picked her up and held her over the basin to behead her, I ran away.

I walked along the seashore for a long time. She was just a chicken, I repeated to myself. It shouldn't matter; that's the fate of chickens. We couldn't very well continue feeding her when she wouldn't even lay eggs, could we? No, we had to measure everything carefully so we would get something back in return. Her clucking about the yard was poor return for all the feed we gave her. I found a stick and drew a picture of a chicken on the sand. It was a pretty drawing and briefly my sadness eased because I had captured the chicken's image. But a wave washed my drawing away, and I solemnly reflected that living things were a lot like sand drawings.

When I returned home, I saw a pile of red feathers outside the kitchen, and there was a strong scent of chicken stew wafting in the air.

"I'm not happy about the chicken either, Yvonne. I am trying my best! Get rid of that face right now," Mama said when she saw me skulking about with tears in my face. "Why don't you get some flowers for the table, instead of walking around with that sour expression."

I stomped out of the house and hunted for the brown chicken that laid olive-colored eggs. "You had better continue laying," I whispered. I ruffled her feathers to check for lice, then I stroked her several times and set her down. The chicken clucked and hovered near me. She knew me. I fed her every day. She had also come from Mindanao and we had shared many experiences together.

When I passed by the gardenia bush near the front door, I sniffed a pretty white flower—it was sweet, soothing. I took a few deep breaths until I felt better, then I decided I might as well get Mama's flowers. I was cutting gardenias when Martin Lewis arrived. His men joined the other guerrilleros who were huddled around an outdoor table. Martin Lewis, clad in green with a revolver hanging by his side, walked toward the house. When he passed by, he stopped and smiled at me. He looked like a grinning pink pig. "What's your name?" he asked.

"Yvonne Macaraig," I replied, feeling awkward.

He shifted his weight and stared at me in a way that frightened me. "The engineer's daughter." He paused, casually looking around us. No one was there. Gil Alvarez, Papa, Doc, and Max were in the living room winding down their meeting; Mama and Nida were setting the dining table; the other guerrilleros were around the house. Martin Lewis continued staring. "How old are you, child?" he asked, in a silky voice that made the surface of my skin crawl.

"Eleven."

"Pretty," he said. He pinched my cheek affectionately.

I looked at him vacantly, not knowing what to say. Then, not realizing I did so, I made the sign of the cross. He threw his head back and laughed so hard his chins jiggled like gelatin. His expression quickly shifted and he said pleasantly, "Tell your father Martin Lewis is here."

I bolted away, and without telling the grown-ups what happened, I went straight to my room and locked the door. I was shivering. I felt strange, as though I had done something wrong. But I had done nothing bad. There was just something—something about Lewis that made me think of fear, and sin, and darkness. I was still in this state when Mama pounded on the door urging me to come down. "Yvonne, it's your birthday," she insisted. "We've already sacrificed the chicken. You had better come down."

After washing my face, I went to the dining room and sat quietly beside my mother. I worried that Lewis would look at me or that he'd say something, but he did not pay the slightest attention. To make matters worse, Mama insisted on giving me a chicken leg. I shoved it around my plate, but Mama stared at me until at last I picked it up and began eating. I could not help thinking what an undignified ending it was for the old red chicken—chicken stew. If I were a chicken, I'd hate ending up on someone's plate. I didn't even enjoy her tough, stringy meat. As I chewed, the idea came to me that it was like receiving Holy Communion. When you receive Communion, you are taking in Jesus —that was what Mother Ignacia used to tell us in school. This thought made me feel better.

Martin Lewis was talking to Gil Alvarez. "I learned about Admiral Yoshida, and I believe, Governor, that we should hold a military trial, Governor. You know how they pulled out your fingernails and rubbed salt into the wounds? Well, Governor, I think we should do the same to our honorable prisoner—haw-haw-haw. We can even squeeze some vinegar too. Did they do that to you, Governor? I've forgotten. Salt and vinegar ought to make the bastard wince. Here's something else we can do to him—we can cut up the man's guts. Hara-kiri, except for the fact that someone else is doing the cutting—haw-haw-haw." He almost choked on his food from laughing.

Gil Alvarez had an easy manner when he was around us. He was an important statesman with the ability of making anyone feel he was your friend. But tonight, he sat seriously and behaved in a way that distanced him from everyone. Tonight he was not just Gil Alvarez, he was his people's leader. His face twitched as he spoke. "We don't like the Japanese, but we don't relish torture."

Martin Lewis's piglike face became mean. "The heathen Jap's killed many people. He deserves a slow death. Hanging's too good for him. Gentlemen, we have here the rare opportunity to tell the Japanese to go fuck themselves."

The muscles in Alvarez's face jumped all over when he spoke. "That's not what we have in mind. The Japanese know we've got him and they've started punishing the civilians. In my area alone, they've gone through six barrios. They've killed the men, including boys, and they've burned the fields. They're going through each place like a fine-toothed comb. If Yoshida hangs, there's no telling what the Japanese will do to the people."

"What do you gentlemen propose?" Lewis asked.

"We're on the same side, Martin. It's just not right for the civilian population to suffer," Gil said cajolingly.

"Tell that to the fucking Nippon bastards," Lewis snapped.

Alvarez said, "If they'd listen, I'd tell them more than that. Martin, they killed my wife and four of my children; I'm not a Japanese lover, but I think we need to consider this case very carefully. If Yoshida hangs, how much would the people of Ubec suffer? I wager it'll be a lot. I'm afraid that as much as we hate to do so, we may have to negotiate with the Japanese."

"Negotiate? You're talking treason, Governor."

"It's not treason, Martin. Call it common sense, but not treason. If we hang Yoshida, the Japanese will try to kill every civilian in Ubec. Yoshida's their top man; they're not going to hold back," Alvarez said.

"Over my dead body are we going to release Yoshida!" Lewis slammed the table with his fist.

Gil's voice shook as he spoke. "They've killed 513 civilians in three days—women, old people, infants—and they're all from my territory. Just this morning a young boy lost both arms. It's not fair to the people. I hate the blackmail aspect of it all, but we can't let the people die this way."

Lewis suddenly shoved the table, shouting, "I'll have no part in this. We're in a war, this isn't a little game where we trade people around. Yoshida's responsible for countless deaths—he deserves to die."

Trying to stay calm, Gil Alvarez said, "That's correct, Martin, we *are* in a war, and people are dying. We can't ignore that. We can't take things personally. We have to look at things in a calculated way. Put bluntly, we have to count bodies. We have an obligation to keep civilian deaths at a minimum. Yoshida's my prisoner and I have the authority to deal with him. Check that with MacArthur if you wish. Go ahead and use our radio."

Martin Lewis kicked the chair and stomped out of the house.

# Deception

༄༅༈

The night Martin Lewis came to our house, I could not sleep. From my bed I peered through the window at the jackfruit tree, trying to conjure up an image of the enchanted black giant, but unable to do so. Usually I could imagine him as an enormous being, clothed only in loin cloth and shining like carved ebony in the moonlight. I kicked up my feet and spread my toes so that side by side they fanned out ridiculously. This used to make me and Esperanza laugh. "They look like little peanuts," she used to say. She would then wiggle her ears, a feat I never learned. "Watch this," she used to say, and she'd pull back her hair and move her ears. They'd flap ever so slightly from front to back, making her look like some wild animal. This was what we used to do at night, fooling around instead of going to sleep. But that was a long time ago, when we were children, before the war. I studied my toes that were all stretched apart, and tried to feel the spontaneous joy that used to possess us over such a silly matter.

I felt nothing. The best I could do was to remember two children whom I now scarcely knew. I watched the moonrays streaming into my room. The same moonrays used to enter our room in Ubec. My cousin used to be frightened about moonlight hitting her head while she slept because she had heard that it could turn you into a lunatic. Esperanza had so many ideas. She was not always good, but one thing with Esperanza, you felt her lively presence. I missed her. I tucked my feet under the sheet and sighed. Finally I fell asleep.

At dawn I awoke with a start. There were rustlings and movement outside. Were the Japanese going to burst into our house and kill us? I crept to the windowsill and peeped out. I saw the figure of a man near the chicken coop. I stayed frozen, uncertain about what to do, but when the man moved, catching the bit of light filtering through the leaves and branches, I saw that he was my father. Relieved, I ran outside to be with him.

"What are you doing, Pa?"

"Yvonne, it's too early, child. Go back to sleep."

"I'm not sleepy anymore. What are you doing?"

"Looking for eggs. I thought I'd make flan. Are you still upset over the red hen?"

I nodded.

He stroked my hair, saying, "Mama tries hard. She says the chicken was old and would die soon anyway." He sighed. "She tries, like all of us. 'Strive, for we are here not to succeed, but to strive,' I think Santa Teresa of Avila said that."

"I know she was just a chicken. And she wasn't even very smart; she used to eat droppings. It's just that I knew her. And—and I had to eat her." Tears began forming in my eyes.

"I know. I know, child."

Trying to compose myself, I took a deep breath and wiped my tears away. "She was just a chicken, wasn't she? She wasn't that important."

"She was important to you."

The tears started falling. "I can't help myself. It's just so sad."

"Life is like that."

While I cried, he stroked my hair consolingly. Later I sighed. "How many eggs do you need?" I asked.

"Six," he replied. Then he added, "Do you feel better?"

I nodded.

"I'm so proud of you, Yvonne."

The brown hen that we brought all the way from Mindanao clucked patiently as I lifted her to get an olive-colored egg. "Good girl," I whispered to her, then I held up my find. Papa nodded admiringly at the beautiful egg. We checked the other hens and found six eggs altogether. Since the war started, we had spent little time together. The eggs were still warm and they gave off an earthy smell that made me feel good.

Back in the kitchen, Papa proceeded to crack the eggs and beat them with milk and sugar.

"What are you thinking about, Pa?"

"Well, it's really strange, but I woke up thinking of Mr. and Mrs. Bowles, the couple I lived with in America. Mrs. Bowles used to fix corn bread. She had white eyelashes and wrinkled skin, but she was lovely. She taught me how to eat corn bread with butter and honey. She and her husband were farmers, good people—decent people. That's all anyone can ask of people—to be decent. It makes me sad that the governor feels differently about Americans. You see, child, I knew them, person to person, as people. I have difficulty looking at Americans as some kind of demons when I knew them so well."

"Lolo Peping hated them also."

"I know. But I can't lump all Americans as bad. It is impossible to do that when you actually know people. You can't make generalizations anymore. People become specific—you remember their mannerisms, the color of their hair, their crooked teeth, the kindness they do to others. Last night I could not sleep. I kept thinking of what the governor said about Americans as a whole. And no, I just can't agree with what he says.

"And here we have Lewis getting involved with the business of Yoshida. It's all one big headache. I'd much rather have a class full of eighteen-year-olds eager to learn calculus than all this."

"So what's going to happen, Pa?"

"As much as I hate the idea, we must, for the sake of the civilians, return Yoshida to the Japanese."

"Nida says he should die. People want him dead."

"Yes, yes, people hate him—except for the Japanese. The Japanese want him so much they're killing our people. Entire barrios are being destroyed. They come, kill the people, burn down houses and fields. They will continue killing until we surrender Yoshida to them."

"There are Japanese spies hiding bombs everywhere. The Japanese Army rewards Filipino spies. Mama says she's never buying another coconut."

"There are many rumors, Yvonne. So many things have been happening, my mind's in a whirl. Gil is right; civilian lives are of utmost importance. But the same civilians you try to save would be furious if the guerrilleros turned Yoshida back to the Japanese. Just look at how angry Martin Lewis was. Then if we do give the Japanese the admiral, what guarantee do we have that they will stop this rampage. Yoshida's all we have; he's our hostage. Without him, we have no negotiating power whatsoever."

"What's negotiating mean?"

"Bargaining, making a deal. You give them something for something in return."

"I see. You would give them the admiral and they would leave the people alone."

"That's right. But it's a one-sided deal, child, because once they have Yoshida, there's little we can do to actually keep them from doing what they want to do."

"Isn't a man only as good as his word, Pa? Wouldn't they be giving their word that they'll stop hurting the people if they get the admiral back?"

Papa grew excited. "That's right! That's precisely it. We have their word, and the Japanese are so bound-up over their honor, they wouldn't think of breaking their word. Especially if it's Yoshida's word."

The feeling of something's being "not right" came to me as I looked at the army jeep outside the house. It was the vehicle that Papa, Gil, and Max would be taking to headquarters. The jeep was green with bulletholes on the side. There was a malevolence in the way the holes lined up. Things that lined up that way were abnormal. Something was askew that day. I could not tell what was wrong, but I could sense evil in the atmosphere. There was a kind of crackle in the air and the hair on my arms prickled. I used to get this feeling in Ubec, at dusk when the dogs howled. One dog would start, and a chain reaction of howling would spread among the neighbors' dogs. I used to make the sign of the cross to ward off evil.

I watched Gil and Max open the front door and head for the jeep. My father paused by the doorway and called to my mother, "I'll be back in a few days."

He turned and in his haste almost missed me, but I chased him, calling, "Pa."

"Yvonne, I didn't see you," he said. "Give your Papa a kiss. Don't give Mama a difficult time."

I don't know why I did it, but I ran to him, threw my arms around him, and said, "Don't go."

Papa was surprised at my behavior. "Why, Yvonne, I'll be back in few days. We have to take care of Yoshida. I'll soon be back."

"You can't go. No, you can't." I tightened my grip around his neck and began crying. This was "making a scene," something Mama disliked, but I didn't care; all I knew was that he should not go.

Papa was taken aback by my sudden burst of emotion. When he tried to say something, I interrupted and said, "Don't go." He tried to unlock my fingers but I would not let go. Gil Alvarez finally told him to stay and take care of me. "I know how it is, Prof. Cris gets upset too."

Papa released himself and held my shoulders. "Yvonne, you know I must go. You're a big girl now, and you must behave like one. You know that we have things to do before more civilians are killed. I've already explained it to you. Go help Mama with the chores." He turned, then paused and looked at me once again. He chucked my chin and said, "Yvonne, if something should happen, always remember that I love my little girl."

My mother, who had come to check on the commotion, held my arm as Papa got into the jeep. "She'll be all right, Nando. Maybe she has a tapeworm. Cris Alvarez had a twenty-eight-centimeter tapeworm." She waved Papa good-bye. "It's just the war, Nando," she added. To me she said, "Yvonne, what is this all about. We don't have time for this kind of foolishness."

I felt a chill travel up my spine as they drove away. I kept to myself. I tried to recall Laydan's stories, but my mind kept getting distracted. My mind was whipping here and there when I overheard Mama and Nida discussing me.

"She's just impossible, Nida," Mama said. "You tell her to do something, she won't do it. If she does it, it's not done right and I have to do it all over again. All she does is sulk. Last night she locked herself in the room; then this morning she made this scene with her father. I never thought having a child would be so difficult."

"Maybe she's going to have her period," suggested Nida.

"She's too young," Mama said.

"I don't know, Angeling. I was eleven when I had my first mense."

I hated when they talked about me like that. I grabbed an old hunting knife and climbed the jackfruit tree. After asking the enchanted giant's permission, I carved my initials on the trunk. The initials were wide and deep and a bit of the tree's sap leaked from the Y and the M. I was watching the sticky sap congeal when a jeep roared up in front of our house. Doc hopped out of the jeep and rushed into the house. His movements were frenetic. Something was wrong. I clambered down to find out what was happening.

"Angeling, I'm sorry to tell you this . . ." Doc began. He had a familiar wild look in his eyes.

Mama dropped the sewing kit. "Nando's dead, isn't he?" Mama asked. Her words made me think of Papa that morning. Why did he say: If something should happen to me? Did he sense something? Did he have an instinctive feeling that things would not go all right, that he and the others would die?

Doc's voice sounded hollow. "We don't know."

Mama's eyes grew wild. "What do you mean? What's going on, Doc? Tell me!"

"The men are missing. Either the Japanese have them or Martin Lewis does."

I stared down at the spools of thread rolling around the floor; the steel needles glinted from where they lay.

"What happened?" Mama demanded.

"We contacted the Japanese and made a deal with them. Gil, Max, and Nando left with Yoshida to hand him over to the Japanese. They were supposed to return this afternoon. When I checked, I heard that Lewis had set up an ambush for them. Lewis wanted Yoshida."

"Speak slower, Doc. What do you mean?"

"The three are missing. We think Lewis has them."

Nida, who had joined us, clutched her belly. "That murderer will kill them. I should have guessed. I know death. I smelled it—that terrible gaddam odor—"

"Nida, be quiet!" Mama ordered. "How do you know all this?"

"A boy saw Lewis and his men block the mountain trail. He tried to warn them at headquarters, but they'd already left."

Mama's dark eyes lit up. "What are we going to do? What should we do?"

"I'm not sure. I'll call Lewis and find out if he's got them. Then I should contact the Japanese, make sure they don't think we're double-crossing them. MacArthur should know what's going on. And Angeling, it's probably better if all of you go to the Virgins' house, even just for the night. We just don't know."

In the evening, we left for the Virgins' house. Mama pulled me along, while Nida with her big stomach huffed and puffed beside us. We pounded on the Virgins' front door and Meding cautiously peeped out the window before unbolting the enormous door.

"Well, I . . . I . . ." Meding stammered, not knowing what to make of the three of us. Before Mama finished explaining, she quickly said, "Come in, come in. Cris is asleep. We're just getting ready to say our prayers." She locked their doors once more—three bolts per door, and they had elaborate wrought iron on their windows.

While the grown-ups pursued an elaborate discussion, I sat on a bench near the windowsill and peered outside. The large moon shone on the narrow street. For a long time I remained still, as if waiting for something to happen. Maybe Papa, Gil, and Max would drive up in the army jeep looking just as they did when they drove away that morning. Maybe the whole thing was a mistake. Maybe Doc went crazy again and made the whole thing up.

A cat scampered across the road, startling me. I suddenly felt cold, so cold I began shivering. My teeth began chattering. I got up, walked around to feel warm. I tried once again to think of one of Laydan's stories, but all I could think of was the time I caught a splinter in my pointer finger, and Papa carefully poked it out with a needle. "Well now, we got it out," he had said, kissing my finger. He was good and gentle. He was patient with me and Esperanza. He never made fun of Lolo Peping's mixed-up conversations; he pampered Mama. I loved my Papa and he was gone.

In the kitchen Nida cursed: "*Puta*, I'd like to cut off their balls and feed them to the pigs as slop." Nida let her tongue loose with wild abandon.

I could tell from the way Petra ran her hands through her skimpy hair that she did not appreciate Nida's language, but Meding calmly rummaged through her cabinet. She pulled out a bottle. "Medicine," she announced. "It'll calm you down, Nida."

One tablespoon of the pink syrup knocked Nida out. Before long she was on her side snoring.

"We might as well say the rosary," Meding said.

I had just knelt down when Cris howled, his loud voice echoing all throughout the house.

Meding stood up. "What is it this time? I thought he was asleep," she grumbled as she went to check on Cris.

We heard Cris scream, "Their heads. I saw their heads . . . blood all over . . . oh, Papa . . ."

"It's just another nightmare," Petra explained, as she hurriedly got the pink medicine and teaspoon. She followed her older sister to Cris's room. In a little while, there was silence.

"He's asleep," Meding said when they returned. "He gets excited; he can't forget."

"He's too young," Petra said.

"Yes, just a boy," Meding continued.

"Only twelve," echoed the younger Virgin.

We were saying the first decade when Nida woke up and began screaming. Meding and Petra looked at each other and rolled their eyes heavenward in exasperation.

"There's water," Nida frantically told us when we reached her room.

At first we were puzzled by what Nida meant. Then Mama checked her. "The bag of water. You'll have labor pains soon," she said. We barely finished cleaning Nida when her labor started.

Mama consulted with the Virgins about whether they should call the midwife. The younger one said we should send the maid to the midwife's house immediately. Meding thought it would be dangerous to do so. Lewis and his men might come to town; there might be a gun battle; no telling what would happen.

The women hemmed and hawed while Nida's labor pains grew stronger and closer together. "It's here," she finally said, panting.

There was some confusion when the Virgins thought someone was at the door.

Petra glanced at the door. "Are they here?"

"Don't open the door," Meding warned.

"What are you all talking about?" Mama demanded.

Nida yelled, "The baby's here."

There was Nida on the bed, skirt hiked up, enormous stomach heaving, legs apart, and right between her legs the baby's dark crown peeked out.

"*Susmaryosep!*" Mama exclaimed. "It is here."

Between her huffing and puffing, Nida said, "Angeling, that's what I said in the first place."

"Well, it is here. *Susmaryosep!* Here it comes!" Mama said.

And thus was Nida's baby born, with Mama there to catch it, and the Virgins and I frozen by the doorway as we gazed in wonder at the small writhing wet creature with a laughable wrinkled face that gave a lusty "WAH!!!"

After Nida and the baby were settled on the bed and we had cleaned up, we resumed our prayers and waited for news. We were in the middle of the Our Father when someone knocked on the front door. We held our breath. There was no time to think, to be afraid. I felt frozen and tense as I waited for the external cue that would tell me what to do. Meding stalked to the door with her rosary in front of her as if it were a mighty weapon. When she peeked outside, she released a sigh of relief. "Just a fruit vendor," she said. After she dispatched the vendor away, we continued praying.

At midafternoon, some jeeps roared outside. Once again we tensed—was it Lewis and his men? Meding checked the door, then she quickly unlocked it. It was Doc. "Our men killed Lewis," he announced, "but there's still no word about Gil, Nando, and Max."

# Waiting

$\mathcal{T}$he only thing certain was that our men killed Martin Lewis. Doc took off to contact Lewis's men and the Japanese, to try and work out the safe release of the three men—if they were still alive.

Back in our own house, Mama prayed in front of the altar, while Nida lay on her bed exhausted from childbirth. I watched her holding the baby in her arms. The baby sucked on Nida's enormous breast, then she pulled away and screamed in frustration.

"I just don't have enough milk," Nida said. "I didn't know they nursed so much milk. I thought they slept a lot."

I had been hanging around, not knowing what to do with myself. I had been avoiding Mama because she was so nervous, all you had to do was spill something and she'd be all over you. I offered to take care of Nida's baby while she rubbed coconut oil on her cracked sore nipples.

I placed the baby in a hammock and rocked it a few times. The baby continued whimpering and sucking on her fist. I remembered how the Japanese shopkeeper Sanny used to make sugar water for her infant and after watching the baby for a while, I finally boiled some water and added some sugar to it. I sterilized the bottle and nipple which the Virgins had given us, and I carefully poured the sugar water into the bottle. I offered the sugar water to the baby, who took it eagerly. She still had tears in her eyes and she was drinking so fast I was sure she'd get gas. Later she dozed off, with the bottle still in her half-open mouth. Very gently, I pulled the bottle away. Her face was tear-stained, her eyelashes damp, and sticky liquid dribbled down the corners of her mouth. I wet a clean rag and cleaned her face. She was small, like a chicken; she just broke your heart. Her face was red and wrinkled; and when she made faces in her sleep, she looked like an old man. I laughed softly at how cute she looked. She had a faint smell of a kitten that made me feel like hugging her tight and protecting her from every bad thing on earth.

Not an hour passed when the baby stirred, shoved her fist into her mouth, and began whimpering once more. She was hungry again. I went to Nida, woke her up, and handed her the baby.

"What, again?" Nida said irritably.

She bared one breast, held the baby against it, and the infant rooted wildly for the nipple. The baby sucked quietly for a few minutes, but then she started whimpering again.

A wild expression crossed Nida's face. "I don't know what to do! She won't stop crying."

"Maybe you should drink water," I suggested. "Sanny used to drink lots of water and juice."

"I'm sore, and I can't stop thinking about Max."

"Doc said it's a good sign if we haven't heard about them. It means they're not dead."

"Not dead! Those savages shove waterhoses into the mouths of their prisoners and fill their stomachs with water. Then they jump on the bloated stomachs. They pluck out eyeballs for the fun of it. Max is too old, and he has malaria. He can't take much."

The baby screamed louder and Nida pressed her hands against her ears. "She won't stop."

I took the baby away. I was jiggling her on my shoulders, trying to pacify her, when Mama walked up to me.

"She's hungry," I explained.

"That baby'll die," she muttered. She strode toward Nida's room. Her voice was strident as she continued, "Nida, if you keep this up, that child'll die."

Nida, who had been resting on her side, was taken aback. "I . . . I don't . . . I can't help it."

"What do you mean, you can't help it. That's your child. Take care of it. Why should Yvonne be the one taking care of it. She has enough things to do. Yvonne, hand that baby over to Nida."

Reluctantly, I placed the baby in Nida's arms.

Even when Nida resumed nursing the baby, Mama didn't leave. She had a lot of nervous energy and she was going to get rid of it right there, at Nida, at me, at anything that crossed her path. "If you were just going to maltreat that child, then why have a child. That's what I have to say. You thought having a baby was like having a doll. Well, it's not that way. That's not how things are. It's a lot of pain and tears, having a child. You can't treat it like a rag doll, hand it over to Yvonne when you're tired of it, you just can't!"

"I didn't do that."

"Then why was Yvonne taking care of that baby? Sugar water isn't good for that baby. What sustenance does sugar and water have? Sugar and water—you might as well give it air. I cannot tolerate ignorant women who have babies and don't take care of them."

Nida's eyes glinted in anger. She sat up, adjusted her baby to her breast, and glared at Mama. "You think you're somebody, don't you, you with your education and name. I have always held my tongue because of Max and Nando being friends and all, but you and your kind are leeches. You've been leeching on others all your lives. You never did a thing before this war. Nothing. Never worked a day in your life. All you ever did was be the society matron. Servants did everything. I wouldn't be surprised if they had to wipe your ass. I'm glad this war came along, to teach you leeches a thing or two.''

Mama, horrified at Nida's vile words, put her hand over her mouth. ''Why, Nida, how could you . . . ?''

''Leave me alone! Get out!''

Mama, now in tears, fled to her room.

I thought I should follow Mama, but the baby started whimpering once more. I went to the kitchen for a glass of water instead. ''You have to drink, Nida,'' I said, handing her the glass.

Her left forearm was flung over her eyes and she moved her arm away so she could see me. She remained quiet for a long time, her face serious as she weighed my words. She sat up and drank the water.

''Don't worry about all that . . .'' She waved her hand vaguely, so I understood that she meant the quarrel with Mama. ''People say things they don't mean. Your mother's upset. Everybody's upset. It's just terrible to think they're dead.''

''Doc says—''

She interrupted me. ''I know he is dead. I lived with Mama who was dying for so long that I can detect the scent of death in the air. Death has a sweet smell like flowers. Before they left I caught the scent of death.''

Nida gritted her teeth in rage. Then calming herself, she continued, ''I have been thinking of my life without Max and I considered taking my own life. It is very easy to do. You get a razor blade and cut your wrist. One of the girls who worked at Slapsy Maxie's did that—some business over a man. She was very neat and she even placed a bucket under her wrist. They say that loss of blood makes you faint before you actually die. But then I thought of this child. Max would not want me to leave her alone. She fell into our hands, like a gift from nowhere. Mama, for all her faults, always took care of me. She accepted me for what I was, no matter what my mistakes. It never mattered to her that some people called me names. She loved me. I cannot do less for my own child.''

The baby screamed, demanding Nida's breast; and Nida took her.

When the baby was suckling, Nida stroked the baby's cheek, but the baby was so intent on nursing, she was even perspiring.

"What will you name her?"

"We thought we'd have a boy, and we wanted to name him Fernando, after your father. But a girl—I don't know."

"You could name her Fernanda."

Even though her nipples were red and cracked, she continued nursing the baby. "Mama called me Bienvenida because I was her good news. I'm going to call her Dolores for all this pain," she said.

We used to have good times in Ubec, before the war. We used to sit out on the verandah, on pleasant afternoons while the soft breeze stirred the leaves of the bougainvillea vine trailing above us. We used to be happy as we talked of this or that: Did you hear that the neighbors heard the condemned man rattling the chains the other night? And did you notice the twinkle in Antonia Cabasa's eyes when she spots the American consul? And did you hear the episode of *The Triumphs of Love*, the one about the doctor asking Ben to choose between his wife or his unborn child? And wouldn't you know, Bitong's been to the Big Dance again?

We used to be happy. When Laydan and Lolo Peping were alive. When Esperanza and I scampered about joyfully. Before the war. Before Papa's conscience carried the burden of a dead Japanese teacher, before Mama's obsession with giving her infant son a decent burial, before all this torment of not knowing where the men were. Before the war, we used to have good times. It had been very different then.

I believed in Doc and Doc said that no news was good news.

"What does that mean?" I had asked.

"That if something really bad happened, we'd hear about it."

"If they're dead, we'd hear about it?"

He nodded.

Despite Mama's and Nida's upset, I clung to Doc's words because they meant that Papa, Gil, and Max were not dead. Doc never lied. Mama and Nida were overreacting. Why, in a few days Papa, Gil, and Max would drive up in their jeep, and everything would be all right. It would be just like when they went to headquarters for weeks at a time, and returned roaring into Taytayan.

I tried to find comfort in these thoughts and I shied away from the women whose hysteria made me doubt Doc's words. When the Virgins dropped off Cristobal, I stayed with him under the enchanted jackfruit tree. He had his hand in his pocket. "Guess what I have?" he asked.

I could tell from his expression that he was up to something no good. "What?"

He pulled out his closed fist, turned his hand upward, and opened it, revealing a coconut beetle in his palm.

"So?"

"Watch," he said, as he pulled out a half-meter length of string from his other pocket. He tied the string around the segmented portion between the body and head. When the string was snug, Cris held the other end of the string so the poor creature hung down. It was flapping its wings frantically, and as it did so, it emitted a whirring sound.

"You're hurting him!"

"It's just a game," he insisted. He began swinging the beetle around and around. The coconut beetle spread its wings and tried to fly.

"Stop it, Cris."

"No, I won't."

He continued and I could see that the beetle was getting weary and was dying.

"That's cruel. He'll die."

"So what, it's just a beetle."

I thought hard about how to let Cristobal free the beetle. "Let him go and I'll tell you a story," I finally offered.

He swung the beetle a couple more times, then he handed the string to me. "All right. Here."

I removed the string. The insect was still alive and it quickly spread its wings and flew away. I watched it land on a branch far away.

"So what's your story?" he asked.

I was tempted to walk away and not tell Cris a story. He was always making fun of Laydan's stories anyway. But I had given my word.

Since Cris was always giving his father a lot of headaches, I told him the story about the young man named Banna who disobeyed his father.

Banna was betrothed to the beautiful maiden Laggunawa. To celebrate, Banna's friends invited him to the bamboo grove to cut lime tubes for their betel chew. The bamboo grove was a restful place, but unfortunately it was inhabited by evil spirits that occasionally caused havoc.

Banna's father warned him not to go. "I cut my hand at that place," he said, "and the wound festered for days. It was only the juice of the magic betel nuts from Gowa that healed the cut."

But ignoring his father, Banna left with his companions. It was indeed cool and pleasant in the grove. The bamboos were tall and lithe and a gentle breeze sang through the leaves. Feeling no fear, Banna chose the tallest bamboo and swung his ax. As soon as metal touched wood, blood spurted out from the bamboo. Banna dropped his ax and jumped back. Blood continued flowing from the bamboo, soaking his feet. "Help me!" he called out to his friends. "My father was right! This is an enchanted place!"

His friends were horrified to see Banna's feet transformed into the tail of a python. They quickly removed him from the pool of blood, but the rest of Banna's body continued changing into a snake. By the time they got him home, Banna was a python.

All they could do was take care of Banna the Python. Laggunawa, his betrothed, fed him chickens, field mice, and an occasional piglet. At night, she covered him with a woven blanket.

It happened that soon after, the evil giant, Gittam, attacked the village and stole the people's gold rings. In the midst of all the commotion, Banna the Python disappeared.

While the villagers searched for Banna, he slithered away toward the house of Gittam the Giant. There he wound himself around the giant's neck and strangled him. He searched for the gold rings, swallowed them, and left.

In the forest, Banna the Python confused the landmarks and he became lost. He wandered from place to place until he found himself in an areca palm grove where, weary from his travels, he curled up under the shade of a palm tree and slept.

The frantic cry of a man awoke him. "Ay, ay, go away! I'll give you all my gold rings and my water buffaloes, too. Just leave me alone," said a man clinging to the palm leaves above Banna.

Banna uncurled himself and the distraught man, certain of death, took out his prized betel nut from Gowa for a last betel chew. Shortly, the man spat out betel juice that landed right on Banna's head. Surprisingly, Banna's snake head turned human.

"Spit once more," shouted Banna.

The man spat a second time and this time, Banna changed into a human being. After thanking the dazed man, Banna gathered the villagers' gold rings and, being a man once more, made his way home with ease.

Everyone was overjoyed to see him and to have their gold rings back. The maiden Laggunawa was the happiest of all of them. She and Banna married soon after, with a wedding feast that lasted for days. They had many children and grandchildren and they lived in deep contentment for as long as the sun rose and set above their heads.

When I started telling the story, Cris had picked his nose just to annoy me. But he soon settled down, and I knew he was interested. When I finished he declared, "That's a dumb story."

"You listened to it. It's not dumb. What's dumb about it? Laydan used to tell me that story."

"It's dumb, and your Laydan was dumb too. And she even had goiter!" He strode away from me.

"You're the one who's dumb, Cris!" I shouted. "I hope you . . . you turn into a python!"

He turned around, made a face, then sauntered into the house.

I took a deep breath. Cris was the one who was dumb. Anyone who went around chewing dirt was strange. Whatever feelings of sympathy I had for Cris vanished. He had no excuse, none whatsoever, to behave badly. Just because his mother and siblings were killed by the Japanese did not entitle him to be as mean as he wanted, whenever he wanted. While it was true that some suffered more than others, we were all suffering. I myself did not know what had happened to my father. For all I knew, he was dead.

# The Ring

❦

$\mathcal{D}$oc left two men in Taytayan as our guards. One possessed a wandering left eye and the other was deaf— reasons why Doc left them in Taytayan in the first place. The wall-eyed one almost shot one of our men once, and the deaf one could not tell where gunshots were coming from and was constantly getting into situations where he'd get himself blown to bits.

Mama and Nida were still not talking to each other, and they confined themselves to their rooms. It was almost noon and the two men hovered outside the kitchen, hoping for lunch. No one had given them breakfast, and the past few days they had been eating boiled bananas and salted shrimp fry. I knew they were hungry and I boiled some rice and fried some dried fish. They devoured that and I realized that they would not be satisfied with that same meal for supper. I double-checked our pantry—we still had half a sackful of rice, but we lacked viands. I thought of asking for some guerrilla notes from Mama so I could go marketing, but I couldn't bear the thought of getting her excited over this matter. She'd start screaming and getting everybody nervous; it was better to leave her alone. I considered buying a few items on credit, but I couldn't do that either. My family never believed in borrowing; you paid for anything you bought on the spot. I finally looked at the brown hen that we had brought from Mindanao. Of all the chickens scurrying about, she was the oldest and would soon die. While it was true that she still laid pretty olive-colored eggs, the yolks of her eggs were pale and tasteless. After contemplating her for half an hour, I told the men to catch her and to kill her. I did not watch her get slaughtered; I did not listen to her frantic squawking. I told myself there was no choice, no choice whatsoever; we needed food. Later I made chicken stew, making sure it had enough vinegar and salt so the food would last us for several days.

Papa was not really a native Ubecan. He came from Batangas in Luzon, but after the death of his first wife, he moved to Ubec and taught at the university. His family had been wealthy, but after his mother's death, his father remarried a woman who gambled their belongings away. By the time Papa finished high school, they could not afford to send him to America where he had wanted to study engineering. That was why he had stowed away on a freighter, and why he picked fruit during the summers.

Perhaps because of his various experiences, or because he had been both rich and poor, Papa had a great understanding of people. He possessed a steady quality about him, an I'll-take-care-of-it attitude, that was perfect for my high-strung mother. Until this moment I had not realized how much we had depended on Papa emotionally. Although he was often away, his presence persisted at home and in our lives. And now the possibility that he was actually dead shook the very foundations of our lives.

A kind of practicality possessed me at this time, and I wondered what we would do if Papa were really dead. Would the guerrilleros cast us aside, leave us on our own, stop providing us with guerrilla notes? That was one thing to occupy my mind with. Then I wondered if Nida's baby would live. And what about Mama? Would she cross the thin line separating sanity and insanity which she now skated? That was another thing that I could worry about for hours. In this way I filled my mind with thoughts that seemed to have a numbing effect.

I also learned how to will my father to live. It was like a little game. I did it inside my head and guts, centering my energy on keeping Papa alive. It was a difficult thing to do, but I did it all the time. This preoccupation preserved an outward manner that appeared normal. And this was important to me; the one thing I truly dreaded was to lose touch with reality as Doc had.

The few times Mama left her room, she would come flying at me. "Pray, Yvonne, pray," Mama said as she grabbed me and planted me in front of the altar. She looked wild, her hair disheveled, and she had not changed her dress in three days. Papa, Gil, and Max had been missing for two weeks now, and the longer we waited, the more desperate Mama became. "Pray, that Papa is not dead."

I looked at the figures of the Child Jesus, the Sacred Heart of Jesus, and the crucifix. They were adorned with flowers; candles burned in front of them. I prayed: "Dear God, I do not understand You. I have not seen You, although Papa says that the beautiful things around us are reflections of You. But God, even though I do not know You, please do not let Papa die. Please save Papa, Gil, and Max. Keep them alive. Let everything be all right, please."

The thought entered my head that if Papa were dead, we would have to find his spirit, just as Bolak Sonday did. Laydan had a story about this brave and faithful woman, Bolak Sonday. Her husband, Sandayo, died on their wedding night. He had gotten a wicked witch angry at him, and she had put a sleeping potion in his rice wine. The moment he tasted the wine, he felt life flowing from him. He fell into a deep sleep. He stayed asleep for days and no one could wake him, not even his bride, Bolak Sonday.

She stayed by his bedside day and night, calling out his name at intervals, hoping his spirit would hear and return. When a week had passed, Bolak Sonday ordered the servants to cover his body with eight tiers of net. She announced that she would set out to find Sandayo's spirit. Bolak Sonday searched the earth and she searched the underworld. Days, weeks, months passed. She grew gaunt and pale. When the gods and goddesses saw her thus, they felt sorry for her and they led her to a bolongis tree, a tree favored by the birds of the underworld. Bolak Sonday lay under its shade to rest.

She was half asleep when two birds landed on top of the tree. One bird was yellow, the other was small and black with red eyes. Unaware that Bolak Sonday was beneath them, the birds started talking.

The black bird said, "It's a pity that Bolak Sonday has grown thin and pale."

Said the yellow one, "What happened? She was never that way."

"Haven't you heard? For two years, she has been looking for her husband Sandayo's spirit."

The yellow bird said, "She'll never find him. It's a well-kept secret where his spirit is."

"That's right. She'll never figure out that he's with the Amazon Woman, Tinayobo."

"And she'll never know where she lives."

"And even if she knew, she'd never find the waters of Piksiipan, where the rivers meet, without our magic feathers."

Just then the gods and goddesses sent a gust of wind, ruffling the feathers of the birds. They preened themselves, then flew off to some other part of the underworld. Two feathers, one black and one yellow, fluttered down to Bolak Sonday's lap.

She held both feathers in her hands and said:

*"Magic feathers, bring me quick,*
*Sandayo's spirit I must seek,*
*To the waters of Piksiipan now,*
*Where the rivers meet I must scour."*

Faster than lightning, she found herself on the waters of Piksiipan near a house made of gold. She knocked and the Amazon Woman, Tinayobo, opened the door. Tinayobo was big and foreboding, but without flinching, Bolak Sonday said, "I am here for my husband Sandayo's spirit."

"He belongs here in the underworld," bellowed Tinayobo, and she started to shut the door.

Bolak Sonday shoved open the door, and pushing Tinayobo aside, she searched the house. The house was dark and slimy, and it was difficult to move about, but Bolak Sonday managed to find Sandayo fast asleep in a back room. She started to pick him up when Tinayobo came rushing to her with a dagger in her hand. Bolak Sonday drew her own dagger, and the women started fighting. While Tinayobo was big and strong, Bolak Sonday was agile and quick. Sometimes it seemed as if Tinayobo had Bolak Sonday in her firm grasp, but then Bolak Sonday would twirl away, escaping her. And other times Bolak Sonday pinned Tinayobo against the wall, but the Amazon Woman would push her away. Their battle lasted for days. Underworld creatures gathered around them to witness this spectacle.

In the end, Bolak Sonday triumphed. Quickly, quickly, before the underworld creatures could stop her, she picked up Sandayo. Grasping the magic feathers, she said:

"Magic feathers, I am done,
Sandayo's spirit I have found,
Transport us quickly home we pray,
In the underworld we can no longer stay."

Instantly, they found themselves back in their home, where Sandayo became his normal self once more. One of the first things they did was thank the kind gods and goddesses. Bolak Sonday and Sandayo lived a long and happy life together and they shared many adventures.

How I prayed that Papa was not dead, that he would return soon to share other adventures with us.

Right on top of the piano in Ubec, framed in silver, was a family photo of Mama and Tiya Lourdes, with their parents Lolo Peping and Lolo Beatrize. It was a daguerreotype taken at a studio, with a river and bridge in the background. Mama and Tiya Lourdes were six and eight years old, lovely children, with ringlets of hair surrounding their chubby, smiling faces. Mama had explained at one time that the ringlets were called tribuson and that Lola Beatrize used to spend hours twirling locks of their wet hair around her finger until the hair dried into the spirally curls. It was very tedious, but Lola Beatrize insisted on doing it, instead of handing the girls over to their nanny. She had been a practical and hardworking woman who thought nothing of manual labor, even though the other women of her social class put on airs, pretending they had never lifted a finger in their entire life. "I've embalmed dead people, put makeup on them," Lola Beatrize often said, "I see no point in putting on airs when we're all going to end up on an embalmer's table some day."

Taytayan's mortician had a gray pallor, as if death itself stalked him, but my Lola Beatrize, at least in that picture, gave no hint of her close association with the dead. She looked radiant, standing beside a handsome and proud Lolo Peping, he standing erect with a cane elegantly slung over his arm. How happy the four of them looked. It was a wondrous moment, frozen onto that piece of paper; a perfect second caught, when the four had had no cares, had only joy and love and peace.

The Mama I saw in Taytayan while Papa was missing had no resemblance to that happy girl in the photo. Mama had developed lines on her face; she did not eat. She cried as she prayed. Once in the middle of a litany she started running outside because she thought she heard Papa's voice, and finding only the chickens and piglets outside, she collapsed, weeping.

Then, curiously, one morning she announced that she wanted a haircut. She knocked on Nida's bedroom door and asked Nida if she'd clip her hair. Relieved that their quarrel was over, Nida gladly did so. Mama bathed and changed into a freshly laundered dress. She spoke in a voice devoid of feeling: "I am weary. I've run out of tears. It's not just these weeks I have been crying, I have been crying for years now. And I have said enough prayers to deafen the entire heavenly hosts. There is nothing we can do, not anything you or I or anyone else can do at all. We might as well go about our business in the best possible way.'' She kissed me, then went outside to count the piglets and chickens.

The most mournful time in Taytayan was sunset. As the sun sank into the sea, it shot forth brilliant hues of red, splattering the sky, making your soul catch at your throat. Then you blinked and the sun was gone, and the world that had been aflame was suddenly plunged into a somber darkness. The sounds of the crickets would crescendo in the darkness and your spirit quaked at such sadness.

I was at the seashore one afternoon, collecting seashells and pebbles which I used to write my name on the sand—YVONNE. The pearly shells and alabaster-colored pebbles seemed to sparkle. I, Yvonne Macaraig, existed. I *was*. Esperanza and I used to talk about how there could be other girls just like us in some other part of the universe, that this possibility could not be refuted. But there was no certainty about their existence either, while there I stood, beholding my name and the fiery sky as the sun prepared to sink into the sea. When the sun disappeared into the horizon, the thought came to me that this sight was akin to life, where one is alive one moment, then gone the next. There was only a slim thread, a thin line separating daylight from nighttime, life from death.

Papa was gone, and Mama had reconciled herself to the situation. In doing so, she left me alone. I (who *was*) was the only one left *willing* my father to stay alive. I alone willed him to survive. I could close my eyes, grit my teeth, tighten my muscles, and will life into him. But I was getting weary. Like my mother I was beginning to feel there was nothing I could do, that anyone could do.

I returned home in the darkness, and I sat at the outdoor table with the lantern, which attracted moths and other bugs. A coconut beetle flew and landed in front of me. I wondered if it was the same coconut beetle that Cris had played with and whom I had talked him into freeing. I stroked it, studied its crisp brown shell covering. How nicely everything fitted—the wings, the head, the body. It was perfect —one of God's fine creations. But was God so perfect? Could He be so wonderful when He had subjected all of us to suffering that could never be described in words? It was a sinful thought—but God made mistakes. I put the beetle down, clenched my fist, and smashed it.

That night I dreamt that I had become the Giant of Pangamanon, and I went about slaying people. My feet were soaked in blood and like Banna I began transforming. However, instead of turning into a python, my skin slowly turned red from absorbing all that blood. I had turned completely red, from head to toe, when I awoke with a start.

Mama wore a ring on her little finger. It was a pearl ring, set in bright yellow Chinese gold, which my grandmother had given to her when she was eight. Lola Beatrize had acquired the ring from a former client, a woman whose husband had been a pearl diver. The husband could hold his breath underwater for eight minutes, and he was revered by the other pearl divers for his enormous stamina. One day the man put on his eye and nose piece fashioned from a coconut shell and went diving in the deepest channel where the finest pearls could be found. The husband did not surface until the waves washed his corpse ashore the next day. The woman had brought her husband to my grandmother and pleaded with her to embalm the man and make him look presentable. The man was terribly waterlogged, but my grandmother prepared the body. The woman, being poor, never paid my grandmother in full. Eventually, she offered her the pearl ring as payment, and Lola Beatrize accepted the ring without begrudging the unfortunate widow. Lola Beatrize always told Mama it was a lucky ring. "Why is that, Mama?" my mother had asked Lola Beatrize.

"Because, little Angelita, your mother did a charitable act, and this ring proves it. It is a symbol, and God will always remember that kind act," Lola Beatrize had replied.

Mama woke up the next morning with more energy than usual. She spent the morning cleaning the house. While she waxed and polished the floors, she made me dust the wooden furniture with the intricate carvings, which turned out to be a tedious job because I had to slip the rag in between holes and around curves. Later, she told me that we had to go marketing. It was very late in the day to do the marketing and I wondered why she was doing this. We walked to the central part of the town, but instead of going to the open market, she headed for the pawn shop. I followed, curious about what she was going to do. Once there, she and the pawnbroker became involved in a lively pricing of the gold pearl ring. My mother related to the man the story behind the ring, emphasizing that it was indeed lucky. At last, the man gave my mother the price she wanted, although she later said that the price wasn't good because many people were pawning their jewelry.

She said, as if it were an explanation, "We have to buy meat today."

She wouldn't elaborate. We bought two enormous pieces of beef, and before going home, we stopped by the Good Shepherd Convent, where Mama handed one of the hunks of meat to Mother Socorro. The nun, who moved about like a whisper, was overwhelmed at such luxury. Clutching the crucifix that hung on her chest, she asked, "What can we do to thank you, child?"

Mama told her about the missing men. "Pray, Mother Socorro, and tell the other nuns to pray for them."

"We will not stop praying until they return," the nun assured her.

At home, Mama marinated the meat. Nida was aghast at such extravagance; and she and I looked at each other with concern. Before we ate, Mama saved a huge portion of the beef stew.

"I'm not crazy," Mama said, understanding our expressions. "I am perfectly fine. Nando and I have been married for a long time, and his heart and mine practically beat at the same time. I know he's on his way home. I just know it."

We kept quiet during the meal and while clearing the table. Mama refused to put the food away even though it was getting to be bedtime. She sat on the verandah and waited. Nida brought her baby to bed with her, and I too went to bed.

Lying on my bed, I remembered how some people celebrated the day of the dead. They would prepare an elaborate meal, bring the food to the cemetery, and lay it in front of the graves as offerings to the dead. The next day, the plates and bowls would be empty, and the people who made the offerings would be glad that the spirits of their dead had partaken of their offerings.

As I watched the shadows of the enchanted jackfruit tree, I wondered if the spirits did eat the food. Or did the poor people who lived near the cemetery—the same ones who reportedly pried open coffins to steal the gold from corpses—creep into the cemetery and eat the food?

My mind was swimming with images of burning candles, bowls and platters full of food, people clothed in black, when I heard sounds —men's voices. These were not the voices of our guards. There was something urgent about their tone. Could that be . . . ? I listened carefully. Male voices. Female voices. Crying—was that Mama or Nida? I caught Doc's voice, then the door slamming and a jeep roaring away. Mama talking rapidly. Then the low and weary voice of a man saying, "Don't—I don't want her to see me like this."

It was Papa!

My palms were sweating. I started to get up, then lay down once more. My legs developed that jumpy feeling. To try and calm myself, I stared at the walls and counted the lizards and geccos skittering about. It seemed like a long, long time before I heard tired footsteps with an unfamiliar dragging. The door of my parents' bedroom creaked open and closed, then there was a slumping sound as if someone sat on the bed. Then I heard him howl—long and steady like a wild animal, but filled with an unfathomable pain. When he stopped, he was sobbing. Mama's voice droned soothingly, but Papa continued weeping. Later, I heard him washing himself. I got up from bed, waited just behind the door. When he passed by my bedroom from the bathroom, I opened my door. He paused, looked at me, and opened his arms. I went to him. I could feel his bones. During all the time Papa was missing, I had not cried, and now the tears I had dammed up inside burst forth in babbling abandon. A tiredness possessed me, so much so that my head spun and I felt like swooning. Mama laughed and cried at the same time. They finally brought me to my bed. Before I fell asleep I overheard Papa telling Mama to burn his clothes.

Papa would not say much. It was clear that whatever had happened pained his soul. For unclear reasons, the Japanese army had sent spies into Martin Lewis's camp to help Yoshida, Papa, Gil, and Max escape. Just when they had almost reached safety, Lewis's men caught up with them and shot them. Gil was dead. Max was alive. Papa's leg was hurt. And Admiral Yoshida was back with the Japanese.

# The Funeral

※

$\mathcal{T}$he mortician complained that he had a most difficult time making Gil Alvarez's face presentable for viewing. Gil's face had three bulletholes. The pale mortician related how he tried wrapping a handkerchief around Gil's neck and pulling it up to cover the blown-off jaw. He combed Alvarez's hair over the bullethole on the forehead. But he couldn't do a thing about the neat little bullethole in the cheek. He tried bandaging Alvarez's face, but that made him look like a mummy displayed in some cheap carnival. Besides, it only called more attention to the fact that the poor governor's face was riddled with holes. From sheer desperation, the mortician had even tried putting a flower into the hole in the cheek, which covered the hole all right, but a gardenia sitting in the middle of a man's face was disconcerting to say the very least. Finally, he threw his hands in the air, sighed *"Bahala na!"*—what the hell—and he applied makeup and powder on Alvarez's face. He covered up the holes in the neck and forehead as he had planned, and he left the hole in the cheek exposed. Gil Alvarez appeared that way in his open casket that sat in the middle of the aisle of San Antonio church.

To symbolize Gil Alvarez's spilled blood, the Virgins had said they would decorate the church in red and white. They discussed what sort of flowers they would use on the altar, along the aisle, and on the church pillars. So caught up were they with the arrangements—a job they were often called upon to do—that they completely forgot they could not order roses, dahlias, daisies, and chrysanthemums from the distant place of Baguio. They scoured the town and came up with white gardenias and ferns; but they had an impossible time finding red flowers. Stuck with what Taytayan had to offer, which wasn't very much, the Virgins eventually figured out a way of stripping the green portions of the gabi leaves so only the red part showed. While the women fluttered about installing the bouquets in the church, they talked about Cristobal. It seemed, according to the scandalized Petra, that he had started touching certain parts of his body. "I caught him in the act," she said, indignation dripping from each word. "Fondling himself."

Mama and I were helping them and my mother paused and stared at Petra's sparse hair, which stuck up at different angles. "If fondling himself makes that poor boy feel better, let him. He's lost everything, after all," she said, leaving Petra glassy-eyed and Meding philosophical.

I had seen Mama afraid; I had seen her stand up against the Japanese soldier in Mindanao; I had seen her force a cheerful front to weather our difficulties; I had seen Mama harangue God and the saints with her prayers. But Gil's funeral shook whatever composure Mama had. She wept on my father's shoulders. "It's all gone. It's dead; we've lost it. It'll never be back again," she wailed.

I did not know what she meant until I heard the other women during the funeral Mass. Women from all over Ubec traveled through enemy territory to catch a last glimpse of Gil Alvarez, the man they had adored in their teen-age years. Crying, they talked about how Alvarez symbolized their youth, and how his death signaled the unquestionable end of the days when they laughed and rhumbaed and jitter-bugged—

those days along with Alvarez had turned into dust whipping in the dry wind, they cried. They mourned for the death that happened in their souls.

When the women saw Gil Alvarez's face, when they saw Cristobal, kneeling quietly (loaded with Meding's pink medicine)—a carbon copy of his Olympian father, Ubec's demigod if not Ubec's god—the women could not contain their deep sorrow and rage. All the sufferings they had accumulated through the war years, all the humiliation they bore and which they lifted up to God—God's Will be done—welled up and burst like a dam in the ancient stone church. The old Spanish friar— deaf and barely with the living—had never in his entire sixty years of sacerdotal activities witnessed such passion. Fearing the women would tear the casket apart, tear Gil Alaverez apart for pieces of his flesh to use in precious reliquaries, he hastened the funeral Mass.

Later, ten women pushed away the men who lifted Gil's coffin, and they (with black veils covering their faces) carried him all the way to the cemetery, instead of using the tired black funeral car that looked like a worn bat and that often stalled in the middle of DeLeon Avenue anyway. Four women tore their hair and strew strands along the way like black confetti.

It was foolish, but lurking inside of me was the hope that Gil would come back to life just as Doc Meñez had. My intellect knew, just by the sight of the hole on his cheek, that he was dead (Gil Alvarez's corpse really looked terrible). But a part of me clung to the idea that some miracle could happen. All these people, all the tears, surely God could grant us another miracle. But beyond the excessive display of mourning, nothing unusual occurred. When Gil's casket grated its way into the niche and the marble marker was put in place with a dull thud, I accepted that there would be no miracle this time. Gil was dead. This realization was punctuated by the fainting of two women.

Later, spent, so thoroughly spent, the mourners gathered at the Virgins' house for the funeral meal which Meding and Petra so very kindly prepared. Over the wartime extravagance of fine white rice, roast pig, barbecued chickens, and fruit-of-the-gods salad, people spoke unabashedly of Gil's magnificence, while Cristobal locked himself in the bedroom and lay on the bed, wetting himself from grief.

I detected a change in my father. What pained him most went beyond the loss of Gil Alvarez, and the torture they endured as prisoners in Martin Lewis's camp. My father lost faith in Americans. He had lived with them; he had known them and loved them. But now he realized that a lot of what Gil Alvarez had said about Americans was true. And my father realized that Filipinos must shape their own destiny, that they were responsible for their future, that America (for all her professed good intentions) watched out for herself and her citizens first of all, even if this meant using other countries and peoples. And so he and other men continued with the guerrilla warfare with an intensity that had been lacking before. They had always held back, waiting for Mac-Arthur to return, waiting for the Americans to liberate the Philippines. But now no more. If they would have to fight the Japanese for the next decade, or even twenty, then that was how it would be. But they would continue fighting for Filipino freedom.

I myself had developed an insecurity about my father. I was always afraid he'd suddenly disappear or die. I touched him often, hung onto his arm, and sat beside him constantly. Even at night, I would awake with a sudden jerk, then I would go to my parents' room and shake him awake, to prove to myself that he was alive. Once I prayed to God and without thinking said, "Thank you God that it was Gil Alvarez who died, and not Papa." I paused, horrified at my words. And then I felt bad. Deep inside I had sensed that blood would be spilled; I had felt it. But guilty as I felt, I *was* happy it was not my father's blood.

One night I fell into a fitful sleep, but later I awoke to the sound of a rhythmic thudding. I felt disoriented. At first I thought I was back in Ubec. Then I realized I was in Taytayan, but I thought Papa was still missing. I became frightened because the sound came from my parents' room. Hurrying to their room, I opened the door slightly. The sound came from the headboard banging softly against the wall. My father was on top of my mother. They were making love, their eyes closed as they rocked regularly, like the waves lapping the shore. Moonlight streamed into the room and I could see a film of sweat on Mama's forehead. Her mouth was half open with desire. And Papa was on top of her, loving her with a vibrancy I had never seen before. His body moved rhythmically on top of hers. They throbbed with life. I felt a vivid sense of clarity that swept aside all sense of guilt and misgivings: They were alive and I was alive.

# *Liberation*

❧

*While* Papa, Gil, and Max had been prisoners of Martin Lewis, Doc Meñez had taken over the guerrilla leadership. Being basically a nonviolent person, it had gone against his grain to participate actively in the fighting. But he talked it over with God, and there was no one else who could head the Movement. Hemming and hawing would have meant sure death to Papa, Gil, and Max; it would have meant the collapse of Ubec's guerrilla movement and total Japanese control of the Island (and a great loss of civilian lives). And so Doc knew that God wanted him to be Ubec's guerrilla head. "It is strange," he said, "how life shapes itself for you." Curiously, once he became the Movement's leader, he lost his ability to read people's auras. He muttered once about how this loss was "payment"—for what exactly, he never elaborated.

Doc turned out to be as fine a soldier as he was a doctor. Under his leadership, the guerrilleros liberated towns until three-quarters of the island of Ubec was in guerrilla hands. Things were going bad for the Japanese, including a major setback when Admiral Isoruku Yoshida died. It was a strange circumstance—shortly after his return to the Japanese, Yoshida contracted cholera after carelessly eating unwashed fruit. People said, with a note of vengeance, that his death was meant to be. The Japanese found themselves confined to the city of Ubec, but they still possessed superior arms and resisted the Movement effectively. Doc said it would take a long time for the Movement to liberate Ubec City; but with the Americans and their superior arms, Ubec would be liberated in a matter of days. His words proved correct.

In Taytayan, it was quiet from the time darkness set in until the sun rose. At dawn, from my room the first sounds that broke the silence were the clip-clopping of a horse. It was the old delivery man, with his fresh milk and white cheese. This November morning, however, I awoke not to the peaceful clip-clopping, but to the shattering sound of rude gunshots.

I lifted the mosquito net, rolled to the floor, and crawled under the bed. I stared out at the rosy sunlight that filtered into the bedroom to figure out what was going on. There was more shooting. I thought to myself that the Japanese had invaded Taytayan and we would all die. I was making the sign of the cross when I heard people's voices and laughter. Laughter . . . ? I crept to the window and looked out. People were running up and down the sidewalk. There were men and women dancing in the street, and down the road marched a steady stream of American soldiers. There was so much activity, so much joy. I stood up to wave, but I felt a stomach cramp. The pain was sharp and all I could do was crawl back to bed. It was then that I noticed bloodstains on the bedsheet and blood on my nightgown. I had been hit by a stray bullet, and I was dying. I remembered my dream when my feet were soaked in blood and I turned completely red.

"Ma—Ma!" I shouted.

Mama burst into my room. "What is it, Yvonne?" She had on her best dress, the same one she had worn in Mindanao when Gil Alvarez had supper with us. Before I could tell her about my terminal condition, she said, "Yvonne, Yvonne, they're here! The Americans are here!"

"Ma, I'm dying."

My mother's Madonna's eyes glinted when she spotted the blood-stains. She checked me, then smiled. "You're all right. It's just your period. You're now a woman. Everything's all right. And the Americans have returned, with tanks and guns. It took a long time, but the war's over."

When she later left to join the impromptu celebration in the streets, I sat by the window and watched the men shoot their guns into the air and yell out loud profanities and prayers. I saw Mama and Papa, Nida and Max, Doc, Bitong, and all the others laughing, shouting. I saw women—young and old—racing from one American soldier to another, kissing the dazed Americans, who were themselves overwhelmed at being the liberators of Taytayan. Bewildered children stood by doorways not knowing what to make of this human carnival.

A scene caught my eye, and I viewed it as if it were all in slow motion. There was a girl, around twenty years old, wearing a filmy white dress that fluttered about her. Her waist-length hair was braided down her back; her tanned skin shone like gold. She was enchanting, like some creature descended from the sky. She ran from soldier to soldier, handing each a flower, kissing them on the cheeks (but her movements were slow and fluid). She approached a lanky young American soldier, and after smiling at him, she tiptoed and kissed him on the cheek. He became so stunned that he stood frozen with his hand on his cheek while he watched her disappear in the crowd.

The revelry continued for a long time and I imagined the Virgins looking out of their balcony, clucking their tongues and predicting that there would be a rash of half-American babies in Taytayan in nine months.

For that was what a woman did—she nurtured a child in her womb for nine months, then released this human being into this world. And I, my mother had just said, was now a woman.

I stood in front of the mirror and studied the reflection of the scrawny girl with bony elbows sticking out. Was that really me? Had I grown four inches since the war broke out? Had my round cheeks receded to reveal cheekbones that would make me look like Mama one day? I unbuttoned my nightgown and pulled it down so my chest was exposed. There were more ribs than breasts; but yes, they were slightly swollen, no longer the flat breasts of a child. I crossed my arms in front to cover myself. A knowledge filtered into my brain that I was different, that I had changed, that I would never again be the Yvonne of yesterday, of last year, of the past. I stood on some threshold, and where it led, I did not know. I tried to smile bravely even as a lump of fear formed and caught at my throat.

Soon after the liberation of Ubec City, we packed our things in army jeeps to return to Ubec. I had found Inuk's vest, which Laydan had given to me on her deathbed, and I clutched it to my chest as we made our way to the city. The vest's rainbow colors sparkled under the sunlight, reminding me of the delightful story of the Maiden of the Buhong Sky who spun rainbows. The rainbow is the symbol that the sun will shine after a rainfall—that was the promise of the Maiden. Briefly I held my breath—the vest was lovely. It had belonged to the greatest bard of all times. I had never met him, but I owned something that had belonged to him. We were linked together.

Laydan learned the story from Inuk. And I learned it from her. Before the war, Laydan used to say, "Yvonne, Esperanza, do you want to hear the story about Agyu?"

"Which one?" we used to ask.

"The story about Golden Rice from the skyworld."

"Oh, yes. Tell us that story."

And Laydan would tell the story:

Until the messenger from the Magindanaos arrived, the Ilianon people had lived at the mouth of the Ayuman River in tranquility and plenty. The deep sea teemed with fish, crabs, mussels, shrimps, and seaweeds, while the nearby forests had beehives thick with honey and beeswax. The Ilianons bartered their goods for cloth, coconut oil, metal implements, porcelain plates, and betel nut and lime containers. They often thanked the gods and goddesses for these bountiful gifts.

But one day a richly clad and arrogant man arrived and presented five wooden chests filled with salt and dried fish. "These are gifts from the Datu of the Magindanaos to the Ilianon people," he said.

These were not true gifts, of course—the Ilianons had no use for salt and dried fish. The messenger was seeking homage from the Ilianons and he was forcing them to barter with the oppressive Magindanaos.

Agyu, the bravest Ilianon warrior, stepped forward. "Thank the Datu of the Magindanaos for these gifts," he began, "but as you can see we are seafaring people and have a surplus of salt and fish. Please return these goods to your leader with our profound gratitude."

The messenger raised his voice, "Warrior, understand this—the Datu of the Magindanaos commands the Ilianons to accept these things. In return you Ilianons must give him a tribute of one thousand lumps of beeswax."

"One thousand lumps of beeswax! That's a fortune. Why, that's worth a hundred times the goods in those wooden chests," murmured the people in dissent.

The messenger glared at the warriors one by one until he rested his gaze on Agyu. "The Datu of the Magindanaos wants the one thousand lumps of beeswax before the next full moon. He also orders the Ilianons to worship only the god of the Magindanaos. He says your numerous deities are nonsense."

At this the Ilianon warriors drew their daggers, but their leader, Datu Tabunaway, ordered them to put away their weapons. "If we kill him," he explained later, "the Datu of the Magindanaos will castigate us tenfold. They have superior forces."

"But this is extortion—tyranny," spoke Agyu. "We must not pay allegiance to this man. We Ilianons have always been our own people, owing nothing to others, living life as we want to."

"That is true," Kuyasu With the Short Temper echoed. "We must not give tribute."

Bongkatolan the Woman Warrior, who was Agyu's sister, spoke. "We must be cautious. I have heard that for every one of our people, there are ten Magindanaos. They are fierce and cruel. They have forced others to trade with them and they have captured those who refused and sold them into slavery. If we do not give them what they want, then it's war."

"They will either kill us or enslave us, but I would rather die fighting for my freedom," Agyu insisted.

"We will not pay tribute. We also would rather die," the other warriors repeated.

They decided to send Agyu and Kuyasu to the Datu of the Magindanaos. "Bring only nine lumps of beeswax to show that the Ilianons will not be enslaved," Datu Tabunaway instructed. "Be careful. See what kind of man this Datu is, and find out how many warriors he has, then we will decide what to do."

Agyu and Kuyasu sailed to the land of the Magindanaos and they presented the nine lumps of beeswax to the furious Datu of the Magindanaos. "I ordered one thousand lumps!" He flung the beeswax to the floor.

Kuyasu's eyes flickered with hatred. "That is all you are getting from the Ilianons!"

The Datu swung his sword at Kuyasu, cutting his arm. Blood spurted out of the Ilianon warrior's arm. Screaming in pain, Kuyasu drew his own sword and struck down the Datu. At this, the Magindanao warriors immediately jumped on Kuyasu and hacked him to pieces. Agyu was able to fight his way out of the fortress, and he rushed home to report the incident to Datu Tabunaway. "We must leave our land," the Datu sadly said. "The Magindanaos will be here soon."

All except the sick and elderly gathered the things they cherished, and they fled on outriggers up the Ayuman River. They followed the narrow Pulangi River until it became impossible to paddle farther. Then they traveled on foot to the top of the Ilian Mountain. There Datu Tabunaway ordered them to cut lawaan trees and to build a fort. They piled logs and enormous rocks near the fort.

Meanwhile, three thousand Magindanao warriors set out in their warships and they ransacked and burned the homes of the Ilianons. They tortured those who remained to find out where the other Ilianons had fled. An old man whose eyes had been gouged out finally confessed. The

Magindanaos beheaded their prisoners and sailed upstream until they spotted the Ilianon fort on the mountaintop.

From their fort, the Ilianons anxiously waited until all the Magindanaos were on the steep mountain, then they hurled huge rocks and rolled down the logs. Knowing more Magindanaos would follow, Datu Tabunaway once again urged his people to flee.

"We are weary of traveling. Why must we continue wandering in this way?" complained the people.

"We will go to the Pinamatum Mountain," the Datu said. "Perhaps we can build our homes there."

It was a difficult climb, and once there they discovered that food was scarce. While scavenging for food, they spoke of their homes and they talked of finding another river like the Ayuman where they could build their houses at its mouth. They wanted balete trees and bamboos lining the banks, tigbaws laden with golden flowers rippling under the hot sun, and betel nut groves in nearby valleys. They dreamed of building reefs to keep away the sharks. They would build a bamboo fence around a bathing area in the river, and they would line the river bottom with porcelain plates so their women would not lose the gold and silver rings that might accidentally slip off their fingers. They talked of building a huge house with a porcelain court on top of a plateau for their Datu and his wife. They would use brass to decorate their own homes, and the entire place would be well fortified, because the Ilianons would never be subjugated by others.

Some Ilianons grew so homesick that they begged to return to their place by the Ayuman River. After a long trek back, they were horrified to see burned logs and ash where their homes had stood. They found the fly-infested, headless remains of the sick and elderly Ilianons they had left behind. They found blood crusted everywhere.

Gathering their dead, the Ilianons wept and wailed at their deities: "Why have you abandoned us? We have been faithful to you. Why have you allowed this to happen?"

From the skyworld, the gods and goddesses heard the weeping and anguished words and taking pity, they rained golden rice and golden betel nuts on them, which the Ilianons gathered and ate. The Ilianons turned golden, a sign that they were beloved by the deities. They rubbed the juice of the golden betel nuts on their dead, who miraculously came back to life.

An Ilianon messenger, golden from the heavenly food, hurried to the Pinamatum Mountain to inform those who remained behind of the divine food. The Datu led his people back to their ancestral home and they all partook of the food. Still fearful the Magindanaos would return, the Ilianons prayed to the deities. "We want our own home where there is peace and freedom. Give us our own land," they prayed.

It was then that the deities promised the Ilianons a place called Nalandangan. "Our beloved Agyu will guide you," the deities told them. "This land is past the two huge boulders that strike each other like the jaws of the great python."

The Ilianons gathered the golden rice and golden betel nuts, and they boarded the enormous floating ship sent by the deities. After several days, they started to run out of food. They began to weep, fearing they would die, fearing they would never find the promised land. "Do not give up," Agyu urged his people. "The deities themselves promised us Nalandangan."

On and on they traveled and just when they thought they would never reach Nalandangan, Agyu spotted two enormous boulders banging fiercely against each other. When the boulders were apart, the ship floated through with ease. Beyond, the Ilianons saw a river with lush bamboos and balete trees lining the banks. And they knew that the deities had not forsaken them, that they had arrived at Nalandangan.

I should have known that Ubec would be different. We had heard reports about the city. Shortly after the war broke out and it became evident that the Japanese would take over Ubec, the retreating USAFFE had bombed the city. The Japanese took over and rebuilt some of the buildings. But, three years later, when the Japanese realized that they would have to retreat, they too bombed Ubec.

I had seen barrios destroyed by the Japanese—the old houses burned down so only the cement foundation remained; the nipa huts reduced to cinders; the surrounding fields transformed into smoldering

ash. I had seen destruction, and I should have been ready to see what
had become of Ubec. But (I quickly realized) there is a big difference
between the heart and the mind. We had heard of Ubec's devastation
—our minds knew this; but our hearts believed that we would be going
home to the one we had always known. The rocking chair on the verandah would still be there, the comfortable four-poster bed would be
waiting, the four o'clock plants would be blooming beneath the riotous
hibiscus shrubs. There is an enormous gap between heart and mind.

I had never seen a city destroyed as Ubec was destroyed. When
we drove into the city we—all of us—could not hold back our weeping.
"Oh look, that used to be Monay's Bakery," Mama said, tears streaming
down her cheeks. "And look, the city hall's also destroyed. And Slapsy
Maxie's is gone."

I felt as lost as the Maiden of the Buhong Sky must have felt when
the wicked Giant destroyed her castle and robbed her of the starlight
and moonrays from which she spun rainbows.

The church still stood, although one wall was blasted away. As we
drove by, raggedy urchins stared at us from makeshift shelters made of
boards and galvanized iron propped up against the walls. I knew from
their vacuous expressions that they had lost parents, brothers, and sisters.
Most of the houses were destroyed, their jagged walls pointing up ac-
cusingly at the bleak sky. Even the Royal Theater had only two walls
remaining. I could not help remembering the numerous Saturday afternoons Esperanza and I had spent at the Royal, where we sat lulled into
some fanciful world with beautiful women and men as magnificent as
Gil Alvarez, where goodness, justice, peace, and love always triumphed
over evil. Bitong, rifle in hand, wept like a child—another part of his
life gone. The Royal had been the mother he never had, the mother
who told him stories, promised him a good life, told him he could be
anyone at all—a cowboy, if that was what he wanted to be.

With a voice quaking like the branches that swayed in the breeze,
Papa said it could all be rebuilt, and be even better. After all, Ubec had
had no city planning whatsoever; the old city had grown in a haphazard
manner. Even as we gazed at blasted buildings, stone, mortar, glass,
metal on the ground, all the destruction, Papa declared that Ubec could
never really be destroyed.

As he spoke his voice grew stronger, firmer. He told us of how Ubec came to be, and how it would stand long after we were all gone. During the Ice Age, he related, the oceans and seas were low and Ubec was not yet formed. It, like the rest of the numerous islands of the Philippine Archipelago, was connected by strips of land to other Asiatic places. People and animals such as elephants and rhinoceroses traveled over the land bridges to Ubec. Then the ice melted and the waters rose, creating the Philippine Islands, over seven thousand of them, and Ubec was formed, shaped like a sock with a mountain range running down its length. Although the island had many good harbors, the best was located at the upper curve of the heel of this sock; and there people have always thrived as seafarers and traders because this fine harbor drew merchants from as far as China, Siam, India. In more modern times, Spaniards, British, and Americans also found themselves on Ubec's shores. And the Japanese too.

So this war was merely a part of Ubec's rich and long history. Ubec would rebuild the buildings by the wharves, fix up the old churches whose walls had enormous holes in them. And people would replace the stone statues of heroes on the plaza grounds. And before long, the open market near the piers would be lively once more, the centenary acacia and flame trees would flower as always, and the rich smells of sea, jasmine, and horse dung would replace the scent of smoke, dust, and death. Ubec would grow like a mollusk, growing in layers outward, with the new growth approaching the hills and mountains.

I could imagine, as Papa spoke, numerous other people in the past and in the future, returning to Ubec, resuming life in Ubec. I saw people living in Ubec centuries before me and centuries after me—an endless parade of humanity through time. And I knew that invaders could not really destroy Ubec, could never destroy its people.

# Good-bye, Laydan

❧

$\mathcal{L}$olo Peping's beloved flame tree still stood. Part of it was burned and branches had broken off, but new growth defiantly sprouted upward toward the sky. We had known that the upper floor of the house was destroyed and only the bottom floor remained. I was relieved that there was no further damage to the house.

At first we were not sure they were there. In fact, we did not know if they were alive at all. During their final retreat, the Japanese bombed Ubec with great ferocity. And Japanese snipers remained even as people returned to Ubec. As we walked through the debris in the yard, we heard a metallic click. The men drew their rifles. Papa called out, "Lourdes, it's us."

Suddenly the kitchen door burst open and Lourdes, Esperanza, and Lupita, looking like frightened and pale ghosts, rushed out screaming and weeping at the same time. "You're here! You're here!" They touched our faces, our hands, our hair. "Is it true, then? Is it over?"

On the way to Lolo Peping's gravesite, Tiya Lourdes explained that a bomb had destroyed some of the mausoleums at the cemetery. According to my aunt, it had been a gruesome sight with skeletons strewn about. The bones had been put away but the cemetery was still in disorder. In front of Lolo Peping's crypt, we placed our bouquets and lit several candles. We prayed for Lolo Peping's soul and we also thanked God that our mausoleum was intact.

Mama started crying at the cemetery, and she continued crying at home. "It was terrible, Lourdes, just awful. You cannot imagine the kind of life we led. Just like animals. And the boy, I had to leave him in that Godforsaken place, Lourdes. That is my greatest sin, abandoning that poor child in that jungle. A sin, Lourdes."

"There's nothing you can do about it," Tiya Lourdes said. She had grown thin and her hair had turned as white as onion roots. But she still retained the pleasant scent of cinnamon. She was cooking, trying to ignore my mother.

Mama persisted. "We abandoned him. He's out there in that jungle, all alone with the wild animals and everything. Abandoned. He'd be two years old now, Lourdes, two, if only he'd made it."

"Stop torturing yourself, Angeling." My aunt's voice was loud and clipped.

"You don't have to shout, Lourdes, after all, I'm the one who lost a son. There you were, in the city, while we had to live on roots and monkeys. Why, many times we had soup without any meat—"

"It wasn't safe in the city! There was little food. Do you know that we ate rats? Rats, Angeling, rats! I had to cook them in all sorts of herbs to disguise what they were. And the bombing was no picnic. My right ear is still deaf from the recent bombing."

"It wasn't a picnic for us, I can tell you that. I lost two molars. Doc Meñez says it was from malnutrition. And I had malaria. If not for the quinine Doc gave me, I would have died."

"I don't want to hear about your malaria and molars!" Tiya Lourdes slammed a pot.

My mother was quiet for a while, then she asked, "What is the matter with you?"

"Nothing's the matter with me. It's you, Angeling. You are so self-centered, you think you are the only person on all the Islands who suffered from this war. You act as if the world revolves around you. You were always that way. It was always Angeling-this, Angeling-that. It was always you and your problems. You never thought of other people. I was here with Papa when he died, and that wasn't a pretty sight. The things we went through—Angeling, don't you see—we all suffered."

Mama raised her voice. "Don't talk to me about suffering. You always had it easy. You were Mama's favorite. You were the good one, the one the nuns favored. You always finished your potatoes and those bitter vegetables that looked like dog throw-up. You could do things with your hands—cook, sew, everything. I could barely make a running stitch. You were Lourdes the saint, the martyr . . ."

"You're just jealous," Tiya Lourdes said.

"What—me, jealous? Did your sewing and cooking find you a good man? All you had was that good-for-nothing husband of yours."

Tiya Lourdes bristled. "Don't say a thing about him. He's dead, and you have no right to mention his name."

Mama gasped. "Oh, Lourdes, I didn't know he died. I'm sorry . . . I didn't mean . . ."

"It doesn't matter. He wasn't a good husband after all, nor a good father. He died in that camp where they placed him after the Death March. Malnutrition, dengue, something. Tecla—the other woman— came by and told me. It doesn't matter. He doesn't matter. It's someone else who matters. Someone else who was good to me and to Esperanza, and who is now gone. But maybe that's what life's all about. Or maybe it's war, I don't know. He was a decent man, Angeling, a Japanese doctor, who helped us when we needed help, who loved me during the darkest moments of my life. But he's gone. Dead, for all I know." She sighed.

"You mustn't tell anyone. They'll call you a Japanese collaborator. They'll shave your hair off," Mama warned.

"They can do what they want. He was the only man decent to me. I loved him, Angeling. He was kind not only to me, but to all of us. He was good to me, the only man who really loved me. And he's gone, Angeling. I've lost him, and I don't know what to do. I feel lost and afraid. So you see, you're not the only one suffering from this miserable war. Other people have suffered. Other people continue to suffer. I suffer, Angeling. I feel alone. I feel small and abandoned."

Mama put her arms around her sister and kissed her wet cheeks. "Everything will be all right, everything will be fine," she said. "All that's past, all finished, all over."

Esperanza and I had walked far away from the city rubble, away from the destruction, to a corn field where lush and green corn plants were almost as tall as we were.

"Do you remember how we used to pull the silk from the corn?" I said, glancing at my cousin whom I barely recognized. Esperanza had grown two inches to my four. She was thirteen, small-boned and angular, and skinny as a flag pole. She was less prickly though, softer somehow, although she remained dramatic.

"We were children," she said. She tilted her head and looked up at the clear sky. "A long, long time ago."

We sat under the shade of an acacia tree.

"I just thought of something," I said suddenly.

"What?"

"Remember when Lolo Peping turned seventy, and we had the big party at home? Do you remember the gatecrashers?"

"What are you talking about?"

"Remember the three men in dirty barong tagalogs? They came in, got all that food, and sat in a corner and stuffed their faces?"

"Oh yes. The bums. They should have been thrown out of the house."

"Mama wanted them out, but Papa said to leave them alone, that they were discreet and didn't molest anyone. That they were just hungry. It's a terrible thing to be hungry. Can you imagine being so hungry you'd barge into a stranger's house? But it was such a funny sight though.

There were all these politicians and bigshots, and there were the three men in their tattered clothes and their plates piled high. After eating, they stood in line and shook Lolo Peping's hands, to thank him and wish him a happy birthday. It was such a big incident then, but now it doesn't matter. I don't know why it seems so funny.''

We were quiet for a while, then I said, ''Doc Meñez left for Mindanao, to help the people there. I'll miss him,'' I said. ''Everything's different.''

''There'll be school soon.''

''But the building's ruined,'' I said.

''They'll rebuild it. They'll rebuild everything. That's what your Papa said. He's already fixing roads. And Max and Nida have already reopened Slapsy Maxie's. Their baby makes me laugh. Anyway, it doesn't matter. Mother Ignacia's determined to educate us, to make us young ladies of good breeding, even if our classrooms are nipa huts.''

I laughed. ''She's alive, then. I can't believe she's still alive.''

''She's so mean, nothing would kill her,'' Esperanza said. ''They say a Japanese almost raped her, but after a second look at her, couldn't do it.''

We laughed.

''I am in love,'' she announced. She closed her eyes and curved her lips into a half smile.

''With a boy?''

''What do you think? He's a man, actually.''

''You're too young.''

''Anyone who has lived through a war is never too young. He's an American G.I. He was here during liberation. We danced and he kissed me. Full on my lips. He'll be back. He promised. And he'll take me away.'' She placed the back of her right hand over her mouth.

''Was he handsome?'' I asked.

''Like a movie star. And he'll be back.'' She pulled her hand away from her face and studied her fingernails. ''Look, I didn't chew my nails today.''

''It's such a dirty business anyway.''

''There was nothing else to do during blackouts and raids.'' She sighed. ''But he probably won't, you know. Men are like that.''

"You never know," I said. "You just never know."

"It doesn't matter anyway. I'm going to be an actress. Or maybe a pilot. You should have seen the dogfights. Planes all over the sky, chasing one another, shooting, and then suddenly a plane spiraling down."

"Do you really want to do that? Shoot down planes?" I asked.

"I just want to fly."

"Then fly."

We were quiet for a long time, and under the shade of that acacia tree, we dozed off. I awoke to the buzzing of a coconut beetle. I recalled how I had squashed the coconut beetle in Taytayan, but I didn't feel bad. It had happened; that was all. Many things had happened. It was futile to apoligize, to feel regret over events that were now memories. There was so much to do; there was no use wasting time on what had been.

I looked up at the sky and saw a cloud sailing by. I became excited. I stood up and stared at the heavens. "She's there," I said, nudging Esperanza with my foot.

"Who?" she mumbled, not opening her eyes.

"Laydan. I know she's up there."

"Laydan's dead. If she were alive, she'd be a hundred years old," Esperanza said.

"She's up there. I know it!"

The cloud hovered above me, and I knew that Laydan was sitting on that cloud, peering down at me, listening. I shouted: "Hello, Laydan. I haven't fogotten you. And I haven't forgotten my promise to you."

A gust of wind blew and the cloud started floating away. I chased it, waving my hands, saying, "Good-bye for now."

Then I heard Laydan's voice, soft, as if in my heart: "You are the epic."

I was not sure I actually heard her and so I did not tell Esperanza. When I returned, she said, "You're as strange as ever."

Not too long after, during supper one evening, Papa got up from his chair and stood beside Mama. "Mama's expecting," he said. He was happy for the first time in a long, long time.

All of us smiled. Esperanza and I clapped our hands. I felt a lightness inside as I'm sure the others did. Our hopes were suddenly focused on this child that had been spared what we had known. An innocent. And some of that unborn baby's innocence entered our souls.

Later that night, when the only sounds were the crickets outside, Laydan's words came back to me: *You are the epic.* I thought about this with great seriousness. Inuk's bidding to her had been: Become the epic. Now she was telling me that I was the epic? How could I, a young girl, *be* the epic? I wrestled with these words for a long time. It was almost dawn when it came to me.

What she meant was, *All of you are the epic.*

I remembered the time after Laydan's death when I felt compelled to relate the tale about Tuwaang and the Maiden of the Buhong Sky. I could feel a similar stirring inside me. I knew someday I would have to tell still another story, and this time in my own words—not Laydan's nor Inuk's but all mine. We had all experienced a story that needed to be told, that needed never to be forgotten.